THE LONDON AGENCY

Jake Bowen-Bate

1

Mickey was pretty sure that his latest video was the most important he had yet made. He grunted with satisfaction, sat back in his chair, and let his mouse curser hover over the 'upload to YouTube' button. If Pulitzers were handed to people who debunked shitty Kickstarters, then he was pretty sure he'd be in the running. Not that he was naive enough to imagine there were any prizes or awards in his future. But he did harbour a little piece of hope that *this* video might finally attract some mainstream coverage. Perhaps get him invited onto CNN or, if needs be, Fox. With that would come droves of new viewers and subscribers to his channel, and that would mean more advertising, more Patreon income, maybe even a big-ticket sponsor.

He rested his finger on the mouse again, a dilemma beginning to form. Previous videos, shredding the scientifically impossible claims of crowd-funded tech companies, had attracted hate: sometimes from the founders, often from backers of the company unwilling to accept they'd thrown their money away. This one, though, was on a different scale. While he had not identified the true threat that it posed, he was still wise enough to know that there might be risks involved in publishing such explosive claims without the protection of editors, fact-checkers, or in-house lawyers.

Torn between unknown risk and uncertain reward, Mickey hesitated. He pulled himself out of the chair, padded to the fridge and opened a Pepsi. The sound of the doorbell meant the Uber Eats sushi he had ordered was finally here. He gulped his soda and opened the door.

For a second, Mickey only felt mild surprise at the delivery guy's size, beard and tan. He looked less like the average Uber Eats driver and more like one of the ex-military types Mickey saw on Instagram promoting fitness programmes and coffee. Then he realised that whoever was at his door wasn't carrying any food, and the surprise gave way to fear.

"Michael Cook?" The mouth moved but the eyes were hidden behind wraparound shades.

"No," Mickey said, quickly. Far too quickly, really. He wasn't fooling anybody.

The stranger gave Mickey a hard shove in the chest, knocking him backwards into the room. That allowed the man to step in after him and close the door. As he did so, Mickey blinked away the surprise of the blow just in time to see that the visitor was quietly drawing a pistol from beneath his jacket.

2

"It's a great opportunity," said Jamie, "very high profile."

"*Everything's* a great opportunity, Jamie. But I'm telling you I just don't have time to work on this alongside –"

"Course you do, mate. Everyone's just got to put in a few extra hours on this one. It's very high profile, big deal for the agency."

Josh sighed. Even if his manager hadn't been giving most of his attention to simultaneously answering messages on Skype, hammering out a grovelling email to a client to apologise for some missed deadline, and shovelling a sandwich into his mouth, there would have been no point drawing this discussion out. The chances of him being taken off a 'high-profile', VIP customer merely because he was already working twelve hour days was close to zero.

"Alright," he said. "Well, who's the client?"

Jamie hesitated a second before answering.

"Well, that's confidential for now, pal. We're calling it Project Sundown internally."

"Confidential? Why?"

"That's the way the client wants it. Don't ask too many

questions, mate, they're… a sensitive bunch."

Annoying though the secrecy was, it did actually give the assignment some appeal. A secretive, sensitive customer had to be better than working on another banner campaign or social media ad, the banality of which was matched only by the incredible speed at which it had to be delivered.

"Ok, well… I guess it sounds interesting."

"Great, then I'll count you in. Thanks for agreeing," Jamie said absent-mindedly through a mouthful of turkey and avocado. "Just be at the meeting tomorrow morning and then you can hit the ground running."

Josh made his way back to his own desk, a few places down from Jamie's but in the same 'pod' that made up their team of account managers and account directors. Unwilling to wait until the following day to find out what he'd signed up for, he opened his laptop, logged on to the internal server and navigated to the agency's long list of clients. Each was a folder containing project work, research, briefs, cost estimates and the other odds and ends of an agency-client relationship, all neatly filed away. A surprising amount of sensitive information about the marketing strategies and budgets of some big-name companies was pretty much at his fingertips and he'd never been shy about making use of BBA\Rowley's lack of internal access controls to satisfy his own curiosity.

Sure enough, sandwiched between a major soft drinks brand and a well-known accountancy firm, was 'Project Sundown'. Certain that there was bound to be something in the folder revealing who exactly the client was, he double-clicked the icon. To his surprise, he was faced with a message he'd never seen before: 'Access Denied - you do not have permissions to view this folder'.

Well, shit, he thought. For once, they really were serious about confidentiality. That was interesting.

Very little else that Josh had done after drifting into an

entry-level job at London's fourth-best digital agency could have been described as 'interesting'. At least not to him. When he first got the job he'd bought a few books by industry legends and tried to muster up the same enthusiasm that his colleagues appeared to feel for 'exciting' campaigns, 'revolutionary' advertising and 'cutting-edge' marketing techniques, but none of it seemed to stick.

Occasionally, mostly when on one of his infrequent Tinder dates, he made an effort to project the image of a young advertising executive doing glamorous work and living the high-life in London. But it didn't take people long to figure out that his job mostly involved creating PowerPoints and sending emails, and didn't pay enough to offer either glamour or high-life. Perhaps now, he thought, he'd at least be able to spice his conversation up with tantalising hints about a secretive client.

Josh closed the folder, opened Outlook, and scanned the nearly a dozen emails that had arrived in his inbox in the half hour or so while he'd been distracted.

It was nearly 8pm before Josh was finally ready to leave the office. By then most of his colleagues had already gone home, though some of the design team were still holed up in one of the big, glass-fronted boardrooms working on a pitch, and two other account managers worked away in the huge open-plan space the client services team occupied.

Josh took the lift down to the basement and dug his running gear out of a locker. He changed into it, stuffed his work clothes into his backpack, and set off running into the cold London night. It was dark, and had been for hours at this point, but the streets around London Bridge were well-lit and busy. He weaved his way through crowds to Lambeth and along the Vauxhall embankment until he began to get to the quieter pavements of Battersea and Wandsworth, and finally back to his flat. The door opened with just the night latch key, so his flatmate, Dan, must be home.

When he had closed the front door behind him, Josh poked his head into the living room and waved silently to Dan, not wanting to interrupt whatever he was watching on television. Dan and Josh had rented the flat together when they graduated from university and both moved to London. When they'd made that plan, Josh had intended the flat to be a temporary home for him while he pursued training at the Royal Military Academy Sandhurst. It would save him travelling backwards and forwards to his mother's home in Germany, and give him a base in London when he had free weekends.

That plan had all changed when Josh was unexpectedly rejected by the Army on medical grounds before he could even start at the famous academy. The decision had only reaffirmed his view that simply hiding his mental health struggles was usually the better choice. At least if he'd done that since the start, his medical record wouldn't have shown a worrying bout of depression and anxiety, and some associated prescriptions, when an army doctor came to review his suitability for training.

Crushed, Josh had nevertheless moved into the flat with Dan while he applied for jobs in London, and the two had settled into a comfortable routine together. A routine that, Josh suspected, was going to change only when one of them found a serious partner.

Dan was making far more progress on that than Josh, and Josh wasn't surprised to find him curled up on the sofa with the guy – Marco? – he'd met on Hinge a few weeks earlier and who had been gradually spending more and more time in the flat. Josh could hardly complain – he was barely there himself these days and he'd started to wonder if Dan was ever lonely in the evenings. Evidently not, at least not this evening.

Dan waved back, and his companion gave a cheerful grin, then they both turned their attention back to the TV. Josh ducked into his bedroom, emptied his backpack onto the bed, grabbed a towel, and headed for the shower. Afterwards, he sat on the bed for a while, wrapped in the towel, idly browsing through social media and dating apps. He knew he was wasting what little remained of his evening, but struggled to summon up the motivation to do anything as difficult as get dressed, go to the kitchen, and make decisions about dinner.

Eventually, after a few dozen 'one last swipes' on Tinder, he sighed, pulled on a t-shirt and tracksuit trousers, and walked down the corridor to the kitchen. Marco was in there pouring two more glasses of wine. Skinny, with dark hair and a scruffy beard, he had to be ten, maybe even fifteen years older than Josh and Dan. That was par for the course with Dan and his relationships, though. Marco shuffled out of the cramped little kitchen when Josh got there, and then lingered awkwardly in the doorway, evidently torn between whether it was more polite to leave Josh to make his dinner, or to try and make conversation.

"Hey," Josh said, rescuing him, and then immediately losing confidence that the guy's name was actually Marco. It was definitely something Italian...

"How're you?" He finished, lamely, knowing that he'd done a terrible job of hiding his uncertainty.

"Good, yeah, good. Thanks. And you?"

"Good. Long day." Tomorrow he'd just have to check with Dan.

"Of course. Well, I'll leave you to your dinner." Marco, if that was his name, looked at the pack of spaghetti and jar of Sainsbury's basics tomato sauce that Josh had on the counter, and there was an awkward pause. "We're watching

Masterchef if you want to join us," he said, eventually.

Josh just wanted to take his pasta to his bedroom and eat it sat on his bed, with *Bosch* playing on his laptop. And he suspected that Dan's awkward, polite, date also wanted him to do just that.

"Sure. Thanks. Maybe. But anyway, don't let me keep Dan from his wine, he'd never forgive me."

Clearly grateful for the excuse, the guy left, and Josh returned to his food. Once he'd cooked the pasta, stirred some sauce through it, and dumped it into a bowl, he headed quietly back to his room and propped himself happily on his bed.

The next morning, Dan's date was gone. Josh vaguely recalled from a previous occasion when Marco had stayed over that his journey to work from Wandsworth was long, and he had to leave early. That did also have the benefit of avoiding there being an irritating queue for the flat's one shower.

"You have a nice evening?" Josh asked, as he ran into Dan in the kitchen making coffee.

"Yeah, really good thanks. Hope you didn't mind us taking over the lounge?"

"Nah, it's all good. I was knackered anyway. It was nice seeing… is it Marco?"

"Yeah, Marco. He's great," Dan said, carefully swirling hot water over the coffee he'd put into a V60 filter, and then reaching for milk from the fridge. The milk would be oat milk and the coffee, Josh knew without even looking, would be Fair Trade certified, sourced from a worker-owned co-operative with the highest ethical standards. Dan had taken some stick at university for the enthusiasm with which he attached himself to the latest and most fashionable social cause. Mocking voices had mostly quieted when, after graduation, he put his money where his mouth was by turning down tech companies offering him junior developer jobs on salaries that made even the newly-hired trainee solicitors look a little green. Instead, he'd joined a tiny start-up building an online skills and equipment marketplace to support tenant farmers in Africa. Josh had learned to live with the occasional small restriction on his own personal liberties, like not being allowed Nescafé in the flat.

"So what does Marco do?" Josh asked.

Dan paused, for some reason he seemed to be having difficulty saying it.

"He's a, um, penetration tester?"

Josh did his best to stifle a snigger, and failed.

"Don't say it." Dan said, looking mock-aggrieved.

"I didn't say anything! That sounds very interesting. What does a penetration tester do?"

"He tests security. Mostly for big companies. It's actually pretty cool, he basically spends his days trying to break into buildings."

"Well. That beats my job, so I shouldn't laugh. And I guess you don't need to worry about giving him keys to this place, so that's win-win."

"Maybe we should install another lock." Dan said. "Now, you using the shower, or can I get in ahead of you?"

"Go for it," Josh said. "I'm going to run into work and shower when I get there."

"You absolute nutter. Ok, have a great day."

3

Josh had run to the office, showered, changed, and reached his desk by 8am. The Project Sundown meeting wasn't until 9:30, but it was an all-morning session and he wanted an early start. He hoped that dealing with the overnight influx of emails from US colleagues and clients, and trying to tick off a few useful tasks would settle down the ripples of anxiety he'd been feeling and let him feel back in control of his workload.

By the time 9:25 came around, and he'd had another coffee in addition to the one he'd made at home and the one he'd bought on the way to the underground station, he was starting to feel ready to face the day. Jamie had sent him a terse Skype message, *'They're here'*, so he gathered up his laptop and notepad and made his way to the building's largest conference room. Vijai and Rob, who together formed one of the senior creative teams, were already there. They'd helped themselves to pastries from the array laid out on the sideboard at the back, and were doing their usual bickering about football as Josh walked in.

"Hey Josh."

"Hey guys. Clients not here yet?"

"Nope. Or, yes, but Jamie and Susan are showing them round the building first. You know who they are?"

"No idea, you?"

"Sort of," Bob answered. "BluJacket Corp. Some kind of tech start up slash defence contractor slash save the world thing?"

"Ok. Well, that beats yogurt advertising, I guess." Josh had spent the last six months on a particularly dull campaign for a major food brand. He wondered if talking about working for a defence contractor on dates might do more harm than good. Perhaps he'd have to lean hard on whatever the 'save the world thing' was.

"Hey!" Vijai threw a pencil at Josh. "Yogurt advertising paid for my extension. Don't knock it."

Just as Josh reached to the floor to retrieve the pencil, the door opened, and Josh stood up a little too hurriedly, attracting a curious glance from Jamie as he ushered people into the room. With him were Susan — the client services director and Jamie's direct boss — and three people who, despite their similar taste in Patagonia fleeces, could hardly have looked more different. The first to enter was a pale, skinny, man with sandy red hair who appeared to be only a little older than Josh; late 20s or early 30s at most. He looked tired and had the beginnings of a scruffy, patchy beard. He was followed by a young Black woman about Josh's age, although she had an air of relaxed confidence that made her seem older than Josh or any of his friends. The third person was a bulky but fit-looking man in his late thirties with tightly cropped hair, a deep tan, and a thick beard. The three of them took seats around the table and, almost in unison, retrieved MacBooks from their bags and opened them. Jamie turned on the giant screen at one end of the room.

"You can connect to the screen if you want to, a code will

come up in just a second… there we go."

The big, tanned man looked at the young woman.

"Abeke, you want to do the honours?"

"Happy to," she said, and tapped a code into her laptop, making her laptop display appear on the screen.

Josh tried not to stare, but she was striking; dark-skinned with a heart-shaped hairstyle of tight curls. Her outfit of a grey, quarter-zip fleece and jeans would have been generic tech-bro attire on anyone else. On her it managed to look rugged and down-to-earth while accentuating her figure in a way that was somehow far more attractive than conventional business attire would have been.

Susan spoke, snapping Josh's attention back to the meeting.

"Right, shall we do a quick round of intros then? I think everyone knows me; Susan Pierce, Client Services Director here at BBA\Rowley. Jamie?"

"Jamie Lyons-Baker, I'm a Senior Account Director and I'll be leading on the agency's work for you. Uh, who's next?"

There was a second's pause, so Josh went next.

"Josh Collins. I'm an Account Manager. I guess I'll be more of a day-to-day contact." Actually he had no idea what he'd be doing, since no one had told him, but 'I'll be sitting pointlessly in meetings pretending to take notes' didn't seem like quite the line to take.

Vijai and Rob went next, introducing themselves as a Senior Copywriter and Senior Art Director respectively, and explaining that they'd come up with creative marketing and branding ideas. Vijai's momentary hesitation and vague explanation of his work suggested that, like Josh, he didn't have much idea of what they were going to be asked to do for the mysterious client.

"Great, well, guys, I'm really stoked to be here and thanks for taking the time to talk to us." The bearded guy spoke next. He was clearly American, but didn't have one of the four American accents that Josh could reliably place; South, New Jersey, Fargo, California. "I'm Chris Adamson, founder and CEO of BluJacket. Abeke?"

"Hey everyone." She sounded a little more definably Californian. "I'm Abeke Hart, Marketing Manager at BluJacket." Her voice had a friendly, open quality that was, quite apart from the accent, somehow very American.

Finally, the other man introduced himself.

"And I'm Pete Taylor, Chief Technical Officer." His accent was clearly Scottish, and incongruous after his two colleagues. "I, uh, wrote a lot of the early code for our product as part of my PhD, and now I oversee the technical side of things." He rubbed nervously at his beard, and looked back at Chris, who took back over smoothly as Abeke brought a presentation up on the big screen.

"BluJacket was founded five years ago when I left the United States Army," Chris said. "During my service I saw first-hand the ever-more complicated range of threats faced by our personnel in the field, and I saw the potential to use cutting edge technology to offer safety to combat personnel, as well as law enforcement and private citizens at home and abroad. I partnered with Pete, who has spent years studying artificial intelligence and machine learning. Between us, we developed the BluJacket Shield System, a revolutionary AI product that uses the most advanced neural networks and real-time situational analysis to provide unparalleled protection to those still serving in the military and law enforcement, at home and overseas."

Chris paused and looked around expectantly, and then gathered his thoughts and moved on, nodding to Abeke to advance a slide. It brought up a slick, graphical timeline with milestones that started with the company's founding in 2016 and went on to include such technology updates as 'first deep learning protocol trialled'. It also included the logos of organisations providing venture capital funding, as well as an increasing number of government departments partnering with BluJacket on testing their equipment.

"To date we have raised nearly half a billion dollars in funding, and have proofs of concept in place with front-line government bodies in more than a dozen countries. While this is of course enormously exciting, we're not content with this pace of growth. We're looking for the next big step, and that means... next slide please –"

Abeke clicked on again. Stock imagery appeared of worried suburban families with children, contrasted with what were probably news shots of rioters and robbers.

"– that means taking the product to the consumer market. Law-abiding families today face more threats than at any time in history, and are increasingly looking to use the same type of technology available to law enforcement and the armed forces, to protect themselves. BluJacket is able to offer safe and affordable protection technology in the home and out in public, and reaching this new market has the potential to open unprecedented new revenue streams. We're in the process of raising a Series C round to fund this exciting growth. So why, you might be asking, have we come to the wonderful London agency of BBA\Rowley?"

Abeke clicked forward one more slide. It showed screen-captures of what was clearly the BluJacket website, along with a couple of logos and promotional banners. It was dull and corporate, heavy on gradients and faux-metallic textures, and Josh even thought he saw a lens flare in there somewhere. The kind of thing that might have pleased a roomful of Generals at the Pentagon, but was unlikely to take the business far in the consumer marketplace. So, the answer to at least part of Chris's rhetorical question was clear. They'd come to BBA\Rowley because, when it came down to it, selling innovative protection products to frightened suburbanites wasn't really all that different to selling them yogurt.

At that point, the presentation was taken over by Pete, the CTO. The powerpoint itself changed from the previous flood of stock imagery and aspirational statements to animated diagrams. Information was sent from devices to servers to clouds to APIs and back again. Signals bounced between layers of blue dots representing, Josh gathered, a deep learning neural network. It was hardly surprising that, as Pete wrapped up with a quiet, "so, any questions on the technology side of things?" there was nothing but silence for a moment.

"Ah, no, well, I think most of that went over my head," said Susan, finally, to relieved laughter from just about everyone else in the room. "But I'm sure it gives us enough to focus on the branding, positioning and messaging pieces... Vijai, Rob, do you have enough to be getting on with?"

"Sure," said Vijai slowly. "It's certainly a useful intro..."

"Will you be providing some detail on, well, what the product actually *is*?" Rob cut in, bluntly. There was a brief silence, and then Chris laughed.

"Well of course," he said, cheerfully. "We just need the NDA in place, and then we can pull a proper brief together, can't we Pete?"

"Of course." Pete smiled. "I'll get right on it when I get back to the office."

"Ok then," said Susan. "That's great. Anything else?"

There was plenty else, of course. A long discussion about brand identity, consumer personas, marketing channels, KPIs and objectives, and other topics. Those were increasingly handled by Abeke and less by the former US soldier. Abeke appeared to have no end of detail at her fingertips, and no fear of asking direct questions.

"What size team will you have on this?" "What are the timelines for delivery?" "What is your approach to iterating on the brand identity?" "How will you ensure that any new identity can be incorporated easily into existing digital assets?" "What is your engagement model for working with BluJacket?" "How regularly will we meet?" "How will the budget be managed?" Jamie and Susan fielded the queries between them; alternating, like an amateur tennis double desperately trying to hold their own against a single world-class player. Josh took notes, feeling a little relieved at not being the target of Abeke's polite interrogation.

It was Jamie who eventually directed Abeke's attention towards Josh.

"So, on a lot of these questions, can I recommend you engage directly with Josh as your main point-of-contact, and he can work through these items with you."

"Ok, that sounds good. Josh, if you have ten minutes at the end, why don't we hang back and we can talk through some of the detail?"

"Oh, yeah, sure," said Josh, quickly, unsure whether to curse Jamie for throwing him under the bus, or silently thank him for setting up the opportunity to get to know Abeke a bit better.

"Great." The conversation circled back to the more comfortably intangible topic of brand strategy, and eventually Susan brought the meeting to a close and offered to show Chris and Pete out. Jamie, Vijai, and Bob followed them, Jamie tagging along close behind his boss while Vijai and Bob went straight back to their own part of the office. Josh and Abeke were left alone.

"I won't take up too much of your time, Josh, I'm sure you're busy."

"It's fine, really."

"I know we'll be working pretty closely together, so it's

The London Agency

good to finally put a face to the name, actually."

"Oh... really? You knew you'd be working with me?"

"Yes." She looked surprised. "You were shown as one of the team members in the pitch deck. I think Chris found your background quite an important factor, actually."

Josh stiffened. He couldn't believe they'd used him all along for leverage in the pitch, while keeping him in the dark about the client.

"Is everything ok?" Abeke was looking at him, a little startled.

"Oh, yes, fine, I'm sorry. I just felt bad that I hadn't introduced myself earlier. Since we'll be working together. Anyway, talk me through what you need from me."

"Hey, Jamie," Josh walked up behind Jamie, who was standing by the coffee machine. Josh had shown Abeke out, and then gone hunting for his boss.

"Hey mate."

"Why did you pull me onto the BluJacket account."

"We need people on it. Why?"

"Is that the only reason? Why was I in the pitch deck when I didn't even know about them until yesterday?"

"We just knew you'd be good for it."

"Good for it how?"

Jamie finally turned to face Josh.

"What's the problem here? It's an exciting account. You don't want it?"

"Come on Jamie. Apparently Chris 'found my background interesting' and I don't think that means he was excited to talk to me more about my 2:1 in Medieval History."

Jamie shifted slightly from foot to foot.

"Yeah, ok I know about that."

"And?"

Jamie sighed. "Clients value account managers who

understand their product. None of us here know shit about the army."

"*I* don't know shit about the army, Jamie. My dad was killed in action, *that's* why you put me on this, isn't it?"

"Of course not. We just try to align people to accounts that they'll connect with, why does that bother you so much?"

"It bothers me that you used me. You should have just asked. If these guys have invented something that keeps soldiers safe then, ok, I'm invested. I see why that's good. But this isn't something you should use to help you win pitches, without even asking me."

"The client was secret, mate, no one was allowed to know about it until they'd come in for the meeting. I told you that. Look, I'm sorry. I'm genuinely sorry. We knew you'd be good for the account, so we put you on it, and then we were doing everyone's bios for the slides and it just made sense to mention you had a military connection. It was literally three or four words on one slide in a 100-slide presentation, but then Chris asked about it in the pitch so we explained. I promise, mate, we weren't trying to be underhanded."

"Yeah, well. It is what it is." Josh looked at the floor. He already knew he'd regret everything about this conversation later, and he couldn't handle a confrontation with Jamie. The man was adept at making Josh feel like the bad guy no matter what he said.

"I'll go and check in with Vijai and Bob about those initial designs then, huh?" Josh said, finally.

"Yeah, yeah, do that please mate. Nice one. Thanks." Jamie hurried away before the discussion could go on any longer.

Josh walked over to the desks where Vijai and Bob sat. They had a lot more space than the account managers down at the other end of the building. Two desks, facing each other, with a sofa next to them. He dropped into the sofa, feeling suddenly exhausted. He busied himself with opening his laptop and finding the copious notes he'd made during the meeting.

"So, guys. You happy with the brief?"

There was a short silence. Vijai looked more serious than normal, and Bob was drumming his fingers on his desk awkwardly.

"'Happy' probably isn't the word," Vijai said slowly.

"Why not?"

"Are they going to send us legally reviewed marketing claims?" Vijai asked, not answering the question.

"Uh, I guess so, if we ask? Do we need them?" Said Josh, floundering slightly.

"Yup." Said Rob. Josh looked at him.

"What's up, guys? You're *not* happy with the brief?"

"The brief is fine. But you know, if we're making performance claims about a safety-critical product, ethically we need to be sure they're properly approved, right?"

"I guess so. It's not really something that's come up before." Josh wasn't sure any of his previous client work could be described as 'safety-critical'. "But can you make a start on the work in the meantime?"

"We can make a start, Josh," said Vijai, somewhat back to his usual reassuring tone. "But the bigger problem is that right now we don't even properly know what the product is, or how it works. That's a bit crazy, if we're expected to market the thing."

"Honestly," Rob added, "it's just a red flag for me when someone starts making all these grand claims about artificial intelligence this and machine learning that, but won't get specific about how it all works. It might sound good when they're raising their billions in Silicon Valley, but you know how much of this stuff actually works in the real world? Not a lot. Let's be really sure before we start hawking it to the family next door and telling them it'll keep their kids safe walking to school, huh?"

"Look," said Vijai, trying to calm his creative partner down a bit, "they promised to get us some more technical detail. Maybe you can just chase that up? Be clear that we need a proper explanation of what it is, how it works, and how exactly it keeps people safe."

Josh tried to squash his feeling of irritation. He liked Vijai and Rob but they were sheltered from the pressure of demanding clients and tight deadlines. It was Josh whose life was made more difficult when they introduced these complexities. Or perhaps, though he hated to admit it, what really annoyed him was the fact that they cared enough about the work to raise these sorts of complaints in the first place. Josh so often just wanted to shout at them to hurry up and do the bare minimum required to keep the customer happy so they could all get paid and go home.

He walked away from Rob and Vijai's desk, thinking about how he was going to approach this with BluJacket.

4

Josh spent a little too long polishing an email to Abeke Hart to ask for the materials that Vijai and Rob wanted. He wanted to go for breezy but professional, but that wasn't a particularly easy thing to pull off, especially not for someone who tended to overthink even the simplest of emails.

In this case, Josh didn't have an opportunity for that, since Abeke responded almost instantly.

Hi Josh,
   Really great to meet you yesterday!

He re-read that line a couple of times and grinned, despite suspecting it was nothing more than American effusiveness.

Thanks for the follow-up on the detailed technical documents. Pete is just pulling this together and it will be with you by EOD today.
   In the meantime, could we arrange a time to get together and discuss the timing plan. I'm happy to come to your office, let me know a slot that works for you in the next day or so?
   All the best,

Abeke

He left it for a bit. *No one* expected instant responses to emails, and it was far more comfortable having that friendly email from Abeke sitting in his inbox than it was taking the concrete action of drafting a reply.

Trying to distract himself from an interaction that he knew he was over-thinking, Josh opened an email from Rob. It had Vijai in CC, and was a one-liner directing Josh to a YouTube video, with the simple instruction 'check this out and you'll see what I mean!'

The link opened a YouTube channel called 'Mickene Learning', which described itself as 'a channel for the skeptical and curious to learn about AI, and learn to recognise bullshit when they see it'. Just about every video thumbnail was a clunky mess of screengrabs overlaid with bright yellow or red text saying things like 'Debunked' or 'Vaporware'. One of the titles mentioned Artificial Intelligence, so Josh clicked on that.

It opened with a polished, corporate video showing a gently animated slideshow of stock images; smiling couples and families of all possible ethnicities and gender combinations. A female voice with a very slight Indian accent spoke reassuringly over the video.

"Your and your family's health is more important than anything to you, but how can you know what treatments are right for you? Our proprietary machine learning algorithm uses advanced artificial intelligence to analyse and assess every detail of your diet and lifestyle and make customised recommendations so that you can live a healthier, hap—"

"Bullshit." A new voice cut in, and the slideshow disappeared to be replaced with a round-faced man sitting in what looked like his study or sitting room, facing directly into the camera.

"Welcome back to another Mickene Learning video, I'm your host Mickey Cook and I'm here to debunk bullshit, expose scams, and hopefully educate you all about *real* artificial intelligence, *proper* machine learning and how it works." He spoke quickly, with an American accent and a polished ease that suggested this intro, or something much like it, was something he'd said many, many times before.

"What you saw a second ago was the promotional video produced for WellSolve, a company that didn't exist six months ago but now has half a million dollars of your money. If, that is, you were stupid enough to support their kickstarter. Half a million dollars is quite a lot of money for a company with no track record, no functional product, and only two full-time staff but it's hardly any money if you want to build a machine learning algorithm that analyses —" at this point the pitch of his voice raised as he pointedly quoted the previous clip "'—every detail of your diet and lifestyle'. No big deal folks, just let me quickly analyse every *single* detail of your lifestyle, shove it into my magic computer and then tell you what brand of hot dogs to eat. Ladies and Gentlemen, I don't know how many times I have to say it, but Machine Learning is not a magic box." He paused for breath and the screen changed to show a long text document. Areas of highlighting animated in as Mickey Cook went on. "Now, let's analyse their claims in a bit more detail…"

Josh tapped ahead a few times in the lengthy video and watched bits and pieces of Mickey's dissection of the start-up's business. Then he watched the intros of several more videos from the channel. Quite a few were about kickstarters or start-ups that had recently raised eye-watering amounts of funding. Almost all were claiming some sort of use of artificial intelligence, machine learning, deep learning, neural networks or other cutting-edge jargon to make impossible-sounding promises possible.

Mickey, it was clear even to Josh, was both highly knowledgeable about artificial intelligence, and not inclined to let the smallest mistake or questionable detail go unchallenged. He painted a compelling picture of a rash of start-ups that liked to use AI terminology to make their products sound more impressive and their promises more credible. All the same, he never gave the impression he thought *all* AI-based technology was nonsense. So, thought Josh, with more than a little irritation, he wasn't really sure what Rob's point was in sending it over. It told them nothing about BluJacket either way.

On that note, Josh realised he probably couldn't delay replying to Abeke any more. He managed, after only three redrafts, to express an appropriately professional delight at the prospect of a meeting and to suggest a couple of options the next day or the day after. He sent it and, when he received no response other than a meeting invite for the following morning, with the subject line *'Josh <> Abeke | BluJacket Digital Campaign Timelines'* he wasn't sure whether to be pleased or slightly disappointed.

When Josh eventually got home, Dan was out, and the flat was locked and dark. Grateful, for once, for the peace and quiet, he cooked himself a supermarket pizza and sat cross-legged on the big corner sofa in the living room with his laptop.

Josh opened a new Google tab and began searching for information on BluJacket Corp. A simple search for the name returned news articles in technology publications, along with a profile on Crunchbase showing their meteoric rise in funding and valuations. There was also a Wikipedia article that even a cursory glance suggested was mostly a puff piece written by someone working for BluJacket. Perhaps, Josh thought suddenly, it was written by Abeke, given that she was responsible for their marketing.

Resisting the temptation to read further into the author's contribution history, he opened up some of the news articles. Almost all were clearly based on the same handful of press releases, each pushed out following another successful round of venture fundraising. The same few quotes from Chris Adamson appeared in all of them; forever delighted to be working with another terrific VC fund, always excited about the future of AI-enabled defensive solutions, never specific about exactly how the technology worked.

Only one of the articles appeared to be even slightly curious about the precise details of what BluJacket had built to justify their eye-watering valuation. The profile of the company in that article was a little less slavishly positive than the rest and ended with a final paragraph pointing out that, 'while BluJacket tells a compelling story about the power of artificial intelligence and machine learning to provide situational awareness to soldiers on the battlefield, police officers in the street, and even families on their weekly shop – it is less forthcoming when asked to provide details of just how it proposes to do so.'

Feeling no more certain of what to believe about the unusual new client, Josh eventually closed his laptop and turned on the television in the living room, bringing up Amazon Prime and another episode of *Bosch*.

Josh was debating whether to watch one more episode when he heard the door open. A second later, Dan appeared in the doorway of the living room.

"Evening mate. Mind if I join you?"

"Go for it." Josh hit the back button on the remote, stopping another episode from playing automatically. "How was your day? You been out with Marco?"

"Yup. He had to head up North for a job, so we had drinks

in town before he left. And, yeah, day was good thanks. Nearly got the first version of the app ready to go. I might be going over to Mozambique at some point to work with our team out there on launching it."

"That's pretty exciting." Josh tried to sound like he meant it and, in a way, he did. He'd never begrudged Dan any of his success but sometimes he did, just slightly, begrudge him his sense of purpose in life. Josh had had that once, and when it had suddenly vanished along with his offer to train as an Army Officer, he'd struggled to replace it.

"Yeah, it's cool," Dan said, dismissively. "How's work with you?"

"Oh, not bad. I'm working on a new client, it's pretty crazy."

"Crazy how?"

"Oh, well, the company's this American defence tech start-up. It's all weirdly secretive. But also, you should see their marketing manager. Honestly Dan, even you'd fancy her."

"Oh really," Dan said, elongating the 'really' with exaggerated curiosity. "Tell me all about her."

Dan and Josh had long had a habit of talking to each other about the ups and downs of their love lives; moping about a hopeless crush, boasting excitedly about a successful early date, or venting about heartbreak. Settling back into that routine was easy, and Josh enjoyed the feeling of regressing to university days when he'd come home and tell Dan about some beautiful girl he'd met after a lecture, or in the cross country team.

"I mean, she's definitely hot. But she's smart as shit, too. She made Jamie and Susan look like idiots when she was grilling them at the end…"

"Sounds out of your league, pal," Dan said, with a smile.

Josh looked for something to throw at him and, not finding anything suitable, made do with a lighthearted "fuck off".

"I'm kidding," Dan said. "She'd be lucky to have you. And, apparently Americans just love a British accent…"

"I might need more than that going for me."

"Sure. It's a start though, isn't it."

"It's a start," Josh agreed.

5

Amber watched the cops pull up to the kerb in two black SUVs. The wheels barely stopped turning before every door on both vehicles opened, and the street was full of dark green uniforms, body armour, and rifles. These weren't the local Fort Pinebec police, and they weren't the regular county cops either — their bulky body armour had black and yellow patches on the back saying 'SWAT'. Amber knew all about them; she'd lived in this neighbourhood more than long enough to have seen a few SWAT raids. A lot of shouting, a lot of destruction, and some startled looking guy — it was always a guy — dragged out of his home in his underwear. There was never any gunfire; at least not that she recalled. Though she'd certainly heard stories of people shot dead in their homes by police serving an early morning warrant and reacting a little too rapidly to a surprised homeowner reaching for a phone, a pair of glasses or, that most common of items in this part of America, a legally-held firearm.

Amber wondered which house they were raiding today. It wouldn't be the one they'd pulled up outside; she knew they liked to park up a block or two away and then move quietly in on the target property so as not to wake the occupants or alert them to the team's arrival. Sure enough, they set off in practised formation; six of them disappearing down an alleyway that ran parallel to the road, and another two moving along the sidewalk, sticking close to the high garden fences so that they couldn't easily be seen from within the houses.

Both of the visible cops were wearing shallow helmets that curved over the top of their heads, leaving the sides open around the ears. Below the helmets, their eyes were covered by bulky wraparound glasses with clear lenses. Amber noticed that each of their helmets had what liked like a wide-lens camera mounted on both front and back. She'd seen the patrol cops with their chest-mounted body-cameras, and assumed this was a more sophisticated version of the same idea. The theory that police officers would behave better if their every move was captured on camera didn't yet seem to be borne out by the evidence, but she supposed it couldn't hurt.

As she watched, waiting to see who was going to be today's lucky recipient of a no-knock warrant, she saw Nate Adams, next-door's teenage kid, come out of the front door of his home wearing trainers, running shorts, and a hoody. He half turned towards the street and, bouncing slightly from foot to foot to keep warm, looked down at his running watch. Amber wasn't sure if he'd even noticed the two cops halfway down the street, and thought of warning him, but they were walking in the opposite direction and he'd see them as soon as he looked up from his watch and set off on his run.

Days later, when Amber would recount events to a confused and curious reporter, she'd say she couldn't remember what came first; the quiet 'beep' as Nate's watch finally connected to enough satellites to locate him on GPS, or the shout of "GUN" from one of the cops down the street.

Both seemed to happen almost on top of each other, and Amber swung her gaze from Nate to the cop. He was still turning round, rotating a full 180 degrees as he brought his rifle up to an aimed stance and then, with barely a seconds hesitation, fired two shots directly into Nate's body.

The silence after the shots was paralysing. Amber felt as if she was wading through treacle as she ran to Nate and tried to stem the blood that trickled from neat holes in one side of his chest and poured from huge exit wounds in the other. She didn't even hear the police officers telling her to stand back, but eventually one of them pulled her away while the other attempted some cursory and pointless first aid. She didn't hear the sirens as more county sheriffs arrived to control the scene, or the roar of the SUV engines as the SWAT team left — their warrant abandoned. But later, long after the shock had worn off and her hearing had returned, and she'd washed Nate's blood off her hands, and was sitting by the side of the road watching an Internal Affairs investigator take notes at the scene, what she mostly didn't hear was anyone asking her for her version of what had happened.

Unwilling to break a painfully-developed habit and voluntarily approach the police with information, she told a neighbour to give her details to the investigator if they asked for them, and then went home to drink three glasses of wine with a shaking hand, and put off the moment when she knew she'd have to walk back over to Nate's house and face his mother.

6

Josh woke up feeling nervous. Specifically nervous, for once, as opposed to the usual ill-defined pre-work anxiety that occasionally chewed at him between waking up at 5am and his alarm going off an hour later.

So, regular old nervousness, and a little excitement, was a pleasant change. As was lingering longer than usual over his wardrobe for the day. Generally, he could get away with jeans and a t-shirt at the office and even most client meetings only really necessitated ensuring the jeans were clean and swapping the t-shirt for a polo shirt or perhaps some checked flannel. BluJacket clearly favoured Silicon Valley chic and wouldn't expect a suit and tie, but he was keen to make a good impression.

Lacking any Patagonia gear, or a gilet of any kind, he settled on a pair of skinny khaki cords and a soft grey shirt, untucked and rolled up to just below the elbow. There would be no running into the office today, even though that was his usual habit on a Thursday morning; a pre-emptive effort to offset the heavy drinking that was more or less mandatory on Thursday evenings at BBA\Rowley. Instead of his running backpack, he slid his laptop into a smart blue shoulder bag that he almost never used, and set off for the underground station.

Fifteen minutes before the meeting, he went into the conference room, set up his laptop and the screen, cleaned off the huge whiteboard wall that took up one side of the room, and called down to reception to check they were sending up the tea and coffee he'd requested. Then he sat at the table, drumming his fingers on the desk and refreshing his inbox to make sure he didn't miss the email that usually came in from reception when a visitor arrived for him.

At exactly 9:55; *Hi Josh, Abeke Hart is in reception for you.* He locked his laptop, speed-walked to the lift, and pressed the button for the lobby, smoothing his hair in the mirrored door as the lift went down.

Abeke was waiting in reception, sitting on one of the angular purple sofas and looking intently at her phone. She looked up as he approached, and gave him a smile that immediately reminded him of the easy warmth that he'd found so attractive when he'd first met her. He'd wondered how much of that was a professional facade but, now that he was meeting her one-on-one, she seemed relaxed and friendly, talking animatedly as they took the lift back up to his floor.

"I love your office, honestly. I thought that when I came here last time - it must be such a nice place to work."

"Ah, yeah. It's got a good vibe, I guess."

"That's it, exactly. Such a creative atmosphere." Turning his limp words into something more polished; you could tell she was a marketing professional. They exited the lift and walked through the cavernous space that housed the account management team; pods of desks surrounded by exposed brickwork and broken up by soft seating areas, foosball tables, and roaming whiteboards. The meeting room was at the far end of the building, and when they arrived Josh was pleased to see that a cart had been wheeled in while he was gone. It had two large pump action thermoses on top, four mugs, and a little plate of biscuits.

"Well this is nice." Abeke commented, as she came in. "Thanks for sorting it. We're using a WeWork while we're in London but getting hold of meeting rooms there can be a pain in the butt."

"So your main office is in Silicon Valley, right? That's pretty cool."

"Oh, thank you. Yeah, we're in Palo Alto which is awesome for sure, although honestly I can't get enough of London. Have you been to California?"

"Yeah. Not Palo Alto, but I've been to San Francisco. I did the San Francisco Marathon a few years ago actually." He felt himself blush slightly, worried that he sounded boastful, and busied himself with the thermoses. "Tea or coffee?"

"Coffee please. Milk, no sugar. A marathon, though! That's amazing, how was it?"

"Well San Francisco isn't exactly flat." He said, pleased to hear her laugh at the comment. "So, yeah, it was a great way to see the city, but not my fastest run ever. Is this your first time in London?"

"It sure is. I've always wanted to go though. When Chris said he wanted to use a London agency for this project I didn't exactly argue with him!"

Josh laughed. "Yeah, London is great to be fair. I've only been here a few years myself, so I'm still loving getting to know it. How long are you here for?"

"Oh, I'm staying a whole month while we get the marketing launch done. Chris and Pete are just here for a couple of weeks, mainly seeing investors I think."

"Nice." Josh hesitated, wondering if Abeke's willingness to pack up and work in London for a month implied that she didn't have a partner back home, and then wondering if he should take the opportunity to ask.

"Well," he said after a second, realising he'd missed the moment. "Here's your coffee, grab a seat anywhere - it's just us for now; the creative team are available later if we want to pull them in, but I think we mainly want to talk timings and project planning?"

"Ah, back to business. Ok, let's go."

She set her laptop up, and they began to go painstakingly through the details of everything BBA\Rowley was expected to deliver. Creative concepts, copy, web designs, website build, digital advertisements, a video script, and various other assets and side-projects. Everything had its own deadline, and as Josh began plugging it all into his word document he was already starting to despair at how any of it would be achievable, but that was another problem for another day. He felt well-prepared with details of how the agency operated and what BluJacket could expect as a client, and the conversation felt collaborative with none of the interrogation that he'd feared.

"One thing, actually, Abeke," he said once all the items were in the document. "You were going to send over the detailed product explanation yesterday. Is there any update on those?"

For the first time since the meeting had started, she looked a little uncomfortable.

"Oh, yeah. I'm sorry. That's taking a bit longer than expected, but we'll get it to you. Can we just move forward in the meantime?"

"We can," he said, but already knowing that that wasn't really true. "It's just that the creative team don't really feel able to work on concepts without know more precisely how the product works."

"Well, we did provide the pitch deck, I think?"

"Yeah... It's just that, honestly, the pitch deck gives us the benefits but there's not a lot of detail. Like, we understand the product uses AI to identify threats, but we're still a bit in the dark about how it works. I mean, even if you can explain it to me, maybe I can reassure them?"

"I'm honestly not sure I can. We definitely have documents, it's just that Chris is kind of obsessive about secrecy."

"Oh really?"

"Yeah. It's probably his army background. Winds Pete up. But then Pete's forever putting stuff in emails and chat messages that he probably shouldn't... I've heard them have stand-up rows about it. Anyway, look, I'll chat to Pete again and I'm sure he'll give me something soon."

She said it with an air of finality that seemed to end that line of discussion.

"Ok, that would be great. Can I refill your coffee?"

"Oh yes, thanks." Her smile seemed to completely dispel the awkward moment, and they moved on to the next topic.

When Josh and Abeke packed up at the end of two hours, Josh had that rare glow of satisfaction he occasionally got at the end of a client meeting where he felt he'd acquitted himself particularly well. The glow was only made brighter by the thought that he'd managed to, if not actually impress Abeke, at least hold his own as they discussed the complex moving parts of the marketing campaign.

It was that, and the release of all the nervousness he'd felt in the morning, that gave him enough courage to ever-so casually make a suggestion as they walked to the lift.

"I hope you enjoy your month in London. If you ever wanted showing around while you're here, do let me know. Not that I'm an expert, or anything, but it's always nice having a local guide, isn't it...?"

He tailed off, trying to gauge her reaction without being too obvious.

"Oh, absolutely!" She sounded enthusiastic, although a tiny cynical part of him wondered if that was just politeness. "That would be lovely, if you're sure. I'd hate to take your time up outside of work as well."

"No, no, it would be fun. I'll email you anyway with the notes from today, and we can set something up if you'd like to."

With that, the lift doors opened and Abeke stepped in.

"Can't wait! See you soon," she said, and pressed the button for the lobby.

7

Chris Adamson, the BluJacket founder, hung up his phone and placed it very carefully on the little desk, taking a moment to straighten it so that it aligned exactly with the edges of the desk. Then he stood up and swore briefly but loudly.

"Fuck."

If anyone in the next-door rooms heard him, there was no sign of it, no banging on the wall or yell to shut up. These fancy London hotels were well-built, he thought. Proper walls.

"Fuck," he said again, quietly, almost plaintively, and sat back down at the desk. He drummed his fingers thoughtfully for half a minute then picked up his phone again and dialled a number.

"Yes?" The voice on the other end answered almost immediately.

"It's Chris."

"I know. What do you want?"

"Have you seen the news?"

"I've seen all sorts of news." The voice said. "Are you

talking about Colorado?"

"Of course I am. You understand the implication?"

"I'm not stupid, Chris. I understand that this absolute cluster-fuck is a threat to all the hard work we've put in. Which is why I'm struggling to understand why you're talking to me instead of. Sorting. It. The fuck. Out." The voice hissed out the last few words.

"I *am* sorting it. It's controllable. But I need to know this doesn't put the pilot at risk."

"This puts everything at risk. If it's 'controllable', then you need to control all fuck out of it, or the committee will drop you like a rabid dog."

"There's no need for any of this. It's sorted, just manage things your end and keep the pilot on track." Chris said, biting back a more violent retort.

"My end is managed. My end has always been 'managed'. Don't call me until this pile of horseshit is back in its fucking box. Good night."

"Good night." Chris said, though he wasn't sure if the call had already been disconnected.

Chris thought for a second, and then grabbed his laptop, checked he had his keycard, and went out into the corridor. He walked three doors down, and tapped lightly on the door. He caught a swish of shadow behind the viewhole as the occupant checked out who was there, and then the door opened.

"Hey Pete," Chris said, stepping in.

"Yeah come in, come in. Was that you I heard effing and blinding down the hall?"

"I have no idea what that means. Have you got some whisky?"

"No. What's the matter?"

"What about the minibar?"

"It's empty," Pete said, sitting on his bed and picking up

his laptop. "They don't fill it unless you request specially. What is the matter?"

Frustrated, Chris dropped himself onto the small armchair in the corner of the hotel room, and rubbed his forehead.

"What's going on with the Colorado pilot, Pete?" He asked.

"What do you mean?"

"Come on. Nothing happens in The Mind that you don't know about."

Pete scratched at the patchy beard on his right cheek. He was trying, not for the first time, to grow himself the most in-vogue accessory at a company with so many ex-military employees. As always, though, it had got to the eight-day point where it neither looked good nor felt good and he would eventually have to give up and shave it off.

"There have been some unexpected behaviours. And perhaps some bugs," he said. "But you know that, that's what pilots are for."

"Not this kind of bug. Jesus Christ, Pete. This could be catastrophic."

"Obviously I'm not happy about this. We're running a root cause analysis as we speak, but this wasn't entirely unforeseeable."

"Not entirely unforeseeable?" Chris's voice rose an octave. "Are you shitting me? It was unforeseen by the committee, or they'd never have given us the go-ahead on Aleppo."

"Chris, calm down. The real problem here wasn't a bug, anyway. The problem was user-error. It's no different to anything that's happened a hundred times in testing —"

"It fucking is. No one died in testing." Chris interrupted.

"Ok, but that's my point. The difference here is entirely down to the action by the end user. Our system in the hands of a responsible user, creates no risk to the user or the public. That hasn't changed."

"Dude," Chris raised his arms in a pleading gesture. "Don't talk to me like you're writing a press release. That is not how the public will see it. It's not how the committee will see it. Or the investors. We *cannot* afford problems at this stage. There's too much money and too many careers on the line."

"Well, then, maybe it's best if the public and the investors don't gain too much insight into this for now."

"What does that mean?"

"That's your department, Chris, not mine. I have an RCA to run and some system bugs to iron out."

There was a long silence. Finally Chris spoke.

"Ok. I'll speak to Bill."

"I really don't want to know." Pete said, opening his laptop and pointedly ignoring the other man.

8

Matt Ibarra first heard about the shooting of Nathan Adams, as was so often the way with these events, via a breaking news alert from his own newspaper. The information available in the alert was limited but, once he logged on to Twitter, there was a deluge of detail.

Matt's work had led him to follow dozens of accounts that fell into a loose affiliation that he could, depressingly, only think of as 'police shooting Twitter'. Not all of them tweeted exclusively about police shootings, of course. Many were BLM activists, or defund the police activists. Others were local journalists, and a handful were lawyers. Some held the police to account as a hobby, a few as a career. Whoever they were, between them they covered enough of the whole Twittersphere that it was rarely long after a police-involved shooting, especially one as public and as violent as that of Nate Adams, before the first tweets would start to enter Matt's timeline.

By now he'd seen enough of this sort of thing to instinctively be able to parse supposition from evidence, distinguish unreliable source from reliable, and make a fair guess at what had really happened and what was hyperbole. The facts in this case were shocking, familiar, and shocking in their familiarity; an unarmed young Black man out for a run was shot dead by a police officer who appeared to have mistaken an innocent hand movement for a threat.

Matt digested the information that was available, and took a few notes. He didn't investigate or even write about every police shooting that took place in the US. Most barely merited a mention, and when they did justify more in-depth coverage, that would be done by the news desks and written about by one of the many young journalists who worked on them.

Occasionally, though, an incident snagged his interest enough that he'd dig into it further. If it revealed some particularly egregious police behaviour or other fact that made it of wider national or international interest, his editor might be willing to turn it into an investigative piece and have Matt spend a few days or weeks working on it.

This one, despite the bleak familiarity of the facts, seemed like a candidate to attract wider interest. For one thing, there wasn't even a suggestion that the victim had done anything to explain the use of lethal force against him. For another, there was the fact that a SWAT team had been involved; these increasingly heavily-armed and militarised units were the subject of ever-growing scrutiny and Matt was curious about how exactly one came to be in a position to shoot an unarmed man outside his front door on a Sunday morning. He scribbled down some more notes on his pad and scrolled through a few more tweets, then he found one that made him stop scrolling, his pen frozen above his writing pad.

This tweet showed some grainy smartphone footage. The early morning light and the fact that it was filmed from behind a window the other side of the street from the police officers meant that the quality was less than perfect, but it was clear enough to show the two SWAT officers making their way down the sidewalk. At the very far edge of the frame, a figure in shorts and a hoody stepped into the shot and then disappeared again as the camera continued to track the police officers walking away. Another few seconds went by and suddenly, without warning, one of the police officers swung round a full 180 degrees and fired two shots. There was no sound in the video, but the flash and recoil were unmistakable, and the camera footage leapt in surprise, dropping down to show blurred wall and carpet. After a moment, it tentatively raised back up to the window and the scene outside. A crumpled body lay on the sidewalk, and a middle-aged Black lady rushed to his side. Finally, the video stopped altogether.

Matt knew from experience that the sensational footage would spread exponentially as horrified Twitter accounts shared it. But he also knew that there was a good chance that, at least to start with, Twitter would fight to remove it since it showed a young man's death in fairly graphic detail. Already, responses to the tweet argued equally vociferously for it to be removed out of respect for the family, and for it to be spread as widely as possible. Matt had no time at the moment to worry too much about either argument, he wanted the video to analyse in more detail, so he quickly opened up a tool that allowed him to download video from a tweet, and saved the footage to his laptop.

Matt loaded it into Adobe Premier Rush, a free editing tool he occasionally used. It was just consumer software, but it made it easier to click through a video frame by frame, going forwards and backwards at will. It also allowed him to make basic colour and exposure adjustments to try and clean up the dark and grainy footage and make some details more visible. By the time he'd watched it through half a dozen more times, he was even more certain than before that this was a story he had to pursue.

***

Luke, Matt's editor, picked up on the first ring.

"Matt, how are you?" He asked.

"Not bad. Luke, have you seen this police shooting in Colorado?"

Matt had walked to Park Slope, about 40 minutes walk from his little clapboard townhouse on East 2nd Street in Brooklyn. Close enough that on a sunny morning like today, he could stroll along 5th Avenue to where the numbered streets ended and his favourite coffee shops began. It was from there that he'd decided to call his editor. He had a feeling that it might be beneficial to be out in the fresh air for the conversation.

"Saw a news alert, that's all. Tell me about it."

"Seems like a SWAT officer from a county Sheriff's department shot dead an unarmed Black kid."

"Jesus. Well, I'm sure the news desk is all over it. Want me to check who's on it?"

"Nah, actually, I want to go there for a few days myself." Matt paid for his coffee, mouthed a thank you to the girl behind the counter, and took his coffee to an outdoor table.

"Why? If we need someone on the ground, they can send one of the kids." The kids were the young, keen, and worryingly cheap journalists who occupied much of the newsroom and could be deployed to work on fast-turnaround breaking news. Matt was supposed to focus on investigations; slow, expensive journalism that brought in just enough readers and won just enough awards to be worth the cost. For now.

"I think there's more to this. You should look at the video, it's very weird."

"Isn't there something a bit more significant you could be working on? Honestly we've done a lot on digging into police departments lately."

"You said I'd have the freedom to pursue whatever stories I wanted." Matt said, gently massaging the bridge of his nose in frustration.

"No, I said you'd have the freedom to pursue whatever stories you wanted as long as you brought in big exclusives. When was the last time you had something on the front page?"

"It's not my fault if they don't put my work on the front page."

"It is if the work isn't good enough." He paused. "Ok, I didn't mean that, I'm sorry."

"My work is good, Luke." Matt said. His voice was even but his nose-massaging was turning into driving his fingers into the corners of his eyes in an effort to stay calm.

"Yeah, it's good," Luke conceded. "But it's not always something people want to read. I hate to say it, Matt, but we *know* cops are racist, we *know* they're too quick to use force. This paper will never stop reporting on that, I promise you, but what's the value in another in-depth piece? What are you going to find out? Hey folks, here's an exclusive investigation by Matt Ibarra that shows cops are racist, over-conditioned to use lethal force, and not held accountable for their actions." He paused, and his mocking tone returned to normal. "You've got to help me out here. I fought to keep you on staff but there are kids half your age on half your salary who can report on this stuff."

"That's the problem. They'll report on it. I want to investigate it. People need to understand more than just 'it happened', else it keeps happening."

"Jesus Christ Matt, I give up. You want to go to Fort Pinebec, you go. But here's the deal: you do your investigation but you also get me some daily stories. Get us the basics, and I'll back you to go deeper for a few days."

"Alright. Thanks."

"Yeah, you're welcome. Don't make me regret it. Oh and Matt, keep me informed with how things go."

"Um, yeah, ok."

That wasn't a great sign. Matt had always had the freedom to do his investigations and then come back when they were well-formed. He wondered if Luke's desire to be kept in the loop reflected his eroding trust in Matt's journalism.

9

It took Matt nearly a day of travel to get to Fort Pinebec, the long flight from DC followed by nearly an hour in an Uber. When he arrived, he made straight for the Sherrif's department. A handful of local news trucks were gathered around the low, sprawling complex on the edge of town that housed the Sherriff's office and jail, as well as the warrants and probation service. A couple of news anchors and camera crews were stood at advantageous points with the main steps and front doors in the background, but none of them appeared to be currently on air. Matt approached one.

"Afternoon. I'm Matt Ibarra, with the Washington Record. You local?"

The anchor, a trim lady with dark brown hair and wearing a bright blue suit, shook his hand.

"Sure am. KFPC. My name's Chloe Quinn. You just got here?"

"Yup, flew right in. Much going on?"

"Not a whole lot. Sherriff gave a news conference this morning, there'll be another in just about an hour. Until then, not much to see or hear. We were over at the scene this morning, you been there yet?"

"Not yet, that's my next stop. I'd like to see this press conference though."

"Well, you won't be missing much if you don't, but that's your call. What brings the Washington Record here anyway?"

Matt shrugged. He didn't really want to get into it.

"I cover stories about police use of force and, well, this is certainly that."

"It certainly is."

There was a brief silence, then she spoke again.

"You're here because this is a weird one, right?"

"Are these ever not weird?"

"All depends on your point of view. But you know what I mean."

Matt didn't feel any particular rivalry with local TV news. Their priorities and processes, and audiences, were very different to his. But still, local journalists were well-connected and might have allegiances and agendas of their own, so he trod carefully.

"Perhaps," he replied. "What do *you* mean by weird one?"

"I've seen the video online. We've all seen this shit before and thought 'ain't no way you can justify that' but this is something else, right?"

"I guess so."

"You guess? You saw that cop. He hadn't even *seen* the kid, then he spins right round and shoots. What's that all about?"

"Hard to say. Has the department given any explanation?"

The anchor narrowed her eyes. Clearly she wasn't getting the full-throated endorsement from Matt that she'd hoped for.

"Not a word, man. Not a word. Sherriff said it's a tragedy, there'll be an investigation, not to pre-judge, and so on."

"What's he like, the Sherriff?"

She shrugged.

"Has a good rep around here I guess. No-bullshit attitude,

but folks mostly like that."

Matt just nodded. He couldn't disagree with anything that Chloe had said, but he preferred to play his cards close to his chest. He looked at his watch.

"So the next press conference is 6pm?" Chloe nodded. "The Sherriff usually on time?"

"Oh yeah, he's a stickler for timings."

That didn't give Matt time to get to the scene, or to do much else except wait here for the conference. That was ok, Chloe seemed like a talker and he was always happy to soak up some local gossip and then figure out what was relevant later.

Sure enough, the Sheriff strode out onto the front steps at exactly 5:55 pm and, by the time the assembled tv crews had gathered round and set their microphones up, it was 6 on the dot. Matt had imagined some barrel-chested stereotype of a sheriff but he was a small, skinny man with greying blond hair and a deep tan that contrasted with his crisply pressed khaki shirt.

"Good afternoon ladies and gentlemen. Thank you for your patience. For those of you who weren't here this morning," his eyes settled on Matt, "I am Sam Jones, Sheriff of Pinebec County." Sheriff Jones had the sort of quiet voice that's designed to make everybody shut up and listen.

"I will give a brief update on today's events and then I will answer any questions. From the top, let me reiterate what I said this morning; I ask you to show respect for the family of the young man who lost his life, and also for the police officer involved. This tragic situation does not need to be further inflamed. I trust that is entirely clear."

The assembled journalists shuffled their feet like chastened children. Jones continued in the same quiet, calm voice.

"At 06:57 yesterday morning, deputies of the Pinebec

County Special Weapons Team travelled to the unincorporated town of Lawharf to serve a warrant at a high risk address. During the course of proceeding to the address, the team encountered a nineteen-year-old male named Nathan Henry Adams. During this encounter, Mr Adams was shot and killed by one of the deputies. I am of course aware of unverified footage circulating on the internet that purports to show this encounter, and I do not propose to comment on this until such time as my department has been able to review and verify said footage."

He paused and looked down at his notes. Matt took the opportunity to raise a hand slightly and ask a question.

"Sheriff, are you able to explain…" He was cut off by the Sheriff speaking in the same low, calm tone as before.

"Sir, as I stated, I will take questions at the end. Now, since I last addressed you this morning, our investigation has been progressing and we have spoken to the deputies involved, as well as witnesses at the scene, in order to ascertain the fullest possible picture of events. Deputies from the Internal Affairs unit are leading the investigation, and the deputy who fired the shots has been placed on administrative leave at this time. I would once again call for a peaceful and calm response to this tragic situation, and for members of the public and the media not to prejudge this ongoing investigation. I will now take a few questions."

Matt jumped in quickly, raising his voice to be heard over the half-dozen questions all fired off at once.

"Sheriff, are you able to explain why your deputy shot Nathan Adams?"

"Sir, that will of course form part of our investigation. I can tell you that deputies, in common with all law enforcement officers, are able to use lethal force in response to a threat as they perceive it at the time,"

"Sheriff," Matt followed up quickly, "so are you saying that the deputy thought Mr Adams had a gun?"

"I am saying, sir, that a deputy may use lethal force if to do so is proportionate to the threat they perceive, as they perceive it, at the time. Yes, Mr Michaels, go ahead sir." The Sheriff pointedly ignored Matt and turned his eyes to another anchor over to Matt's right.

"Is there any evidence to suggest that Mr Adams was armed?"

"At this time we have not recovered any weapons from the scene."

"So he was unarmed?"

"As I say, Mr Michaels, our forensic unit has at this time not been able to recover any weapon from the scene, save of course for those carried by the deputies. Let's move along. Any other questions?"

This time it was Chloe who managed to get a question in.

"Sheriff, were the deputies wearing body-cams?"

There was a pause before the Sheriff answered, and Matt thought he saw his eyes flicker downwards for a second, before he fixed them back on the KFPC anchor.

"I have not been made aware of any footage. While Special Weapons Teams do wear body-mounted recording devices, it is entirely within the realms of probability that these would not have been enabled until such time as they were in proximity of the address at which the warrant was being served."

The sheriff dealt with the remaining questions, perceptive and otherwise, with the same cool detachment and polished verbosity, and Matt learned little of any interest. Eventually the conference wrapped up with a promise of a further update in the morning, and the TV teams began to pack away their equipment. Chloe, busy untangling a lavalier microphone from her suit jacket, approached Matt.

"I told you you wouldn't learn much."

Matt shrugged.

"Sometimes it's as much what people won't answer as what they will answer."

She narrowed her eyes for a second, and then smiled.

"Alright, Mr Woodward and Bernstein. Well, if you're serious about investigating this properly, and I think you are, I've got someone you're gonna want to talk to."

"Sounds interesting. What about your question, though. Body-cams? What made you ask that?"

"Ah well, come and meet this witness and I think that will become clear too."

10

What, exactly, Josh should do for his day of showing Abeke around London was the subject of much discussion with Dan that evening. Despite some misgivings, Josh had reiterated the offer of playing tour guide when he emailed Abeke back after their meeting and, slightly to his surprise, she had enthusiastically suggested they make a plan for that Saturday – if he wasn't too busy. He wasn't.

So, as Dan and Josh worked their way through a bottle of wine and half-watched several episodes of *It's Always Sunny in Philadelphia*, they proposed various ideas with differing degrees of seriousness. Dan tried, half-jokingly, to push for a plan that would garner Josh some cool points. Street food in Shoreditch, a contemporary art exhibition in a warehouse, and an underground house music gig in East London.

Josh, who knew his limits, made the point that Abeke probably had access to all the street food and contemporary art she could handle in the Bay Area, and might prefer to see some more classic London tourist sites. In the end they settled on a plan involving the Houses of Parliament, 10 Downing Street, seeing the Household Cavalry sentries at Horseguards and then a stroll along the Mall to Buckingham Palace.

By the time Dan and Josh each headed off to bed at almost midnight, Josh was looking forward to Saturday. Playing the role of a guide for an enthusiastic tourist came naturally to him and would be far less nerve-wracking than the prospect of a drink or dinner-date. Not, he reminded himself, that this was a date. Not that he had any reason to believe Abeke had the slightest interest in him as anything other than some company for her first weekend in a new city. And not, he tried to tell himself, that he minded either way.

He wasn't convinced and, despite the wine and the late night, he lay awake for a long time after he'd climbed into bed. He knew he was half-consciously encouraging himself in developing a crush, and that doing so was more than likely setting himself up for a fall. But it was too easy to ignore the warning voices. It had been a long time since Josh had been on a date with anyone who hadn't started out as a carefully-curated series of photos on Tinder or Hinge, and he was struck by just how much more attractive people are when you meet them in real life; when you get to see them smile, and move, and talk animatedly about work and life.

It wasn't just Abeke on Josh's mind as he struggled to fall asleep, though. He couldn't shake a nagging anxiety about the BluJacket work itself. He'd expected to be excited to work on something cutting edge, high tech, secretive, and with a military application. Jamie and Susan might have been crude in their methods by exploiting his connection to the military, but they had a point. He had every reason to be enthusiastic about promoting military equipment that might ultimately prevent other families from going through what he and his mum had.

Which he was, sort of. But Jamie and Susan hadn't considered the other side of it. They probably hadn't even known the details of how Josh's father had died, and that Josh knew better than anyone that military equipment could cut two ways. There was equipment that saved lives, and then there was equipment like the 'Snatch' Land Rover. Originally used by the British Army for patrolling Northern Ireland in the '90s, the 'Snatch' was essentially just a civilian Land Rover 110 with a bit of extra armour and a hole in the roof for a machine gunner. They were light and mobile and a little less aggressive-looking than more heavily-armoured options. The only disadvantage, and the reason they earned the moniker 'mobile coffin' in Iraq and Afghanistan, was their inability to withstand blasts from the improvised explosive devices that had become the greatest threat in both theatres. Josh's father's platoon had been travelling in a convoy of Snatch Land Rovers when an IED had gone off directly underneath the rearmost vehicle, in which he, as platoon sergeant, was travelling. He had joined the list of more than thirty-five British service personnel killed in the vehicles.

So, yes, military equipment cut two ways. And military equipment pressed into service for political expediency even more so. The question that bounced around his mind as he finally dropped off to sleep was which way did BluJacket fall, and how could he be certain?

11

Chloe parted ways with her film crew, and drove Matt in her own car to the small town of Lawharf, about 15 minutes drive north of Fort Pinebec. She pulled into a street that Matt immediately recognised from the video of the shooting, and from some of the photos he'd seen on social media.

"Up here on the right is Nathan Adams's house." Chloe said, quietly, gesturing up the street.

A square white and blue tent sat outside the house. Matt recognised it as the style used to cover crime scenes, providing privacy to forensic teams while they worked. There was no sign of such a team here now, just a solitary deputy standing next to the tent. He watched Chloe's car as it drove past, and returned Matt's curious gaze.

"So, that, obviously, is where he was shot." Chloe said, pointing again as she drove slowly up the street. "The deputies were about a hundred metres away, around about here," she pointed to a spot on the pavement. "And *here*," pointing to one of the terraced houses across the street, "is one of the witnesses."

"One of?"

"Well I know of two. Amber McDade, she's 52 years old, lives right here, and she's coming home from a night shift when she sees the SWAT team arrive. The other is if I had to make a guess, a 17 year old called Kevin Johnson who lives right here opposite where the deputies were. I'd say he filmed that video we've all seen on Twitter, but good luck getting him to talk to you or anyone else."

"I see. But you've spoken to Amber?"

"Sure have. Spoke to her this morning, and then we filmed a little clip of her talking to the camera. Been using that on the hourly news ever since. But, I reckon you'll want to hear her take on things."

"Want to give me a preview?"

"Nah, you might as well hear it from her."

Chloe pulled the car over, walked up the short path to the front door, and rang the bell. It was answered by a thin, Black woman who – assuming she was Amber – could easily have been ten years older than the 52 Chloe had said she was. Her hair was grey and thinning a little on top, and she wore a shapeless dress that did little to disguise her frail frame. Even making allowances for the horror she'd been witness to yesterday, Matt had to assume she was either unwell or struggling to take care of herself or, perhaps, both. She gave Chloe a wan smile, and nodded to Matt.

"You folks come in then," she said, and immediately turned and headed back inside. Chloe followed and Matt came last, following Chloe's cue to slip his shoes off. The hall, contrary to what he might have expected from Amber's appearance, was immaculate. Framed family photos sat on a tidy dresser and a row of coats hung neatly from hooks. The fact they were mostly shades of blue or grey made it hard to be completely sure, but Matt had a feeling they'd been sorted into colour order.

Amber carried on into a small sitting room that was

equally tidy, though homely. A slightly chewed tennis ball next to the sofa was the only item out of place, and that plus a little tartan bed on the floor indicated the presence of an unseen dog. Amber gestured to the sofa while gently placing herself into an armchair near the window.

"You know, you folk are the only ones who've come to speak to me." She said, suddenly, before Matt had even had a chance to take his seat.

"The two of us?" He asked, dropping himself into the sofa.

"Well, you and the other journalists. I mean the sheriffs haven't come to speak to me. They say they're investigating but I'm a witness aren't I? I held that boy after they shot him, and they don't need a statement from me?"

"Perhaps they'll come tomorrow. It's only been a day, I guess."

"What else can they have to do? That cop straight up murdered Celia's boy. I saw it, and they've got it on camera, so there's no more investigation needed, is there?"

"Well," said Matt, gently, "that's something I'd like to hear more about. What makes you say murder?"

She looked aggrieved, but her voice remained steady and quiet.

"No other word for it, is there. He was no threat, he didn't have no gun, he wasn't holding anything that *looked* like a gun, he was out for a run – did you know he was training for a marathon? Raising money for kids with sick cells. And here's the thing, here's the worst part," she wagged her finger at Matt to emphasise her point, "the cops weren't even looking at him! They're just walking away and then boom." Amber mimed spinning round, although as she was sitting in a chair it was little more than a sharp twist of her shoulders. "He spins round like that and doesn't even stop to look."

"That is certainly strange. Did you see anything that might have startled him? Was there any noise?"

"Well, no. Nate's watch beeped but it was so quiet, you know. *I* could barely hear it and I was closer than they was. And anyway I swear the cop was turning before the watch even beeped."

Matt made a quick note in his pocketbook, and Amber scowled, misinterpreting Matt's interest in what she'd said.

"No watch beep is a reason to shoot a boy!"

"Of course it's not, Ms McDade, I'm just making sure I write down everything you tell me. So you didn't see anything else strange? Any other reason for the deputy to notice Nathan?"

"Nothing at all! I tell you, it was all normal and then it's like, bang, he suddenly decides to shoot a boy he can't even see."

"It certainly is odd. I saw the cell phone video…"

"What cell phone video?" Amber asked.

Matt furrowed his brow.

"The one your neighbour took, that got posted on social media. I thought you knew about it, you said the cops had it on camera?"

"I meant on *their* cameras, the ones they wear. Oh, I don't do social media. So someone filmed it? Then what are we waiting for? If someone filmed me gunning a boy down in broad daylight for no reason I'd be in jail like that!" She snapped her fingers crisply.

"The Sheriff says they don't have any footage from the cameras. Perhaps they weren't on?"

"Well their little lights were on! Front and back!"

"Front and back?"

"You know, the front camera and the back camera. So that will show Nate, and it will show he wasn't doing nothing wrong."

"There was a back camera?"

"Oh sure. On the back of their helmets. So why don't they

just look at that video and everyone will know what happened."

"Ok. And you saw they had lights on? What colour?"

"Red. Just like my camera when I'm recording. So of course they were on."

Matt made another note. While he scribbled down just about everything Amber said at the top of the page, at the bottom he maintained a neat list of items that he wanted to follow up on. That list was already getting full.

Half an hour later, as Matt and Chloe drove away from Amber's house, Matt looked down at his notes, and debated where to start with digging further into some of what he'd learned.

"So, what did you think?" Chloe asked, breaking the silence.

"Well, it fits with the video we saw. Interesting what she said about their helmet cameras. You think she she's right about them being turned on?"

"Maybe. That's why I keep asking the Sheriff about video footage. But who's to say what a red light means? Could mean recording, could mean turned off, could just mean low battery. She told me the same when I spoke to her yesterday, I've been trying to find someone who actually knows shit about these body cams who can tell me whether they reckon they were on or off. But, honestly, I'm not paid to do investigations and no one is really interested. They've got their angry quote from Amber to put on the evening news, and that's enough."

"Yeah. Well, there are going to be plenty of angry talking heads to choose from soon. I might know a guy I can talk to about the cameras. What about Nathan? He everything she said he was?"

Chloe looked at Matt sharply.

"What does it matter? Would that change anything?"

"I just want all the details."

"Yeah, well. I couldn't find any criminal history, and you can be pretty sure if he had a record, the Sheriff would have made sure we found it. Besides, I found his JustGiving page, *and* I confirmed he was signed up for the city marathon next month. All that was true."

"Who said you don't do investigations?" Matt said, looking at her, eyebrows raised.

"No one did." Chloe grinned. "I said I'm not *paid* to do investigations. On that note, I got to get home, I'm on air early tomorrow. Can I drop you somewhere?"

"I'm booked at the Holiday Lodge in town."

Chloe wrinkled her nose.

"Good luck with that. Anyway that's on my way, I'll drop you outside."

"Thanks. It's bad?"

"Oh it's fine. As long as you don't eat the food. Or sleep in the bed."

"Wonderful."

As they drove back to the centre of Fort Pinebec, Chloe chatted away, asking Matt questions and, unperturbed by his brief answers, talking cheerfully about her own experiences in journalism. Despite himself, Matt got drawn in to the conversation. He warmed to Chloe; her pragmatic appreciation of the reality of small-town journalism, combined with her unwillingness to fully accept that reality, appealed to him.

As they drove and talked, Matt looked out at the residential streets — wide pavements and well-kept houses and plenty of plants and trees — and wondered if this would all look very different in a few days, or even hours. Would protests or riots rock this neighbourhood as they had so many others, after so many similar incidents? Or would the community somehow find a way to return to normality quickly after the trauma inflicted on it. Matt knew that some of the answer to that question was immutable, preordained at the moment the deputy fired those shots. But some of it might depend on what facts he uncovered and how he, and other journalists, presented those facts. The sense of responsibility didn't weigh Matt down, but buoyed him up, inspiring him to want to know more and to understand more, and to try to provide some answers.

Chloe's judgement of the hotel wasn't far off, Matt saw as they arrived. The entrance was well-lit and welcoming and the night manager greeted Matt with a friendly smile, but the room was tiny with a stained carpet and what looked like cigarette burns on the bedspread. He dreaded to think what he'd discover if he looked any more closely at the bedding, so he didn't. Instead, he pulled a fleece sleeping bag liner from his bag, and spread it out on the bed. Small and light, it had proved a useful travelling companion on many occasions. Whether to provide a little extra warmth when forced to sleep in his car, at an airport, or on a sofa; or just to provide something of a barrier against unhygienic beds.

He didn't get straight into it, though, but sat on the bed and opened his laptop. He searched through his contacts and then, when he found the person he'd hoped to find, dropped their email address into a new message. Next he went back into his video editing app and opened the cell phone video of the shooting. He flipped through frames until he found two that provided a decent view of the helmets of both deputies. Now that he knew what he was looking for, they certainly appeared to have cameras on both front and rear. He peered closer at the cameras and tried to zoom in further, but the footage was far too grainy and distant to be able to make out whether there even was an LED on them, let alone what colour it was. He saved both frames as individual images and attached them to the email, then tapped out an accompanying note.

Carl,

Hey buddy, hope you're well. I'm looking into this shooting in Fort Pinebec, I'm sure you've seen it. Hoping you might know a bit about police body-cams? If so, can you advise:

- What make/model of camera is this?

- What would a red LED showing on the camera indicate?

- Typically what would cause a body cam to start recording, and at what point in an incident might this happen?

- Where is the footage stored?

Thanks! Catch up soon,

Matt

Carl was a friend Matt had made almost five years earlier. Prior to a trip to South America to report on an investigation Matt was conducting into drug smuggling, the Washington Record had paid for him to attend a 'HEAT' course. Hostile Environment Awareness Training. He'd been sent to a remote ranch in Wyoming and put into the hands of a team of mostly ex-military instructors including medics and a former Green Beret. Over four days, they took him and the other students through training and scenarios covering everything from how to offer bribes at checkpoints, to how to give life-saving first aid, and how to escape a kidnap.

The only instructor who wasn't ex-military was Carl, a chatty but intense former bodyguard from the Diplomatic Security Service. With years of experience keeping diplomats safe in some of the most hostile locations in the world, he offered a level of pragmatic insight that Matt appreciated amidst all the testosterone and adrenaline. They ended up talking a lot in the evenings; usually Matt asking a couple of questions and then listening as Carl got drawn into lengthy but fascinating explanations. After the course was over, they had stayed contacts and friends. Carl now ran his own consultancy advising small police forces on tactics and equipment, and he was the best-informed and most up-to-date person Matt could think of when it came to anything to do with law enforcement.

Matt hit send on the email, and then finally got ready for bed.

12

When Josh woke up on Saturday morning, he was relieved to see blue skies, and an online forecast that promised they'd stay that way. The day would reflect London at its best, he thought; sunny but cold, and not quite as busy with tourists as in the summer months. The perfect day to walk through Westminster, and then warm up in a coffee shop or cosy pub.

He selected an outfit that he'd recently decided was his best look. A fleece-lined corduroy trucker jacket over a black cable-knit jumper, with indigo jeans. It looked autumnal, Josh thought, and struck the right balance of well-dressed without trying too hard. He wasn't sure what the expectations of a Californian might be as far as dress-sense went, but he was keen not to let himself down so early on.

Knowing that the exits from Westminster underground were too busy to be convenient meeting places, Josh had suggested meeting at Embankment and then walking down the river to the Houses of Parliament. He intended to get there ten minutes early but, over-compensating out of a fear of being late, ended up being there for more than twenty minutes before Abeke emerged from the tube station. She walked past the flower seller and newspaper stand and then smiled and gave a little wave when she caught his eye.

"Hey Josh! Hope you weren't waiting too long."

"Not at all. Only just got here. You figured out the Tube, then?"

"The Tube? Oh, the subway, right. Yeah, I'm staying near Monument so it was really easy. Straight along the green line."

"Great. It's pretty easy for me too, I'm on the same line the other way. So, I thought we could walk up to the Houses of Parliament, if you like? There's Big Ben and Westminster Abbey, it's kind of a must-see while you're here."

"Sure! You're in charge!"

They walked along the Embankment, Josh pointing out the London Eye on the opposite bank, the rotating blue sign outside the newly-relocated Scotland Yard, and the statue of Boudicca on the corner of Westminster Bridge. He'd forgotten how many famous landmarks were crammed into such a small space, and was pleased at the enthusiastic reception that each one got. Even the last one, about which Abeke knew nothing.

"Ok, so who's Boudicca then?"

Josh, who had been largely educated in Germany and missed out on some of the standard pieces of history taught to British children, wracked his memory.

"Uh, I think she was a queen who rebelled against the Romans, when they ruled Britain? A celt, maybe? Or a pict?"

Abeke took a photo of the statue.

"She looks badass. Look at that spear!"

They turned back to the Houses of Parliament and Big Ben, and carried on walking. Abeke snapped photos as they went.

"So how long have you been at BluJacket?" Josh asked, on a break from trying to remember historical details about buildings they were passing.

"Nearly six months, now. They didn't used to have any marketing team before that, but now things are taking off I think they felt the need. So, I've kind of been growing it from scratch."

"That is really cool. Nice having so much autonomy. What did you do before that?"

"I was at another startup. It didn't work out. How long have you been at BBA?"

"Three years now. I got on a grad scheme here and then ended up in the account management department. It's… decent."

"It seems great. Chris was very keen to work with you guys. I think he saw those glamorous car and liquor ads you do. He desperately wants something like that."

"Well, hopefully we can keep him happy. What's he like? I feel like you have to be a certain kind of person to start a company from nothing, and get people to give you money along the way."

"You're right. He can be intense. But, he's got a vision, and so much energy. And, you know, he served in the army so he's really invested in what we're doing."

"Yeah." Josh remembered the brief, awkward conversation with Abeke at the end of the meeting two days before. "I guess you know my Dad was in the army?"

"Susan mentioned it at one of the pitch meetings. I'm really sorry, I can't even imagine."

"Yeah. Well, it was a long time ago." He saw the usual scrum of tourists at the gates to Downing Street ahead of them, and gratefully seized the opportunity to change the subject. "Ok, so this is Downing Street up ahead, that's where No 10 Downing Street is."

"The Prime Minister's house, right?"

"That's the one. I mean, it's mostly an office really now I think, but there's an apartment at the top that he lives in."

They stopped at the gate, and Abeke peered curiously through the bars, trying to make out the famous front door far down the street.

"It's crazy you can get so close to it, really."

"Apparently you used to be able to walk right into the street, they only put the fence across because of IRA attacks."

As they walked on up Whitehall, Abeke turned the conversation back to Josh again, although he was pleased she didn't pick up on the thread about his dad.

"So what made you want to work in marketing?"

"Who said I *wanted* to work in marketing?"

Abeke laughed.

"You don't like it?"

"I'm kidding," he backtracked quickly, remembering he was talking to a client, so demonstrating at least some positivity about his work might be a good idea. "It's good. I just meant that I kind of fell into it, I guess. It sort of took me a while to find a job after uni, and then the grad scheme came up, so I took it. But it's a nice environment, and when the clients are good it's great."

"Oh I see how it is, Josh. So is *this* client good?"

Josh blushed.

"I mean, any client that lets me show them round London has to be good, right."

"Right! But it's you that's doing me the favour. I didn't fancy a day alone, and you're a great tour guide."

"You only think that because you don't realise how much I'm making up."

Abeke laughed again, and Josh beamed inwardly.

As they crossed Horseguards Parade and began walking up The Mall, there were fewer landmarks for Josh to point out and the conversation turned back to personal topics.

"What about you and your parents?" Josh asked. "You guys close?"

"Mmm, sort of," said Abeke, frowning.

Josh looked at her, raising his eyebrows. "That doesn't exactly sound convincing!"

"Oh well, we get on. It's just that I have high-achieving siblings. It can be hard getting much attention."

"You hardly seem low-achieving…"

"You'd be surprised. It's all relative!"

They arrived at the end of The Mall and walked round the Victoria Memorial to the fence at the front of Buckingham Palace. The two Guardsmen, dressed in their grey winter overcoats, were doing one of their regular marches across the front of the building, and Abeke watched in undisguised delight. When they returned to their sentry boxes, she turned to Josh, grinning.

"How am I supposed to try and make them laugh if they're all the way over there?"

Josh had never really thought of that. He'd seen videos of people interacting with Guardsmen on duty, but maybe that was at one of the other palaces.

"Oh, that's a good question. Maybe that's at Windsor Castle?"

"Well. I'll just have to go there then."

"I'm sure if anyone can make a guardsman laugh, it would be you."

She looked at him, brow creased in mock-suspicion.

"I'm not sure if that's a compliment or not."

"I think it was a compliment," Josh said, glad that it hadn't come across quite as cheesy as he'd worried it might.

"Good. Then maybe I can convince you to take me to Windsor Castle next time."

That, Josh thought, would not take much convincing.

13

When Matt woke up, the first thing he did was set the little coffee maker in the hotel room going. The second thing was look at his phone. There were a dozen new emails in his inbox, two of which were news alerts based on keywords he had set up after he started looking into the shooting. One, which had come in at just after two in the morning, announced that the name of the deputy who had shot Nathan Adams had been released. Myles Weston, age 39, 12 years in the department, four years on the Special Weapons and Tactics team, no prior disciplinary problems. Before his police service, Weston had spent five years in the Marine Corps, during which he had done a tour of duty in Iraq, and had been honourably discharged. It didn't reveal any reason why Deputy Weston might have suddenly decided to shoot a unarmed man, and of course Matt didn't really expect it to.

The other news alert was about a vigil and protest outside the Sheriff's Department headquarters, planned for that afternoon. Matt made a note of the time, thinking both that it might be worth observing, but also that it would be best to plan any attempts to speak to members of the department for well before the protest began.

Most of the other emails were of little importance, but he was pleased to see a reply from Carl.

Hi Matt,

Good to hear from you. Hope you're doing well – that case is certainly a crazy one. Re your questions, will be easier to chat on the phone – call me as soon as you're awake? 202-555-0133

Carl

Matt dialled the number and Carl picked up straight away. He'd clearly looked at caller ID, as he answered with "Hey Matt".

"Hi Carl. Thanks for taking the time to speak."

"No worries dude. Look, easier to talk this through than type up a million-word email, yeah? Ok, I've got your email in front of me. I'm gonna just talk, you fire questions at me if anything isn't clear, ok?"

"Sounds good."

"Ok ok. So, question one. Make or model. Right at this time there are about sixty manufacturers globally that make body-worn cameras. That's enough that I couldn't claim to know every single model, but what I can say is I don't recognise the ones in your photo and I'm not aware of any that currently make front-and-back cameras. Now, most US departments are using cameras made by Axon. It's part of Taser, so they're pretty hooked in – no pun intended – with selling to law enforcement. This definitely isn't one of theirs."

"Ok, that's good to know." Matt set his phone to speakerphone, propped it on his bedside table, and pulled his laptop over to him so he could start Googling Axon while Matt spoke.

"Question two. LED colour. Ok, so what you have to understand about most, and I emphasise most because I really can't speak for all, body cams is that they have three modes. They can be turned off, which is going to be indicated by no light. Next up they can be in what's called 'buffering' mode. That's when they're capturing footage but only keeping it for a pre-set amount of time, let's say two minutes – could be less could be more – that's usually up to the department. So it keeps this two-minute loop and then that's discarded. But when something happens, the officer hits a button and it goes into 'capturing mode'. Now capturing mode is usually a red light, and in this mode it's recording footage just like any camera. But it's *also* saved that buffered footage from the time before the button was pressed. The two minutes, or five minutes, or whatever the department specifies. Am I making sense?"

"I think so. So, if the red light is on, we'd say it's probably recording?"

"I'd say so, yeah. But, again, sixty manufacturers, dude. So, I can't promise that one of them isn't using red light to indicate the damn thing is turned off."

"Ok. And when would it go into recording mode?"

"Coming to that. So that's question three, would they be recording at this point? The technical answer is, recording mode is most likely activated by hitting a button. But then these days there are departments that activate it from prompts – turning the sirens on, getting out the car, raised voices. I mean, could be anything honestly."

"Clever stuff." Matt said, genuinely impressed. He'd seen a lot of body cam footage from previous investigations, but he couldn't remember one where he'd been required to do much digging into how exactly they worked.

"Yeah, clever in a way. Ok, but also you want to know what's the department policy for turning on your camera on the way to kick a door down. That I cannot easily answer, I'm afraid, but I can tell you that the department I'm currently consulting with has all SWAT teams turn their cameras on as soon as they step out of their vehicles. But not all departments are quite so responsible. Or so prone to getting sued. So your mileage may vary."

"I see. But, still, that's helpful, Carl. Thank you."

"Sure thing. And question four, that's an easy one. Where is the footage stored? Same place as everything these days: the cloud."

"Really?"

"Well, most likely. I mean, it's going to be stored locally on the device for a bit too, but most of the time it's either getting pushed up to some cloud storage straight away, or when the officer gets back to base and uploads it. And you know the good thing about things on the cloud?"

"What's that?"

"They're almost never truly gone."

"Yeah. That *is* good."

"Sure is. Hey, Matt, it's been ace talking. Thanks for calling, glad I could help. Hit me up if there's anything else." With that, Carl hung up, and Matt was left staring at his phone, in the wake of this whirlwind of knowledge and information.

Behind him, the coffee machine beeped to indicate it had finished brewing. He poured himself a cup and drank it slowly as he got himself ready to go out.

Once he was ready and caffeinated, Matt got an Uber back to the Sheriff's department. As before, he was dropped off on the street, then walked across the parking lot and through the large front doors to the main lobby. A cool, air-conditioned space with high ceilings and a polished linoleum floor, it housed a long wooden counter that had presumably once been the only protection the deputies working at the front desk needed. Now, it was retrofitted with a high Perspex panel, behind which sat a very overweight man in a deputy's uniform, watching something on his phone. He looked up as Matt approached and smiled cautiously.

"Good morning sir, welcome to Pinebec County Sheriff's Department."

"Good morning. My name is Matt Ibarra, I'm with the Washington Record. May I ask who is in charge of the investigation into the shooting at Lawharf?"

"Oh, the Sheriff is overseeing that personally, sir."

"I understood it was assigned to internal affairs. Is there somebody there I can speak to?"

"Not without an appointment, sir, I don't think."

"Presumably if someone came in with information about the case, they wouldn't need an appointment?"

"Ah, well, perhaps not, sir. But you said you're a journalist."

"That's true, but a journalist with information. Tell you what, why don't you give whoever is running the case a call and ask them if they'd like to speak to me. Tell them," Matt said, almost on a whim, "tell them I'm interested in the cameras."

The deputy shrugged.

"If he's in, I'll ask him. But I wouldn't hold your breath if I were you."

"Sure."

The deputy picked up one of the two phones behind the desk and dialled a number. From the delay before he spoke, it seemed to ring quite a few times before anyone picked up.

"Hey. It's Kurt. I'm on front desk, there's a journalist here to speak to you… I told him that, but he says he's interested in the cameras." He looked up at Matt, and lowered the received away from his mouth slightly. "He says, 'what cameras?'"

"He knows what cameras. He can talk to me now, and we can exchange facts, or I can guess a bit and he can see my guesses in print."

Deputy Kurt relayed Matt's message word-for-word, then

there was a long pause. At first Matt, unable to hear any of the other side of the conversation through the plexiglass shield, wondered if Kurt was getting an earful of abuse. But then the deputy said "You still there, buddy?" and Matt realised he'd been getting an earful of silence. There was another couple of seconds pause, and when Kurt spoke again his tone was different. "You sure? Well, ok. Ok. Yes, ok. Thanks."

He looked back at Matt, a slightly different look in his eyes. Not respect, certainly, but perhaps a newfound wariness.

"Ok. Detective O'Riordan will see you. He's coming down. You can sit over there." He gestured to a row of plastic chairs along one wall. Matt took a step back from the desk and half-turned towards the interior door out of which he assumed Detective O'Riordan would come, but otherwise he stayed where he was.

Detective O'Riordan kept Matt waiting just long enough for him to be fairly sure it was deliberate. Eventually the door next to the front counter opened and a tall, skinny man in shirtsleeves and grey suit trousers appeared. He had a badge and pistol on his belt, and a lanyard with an ID card around his neck. His tie, emblazoned with the emblem of some sort of club or society, was done up tightly, and his sleeves were rolled with military neatness to just above the elbow.

Apparently wanting to avoid having to let himself back through what was clearly a security door, O'Riordan stayed in the doorway and beckoned Matt over. He turned away just as Matt got to the door, partly in order to start leading him down the corridor and partly, Matt suspected, as a convenient way to avoid shaking his hand.

"I appreciate you agreeing to meet with me, Detective O'Riordan."

"This way."

Matt shrugged, and followed the detective up a staircase, along another corridor, through a door accessed via a combination code, and into an office marked 'Internal Affairs'. Half a dozen desks filled most of the room, while one corner had been glassed in to form a small meeting room. The room smelt faintly of coffee and freshly-printed documents. None of the desks were occupied, but a man dressed similarly to O'Riordan was waiting by the meeting room. He raised his eyebrows slightly as Matt and O'Riordan approached, and then silently went into the room ahead of them. O'Riordan gestured for Matt to follow and to take a seat, which he did.

"Again, thank you for taking the time to meet with me –"

"Mr Ibarra, let me be clear. We *don't* have the time to meet with you. We don't *want* to meet with you. We're in the middle of a complex investigation. So let's move this along."

"Sure. Well, Detective O'Riordan and Detective… Cooper?" Matt read the second detective's ID card, hanging around his neck. Cooper scowled, but said nothing. "I'd love to ask you some questions about why a deputy from this department shot an unarmed man who evidently posed no threat. But you're busy, so let me just ask you where is the video footage from the helmet cameras worn by the officers?"

"What footage?"

Matt raised an eyebrow, and very slowly unfolded his notebook.

"Are you sure that's your answer? You're the ones that are short of time, not me. I can play twenty questions if you want, but I thought you wanted to move this along."

"You won't be playing any number of questions if we remove you from this building."

"If you didn't want me here, you didn't have to bring me in. But you did, so we both know that *you* know that Deputy Weston and his partner were wearing cameras, and that the cameras were recording. And that means that your Sheriff lied to me when I asked him about the cameras last night. Which is certainly a good starting point for my next article in the Washington Record, don't you think?"

"He said he wasn't aware of any footage. That's not a lie." Matt sighed.

"Ok. Forget the Sheriff. You're the lead investigator on this, and you don't look stupid to me. So the first thing you did was check if the cameras were recording, and if they were recording the next thing you did was watch the footage. So none of this should be too difficult. Where is the footage?"

O'Riordan leaned back on his chair and studied Matt hard for a few seconds.

"I know about you, Ibarra. I've read your articles. I know you make your living criticising and second-guessing hard-working police officers."

"Detective," said Matt, opening his hands in a gesture of innocent hurt feelings. "You work in internal affairs, you of all people should know that sometimes cops do the wrong thing."

"I'll tell you what I know. I know you come to places where you smell the opportunity to stir shit up. You write your articles, you insinuate and imply and lay blame, and then you go back to Washington or New York or wherever you live, and meanwhile this place will turn into a fucking war zone. We'll have BLM and Antifa and every fuck with a grudge against the police tearing this town apart. *I* can investigate cops without any of that happening."

"If that was the case, Detective, you'd want to help me find the truth, wouldn't you? So why don't you tell me about that video footage?"

"You're wrong, Ibarra. I didn't bring you in here because your empty threats at the front desk worried me. I didn't bring you in here to tell you about any video. I brought you in here to give you a warning. You have, for once in your miserable fucking career, bitten off more than you can chew. Stop digging, stop stirring shit up. Let us do our jobs and, trust me, this will be taken care of."

Despite the words, there was no venom in O'Riordan's tone. He looked steadily at Matt and spoke with the confidence of someone who has spent a career being respected and obeyed simply because of what he wore on his belt.

Matt shrugged. He wasn't surprised that he'd got nothing out of the detectives, but he was surprised at how aggressive the meeting had turned, and how fast.

"That footage exists, detective, and that means that sooner or later it will get out. Maybe it'll be a FOIA request, maybe it'll be a hacker from 4Chan, but personally I'd put money on it being one of your own colleagues seeing a way to make some extra cash or curry a little favour with the local news. I guess we'll see. Thanks again for meeting with me, I'll find my own way out."

He got up and walked out.

14

Josh's Sunday was spent sleeping late, going for a run, slowly making a fry up, and then wondering where most of the day had gone. A quiet voice in his head told him to distract himself from Abeke, while an increasingly loud part wanted to do the opposite; to spend all day thinking about her and basking in the success of their date. If, indeed, that's what it had been.

He had finished their day together with the brainwave of taking Abeke to the *Coal Hole* pub. She had expressed an interest in sampling some 'proper English food' and the old Victorian pub on The Strand was the first thing that jumped to mind. It oozed character from every inch of its old oak bar, mullioned windows and classical plaster friezes around the walls. It also, importantly, served excellent ale and pies and so represented the most stereotypically English supper Josh could think of.

Abeke had seemed genuinely delighted by it all, and they'd eventually walked back to Embankment tube station in high spirits, chatting cheerfully as if they'd known each other for far longer than a few days. They'd parted ways with a hug and, by the time Josh's train regained signal somewhere around Earl's Court, he already had a message from Abeke thanking him for the day and, to his delight, reiterating the jokey suggestion of a follow-up trip to Windsor.

They continued some on-and-off texting that evening and throughout Sunday. For almost the first time since he'd started working at BBA, Sunday evening came round without the usual dread of an approaching Monday and the faint sense of a wasted weekend. Instead, he almost looked forward to getting back into the office. Not for the work, obviously, but at least for the excuse to keep the conversation going with Abeke.

'Are you guys coming into our office at all this week?' He messaged, towards the end of Sunday.

'Not sure. Why, you missing me already?' She replied. That was definitely flirty, wasn't it?

Wasn't it?

'Oh yeah. But of course, mostly can't wait to see Chris again,' he typed, then thought for a second, added a 'tongue sticking out' emoji, and pressed send.

Abeke's response was quick. *'Well, I might have to disappoint you then. He's back in the US this week. But if you could make do with me, I'm thinking of coming in tomorrow afternoon to go over the project plan?'*

'Disappointing, but I guess that'll have to do.' He sent back. She responded with a solitary middle-finger emoji, but then quickly followed up with *'Well,* I'm *looking forward to it.'*

Got to love Americans, he thought to himself, realising he was grinning broadly. Even when they managed to dabble in sarcasm for a bit, they couldn't avoid reverting to sincerity.

When he got to his desk on Monday morning, Josh already had a meeting invite from Abeke for that afternoon. He also had another email from Rob in his inbox, asking if there was any update on the technical information from BluJacket. Josh felt a surge of annoyance. It was partly with Rob for chasing him again, but mostly with himself for not having actually made any real effort to get the information. Seeing an opportunity to demonstrate his value as more than just a forwarder of email, and reluctant to break the chain of friendly banter with Abeke by asking her for the information, Josh wondered if could make a proactive effort to find something to appease Rob by himself.

There was someone he knew who just might have some insight. He wasn't entirely sure if speaking to him about it would breach the non-disclosure agreement that BBA\Rowley had signed, but he also didn't particularly care. He was, after all, trying to obtain information about his client, not give it away. He opened up WhatsApp and started typing 'P-A-U' into the search bar until 'Paul Tickner' appeared, and he clicked into the conversation.

Josh felt a little flash of guilt at seeing that their last conversation was nearly eighteen months old, and had ended with Paul suggesting they meet up for a drink and Josh saying 'sure, that would be lovely'. Presumably they bore equal responsibility for the failure to make the meeting happen, but Josh couldn't help feeling that he'd started taking Paul for granted.

Paul had been Lieutenant Tickner when they'd first met, and Josh had been five years old. Paul was then a platoon commander newly back from a tour in Iraq during which he'd seen his friend, mentor and platoon sergeant, Josh's father, killed almost in front of his eyes. Young, desert-tanned and, in retrospect it was clear, quietly traumatised, Paul had introduced himself to Josh and his mother at Josh's dad's funeral. Since then, he'd done his best to stay part of Josh's life despite continuing a successful military career and starting his own family.

Pushing aside his guilt at his own part in the length of time since they'd last spoken, Josh carefully formulated a message. He started with the expected pleasantries — how are you, how's Julia, can't believe it's been so long — and then *'I'm working on a project for this company'* with a link to their website *'but honestly I don't really get how it works. Thought you might have come across them in your world? If you have time to answer a few questions it would really help, and of course would be great to catch up!'*

That ought to do. He knew that only getting in touch when he had a favour to ask was pretty transparent, but he also knew that Paul wouldn't mind, and might even be pleased. As a self-appointed Godfather, and one still dealing with a certain amount of unresolved guilt, he'd always seen it as his role to do what he could to smooth Josh's path through life and help him out whenever the opportunity arose.

Josh focused back on work. If Abeke was coming in that afternoon to look at the project plan, then he should probably create one. The task was dull but relatively easy, the kind of thing he could do with headphones on and music playing, enjoying being undisturbed for a while. He'd just about finished it when his phone buzzed with a message. For a second he assumed it was Paul responding to him but, when he glanced down, it was Abeke's name on the screen. He tried to ignore the little bolt of nervous excitement, and opened WhatsApp.

'I'm on my way over to you now. I could use a decent coffee - do you fancy doing our meeting in a coffee shop rather than at the office? It's the Silicon Valley way!'

'Sure!' He replied, *'Want to meet in the lobby then walk somewhere? I think I know a place nearby.'*

On the rare days when Josh felt he could afford coffee out, rather than free coffee from the machines in the office, he went to the big Starbucks on the corner. He had a feeling, though, that might not be what Abeke had in mind. He remembered the effortlessly cool Vijai once taking him to an independent coffee shop on one of the side-streets not far away. His flat white had been pretty spectacular, although at very nearly £5 it was also more than he spent on lunch some days, so he'd not been back since.

When Abeke arrived in the lobby, he led her in what he hoped was the right direction, and was relieved to see the coffee shop sign ahead of them; the letters GRND arranged in a circle and divided by two crossed lines. There was a short queue at the counter and Josh looked up at the chalkboard, trying to pre-select a drink, size, bean and milk type before he was put on the spot by the need to order. In the end, he went for the safety of a flat white with the house roast, and Abeke got the same. She paid, brushing off his attempts to stop her, and they sat down at a broad table made of reclaimed wood.

"So, I've pulled together a draft of the project plan," he started, once they were settled, trying to settle his nervousness by making an effort to start the conversation off on a business footing.

"Ah yes. Work. Well, I guess we'd better take a look at that then," she smiled, and Josh wondered if he'd made a misstep by taking Abeke at her word and treating this as a work meeting.

In the end, it took them barely half an hour to review the plan anyway. As in the first meeting, Abeke was focused and precise, teasing out all the small discrepancies or wildly optimistic timings that Josh had either overlooked or hoped would go unnoticed. This time, though, her approach was more collaborator than client – carefully drawing attention to potential problems and immediately proposing solutions. As she began directly moving around items on the complex, interlinked timing plan, she lent across him to manipulate the laptop trackpad, and he felt her arm resting against his. He wondered if she was as aware of the physical contact as he was.

"Ok," she said eventually, "that looks pretty good to me."

"Looks a lot better now you've fixed it, for sure!"

"Ah, don't be silly. Just needed a second eye. You're all over this."

"Yeah, that's the facade I like to maintain."

"And you maintain it well." She said, squeezing his arm. He looked at her and, for a second, their eyes connected. Then he looked away, awkwardly, and fumbled for something else to say.

"So, do we want to get some time booked with Chris to review the concepts when they're ready? Or who's got sign-off on that?"

"Good question." She was back to business again. "I'll check with Chris but he's back State-side and really busy right now. Strictly between you and me, there's been some kind of issue with one of our pilot programmes."

"Oh?" Josh said, raising his eyebrows over his coffee. "What kind of issue?"

"I don't actually really know. The company keeps a lot of that sort of thing confidential. You have to have special clearance to know about the government work."

"Gotcha. That's kind of exciting though. So how does it work having Chris in the US and Pete in Scotland? Do you have an office there as well?"

"Oh, no, it's only Pete. He has an office in a co-working space on George Street. I think him being there annoys Chris, if I'm honest, but then Pete works all night so the time difference hardly matters, and he has everything he needs to access the servers." Abeke paused and then went on. "Hey, it looks as if this place serves wine after 4pm. If we're pretty much done with work, want to get a glass of wine?"

Josh did, of course. The meeting invite from Abeke had been for two hours, so that length of time was blocked out in his calendar with a pretty cast-iron excuse to be away from his desk, and he was more than happy to use every last minute of it.

An hour later, Josh and Abeke had got through two glasses each of the expensive organic wine that the café offered in the late afternoon. The wine, and Abeke's own openness and apparent interest in Josh's life, encouraged him to be a little more forthcoming than usual. In a fairly short space of time they'd managed to cover each of their childhoods, their musical tastes, just enough of their prior romantic history to clearly establish that they were both single, and their respective families.

"So it's just you and your mum?" Abeke asked, carefully, when they'd both finished giggling over her doing impressions of her siblings – a surgeon and a tenured professor, respectively – probing her about her professional ambitions at Thanksgiving dinner.

"Yeah. Well, and three of my grandparents are still alive but I didn't see a lot of them when I was growing up. My dad's parents kind of fell out with my mum, so…"

"Oh, what happened? Do you mind me asking?"

He didn't mind, actually. It was just that people rarely did ask, so that answering the question felt unfamiliar, and he had to quash the instinct to mumble something non-specific and move the conversation on with a joke or a question about Abeke.

"Well, my dad's dad was a soldier too. A former RSM – that's a regimental sergeant major – in the same regiment. And then, after my dad died, my mum got really into some campaigning. Wanting inquiries, prosecutions, people blamed. That sort of thing. It made things a bit tense with the regiment for a while and I guess my grandad picked a side. My mum ended up pretty isolated."

"That must have made the two of you close?"

"Yeah," Josh said.

"No?" Asked Abeke, picking up on the equivocation in his voice.

"No, it did. We're close. But, she never wanted *me* to join the army. For obvious reasons, I guess. So when I started applying, we fought about that. And then, when I ended up not even being able to join..."

"You're dealing with all that disappointment, and she's just kind of relieved, right?"

Josh laughed.

"You're wasted in BluJacket. You should be a therapist."

"You're not the first to say it." Abeke laughed as well, perhaps sensing that Josh was ready to lighten the conversation up and move things along.

It was only when an alert popped up on his watch reminding him that he was supposed to complete a weekly status report that he dragged himself away, apologetically, and returned to the office. Despite the prospect of one of his least favourite activities of the week he felt cheerful.

When the interminable status update was finally complete, and Josh's good mood was at least partly ruined, he packed away his laptop and began getting ready to leave the office. He wasn't sure the update had achieved anything – he wasn't sure it ever did, really. It felt more ritualistic than purposeful, going through the status spreadsheet and adding colour-coding and comments on items that were 'on-track' or 'at-risk', like a religious adherent carrying out a ritual that's been unchanged for hundreds of years. Deep down, not really believing any immediate good will actually come of it, but unable to break free of the group conviction that it somehow, indefinably, *matters*.

Josh couldn't help thinking of the sense of focus and purpose he'd felt when he'd joined the Officer Training Corps at university. Despite only being students, they'd been pushed by their instructors to perform on exercise like soldiers and potential officers. Each weekend away, all other worries had dissolved, replaced by the crystal-clear importance of fulfilling the mission, performing whatever role he'd been given for the two days and, above all, of not letting his friends down.

He'd always assumed that he'd carry that sense of clarity and purpose into his professional life, following the example of several of his friends from the OTC and commissioning into the regular army after university. That he'd enter an organisation where his role, and the importance of it, was clear and he'd understand what he was doing and why he was doing it. Instead, he'd somehow managed to stumble into a job that he wasn't certain needed to exist, in a company he wasn't sure did anything very useful, working for clients who didn't seem to contribute much to society.

He was about to get in the lift and head home when his phone buzzed. He glanced at his watch, where the alert popped up. It was a WhatsApp from Paul Tickner.

'Josh. So good to hear from you, it has indeed been too long. Your question interested me. It would be good to speak. I'm in London tomorrow, can you do lunch at the Cavalry and Guards?'

He sighed. He'd never really had the heart to try and explain to Paul that, in Josh's industry and relatively junior position, taking a two hour lunch at a location that required a jacket and tie was neither normal nor convenient. He knew, though, that Paul felt safe and comfortable in the large, invariably half-empty, dining room of his club. While he would understand if Josh suggested meeting somewhere else, it would be much harder to get him to speak freely.

'Of course. Sounds lovely. What time?'

The response came back straight away. *'13:00. See you there.'*

Josh pulled his laptop from his bag and, propping it on a nearby window-ledge, opened it and went into his calendar. Fortunately he had a day fairly free of meetings, so he blocked out a period from 12:30 to 2:30pm with the enigmatic title 'appointment'. He knew Jamie had access to view his calendar, so hinting at something that could be a medical issue was the easiest way to ensure that no questions were asked. He'd wear chinos and a shirt, hide a jacket and tie in the locker room downstairs, and hope that if it was a working day for Paul there wouldn't be any expectation to share a bottle of wine at lunch.

That job done, he headed for the underground station, and home.

15

When Matt left the Sheriff's office he wasn't particularly surprised to see Chloe and her TV crew setting up outside. There were almost twice as many vans as yesterday. He saw more national crews and even recognised a major London paper's US correspondent amongst the gathering cluster. He gave Chloe a slight wave, and she responded by beckoning him over.

"You went to see the Sheriff?"

"Nope. Went to see IAD. Two nice gents named O'Riordan and Cooper. Know them?"

"I've met O'Riordan once before. He's super old school, he is. Been in the department practically since he was in diapers. Don't think I know Cooper. How did your chat go, then? I'm surprised you managed to speak to them, to be quite honest with you."

"Yeah. Me too. They were… cagey."

"Cagey? Come on, Mr Ibarra. Give me a bit more than that! I'm just curious – we're off the record here."

"They warned me off pretty aggressively. And they really weren't willing to talk about the video footage."

"Are you surprised?"

"I am, actually. For one, it will end up coming out anyway. That kind of thing always does. And for another, there's already video out there. It's hard to see what could possibly be on the police camera footage that would make them so keen for me to stop digging."

"Yeah. I've not known these guys to be so defensive in the past. So, you gonna stop?"

"Of course not," Matt said. "What are you doing today? Covering the protest?"

"You guessed it. Gonna be here all day, I'm afraid, so you're going to have to find another driver." She winked.

"That's ok. I've got a few more things I want to try. Hey, be careful today, these things can turn nasty fast and not everyone likes the press."

"Don't you worry, sir, I'll take good care of myself."

Matt walked back across the parking lot and to the street. As he walked, he opened his phone and tried plugging Deputy Myles Weston's name into a couple of open-source identity tracing services. Unfortunately, and unsurprisingly, he'd been smart enough to keep his home address and phone number unlisted. Matt thought for a minute. It was still early, and Weston's name had only been released a few hours before, practically in the middle of the night. There was a decent chance that word hadn't spread particularly far yet. If he could find someone who might have access to a departmental phone directory and be slightly off their guard, perhaps he could get a number out of them.

Matt brought up the Pinebec County website and navigated to the section about the Sheriff's Department. The Department operated three outposts in small towns where they provided contracted policing services. Matt clicked one. The headquarters was listed as being at the Town Hall, and there was a phone number for it. He dialled the number.

"Good morning, Hamilton Town Hall, how may I help you?"

"Oh good morning. My name is Matt Ibarra. I'm trying to get in touch with a Sheriff's deputy. Myles Weston? I have some important information to discuss with him."

"Oh, well, that isn't the name of one of our deputies, I'm afraid, honey."

"Goodness me, are you sure? I know he's a Pinebec County Sheriff's Deputy."

"Ah I think you have the wrong place, honey. We do have some deputies based here but they just police Hamilton. The main Sheriff's department is in Fort Pinebec. But, I tell you what, I have the county contact list here so let me take a look." There was a pause, and the sound of typing. "Ah yes, Deputy Weston is listed here and I do have a cellphone number for him."

"That's wonderful, it's very important I speak to him this morning."

"Well, I can't go giving out his number I'm afraid. But tell you what, how about I put you through to him?"

"That would be perfect. I'm very grateful."

"You're quite welcome, honey. Putting you through."

There was the electronic sound of a new number being dialled, and then the phone rang. It rang four or five times and Matt started to assume that Deputy Weston was wisely not taking any calls. Just as he was about to give up and hang up, a man's voice came on the line. It sounded strained and cautious.

"Myles Weston. Who is this?"

"Deputy Weston. My name is Matt Ibarra. I'm a journalist from the Washington Record. I'm very keen to speak to you, if you have the time?"

There was a long, long pause. Matt kept expecting to hear the click of the call being disconnected, or just be told to fuck off, but when Weston's voice came back it sounded tired, resigned, and not unfriendly.

"I shouldn't talk to you, Mr Ibarra, I'm not supposed to."

"Has the Sheriff's department told you not to?"

"Of course. But there's a bit more to it than that."

"Well, we can keep everything off the record, or on background. However you want to play it, I can work with that. But wouldn't you like to have your side heard? I'm sure you've already seen what's being said on the news."

"Oh I've seen."

"Well, why don't you tell me what happened?"

"You know what happened. I shot that kid." Matt was taken aback by the blunt statement of fact. Weston's voice sounded hollow.

"Ok, yeah. Well, can you tell me why?"

Another long pause. When Weston's voice came back it sounded as if he was trying not to cry.

"I panicked. I should have waited. Should have checked."

"Checked what?"

"The system. The alert. This fucking BluJacket bullshit."

Matt furiously scribbled notes, his phone clamped awkwardly between his ear and his shoulder.

"What system, what blue jacket?"

"Look, Mr Ibarra, I can't discuss this on the phone, I really can't."

"Can I come and meet you? It sounds as if it's important that I hear what you have to say."

"Yeah, fuck it. Come round."

"Where do you live?"

"160 Laurel Drive North. But wait, don't come here. I'm sure people are watching the house. There's a bar, two blocks down, the Brighton Beach Grill. Meet me there this afternoon, 5pm. Get one of the booths at the back, and I'll find you."

Now, finally, before Matt could ask why people would be

watching his house, Weston hung up.

Matt had most of the day to wait. He fought the temptation just to go to Weston's house now that he had the address, but he didn't want to break the fragile trust that he'd built up. If the deputy was willing to speak to him, he was willing to wait.

He typed 'blue jacket' into Google, not sure what he expected to find. What he found were Google Shopping results for dozens of men's jackets in different shades of blue, maps results for local shops in Fort Pinebec where he could buy such jackets, and page after page of online stores selling blue jackets. None of it seemed to bear any relation to the shooting of Nathan Adams. Wondering if blue jackets had something to do with the police, he tried adding 'police' and then finally 'police shooting' to the end of his search. The only result that caught his attention was a 2005 article about the psychological influence of the police uniform. He scanned through it, but nothing stood out as having any bearing on his investigation.

Frustrated, and all the more frustrated knowing that if he could simply wait until 5pm, his questions would be answered, Matt summoned an Uber and directed it back to his hotel. He planned to distract himself with brunch while he typed up the first draft of an article. He liked to maintain a 'ready-to-print' article at almost every stage of an investigation. Although, this early, it would be far too thin on interesting details to really pass muster, it was good to have something in his back pocket if there ever was a need to rush to press. Apart from that, it helped to focus his mind on what information he had, what needed additional sourcing or investigation, and what gaps there were. Right now, he knew, there were a lot of gaps.

The basic events didn't seem to be much in dispute. The

cellphone footage, Amber, and even Weston himself essentially agreed that the two SWAT deputies had been on their way to serve a warrant when Weston unexpectedly turned and shot a young man who no one, not even the Sheriff's department, could credibly claim was a threat. Matt plugged in a few quotes from the Sheriff's press conference, realising as he did so how bland and generic they were. The unanswered questions were; where was the helmet camera footage, why was the department so reluctant to release or even discuss it, and what had caused a seemingly experienced and well-trained deputy to act with such unexpected violence?

Matt closed the document. It was the sort of bare restatement of facts that, he knew, his paper had already published under the bylines of other reporters. Less experienced and less expensive reporters. He'd have to do better than that if he was to justify his continued employment and freedom to operate.

He idly plugged Myles Weston's name into Google, trying a couple of variations including 'Deputy' and then 'Marine'. Very little came back; a brief mention of him on a local news site from four years earlier when he had been in the department's Traffic Safety Unit and given a dull quote about a counter-DUI operation he'd led one Thanksgiving. The search with 'Marine' attached returned a photo of LCpl Weston, 1st Battalion, 6th Marine Regiment, greeting his girlfriend as the Battalion returned from Al Anbar province in 2007. The article commented on their involvement in the Battle of Ramadi, the heavy fighting and casualties they had seen, but there was no other mention of Weston himself.

Matt's phone rang. It was Luke. Making good, no doubt, on his threat to keep a close eye on Matt.

"Hi Luke."

"Morning Matt. How's Pinebec?"

"Strange. This is an interesting one, I can tell."

"Yeah. I reckon it could all get a bit messy up there soon. You being careful?"

"Of course."

"Good. Look, I know you're doing your thing, but don't forget I asked you to file some daily stories as well."

"Don't you have anyone else on it?"

"No. And I'm not putting anyone else on it. We're paying you to be there playing detective, so you can file some copy while you're at it."

"I'll send you 1,000 words. Just the facts. I'm not going to tip my hand on the investigation."

"That's fine. That'll do. How's the investigation going?"

"It's all pretty thin right now, Luke. But, strictly between us, I'm meeting Deputy Weston, the cop who fired the shots, later today. That gives us a nice exclusive for tomorrow."

"You're meeting him? How come?" Matt wondered if, perhaps, he'd managed to impress the veteran reporter with the speed at which he'd obtained such a valuable interview.

"I got hold of his number. He says there's something he wants to tell me, about what happened."

"Did he say what?"

"Not really. He seems upset about the shooting. Blames himself but, there's something else going on there. He talked about a blue jacket. I can't figure that one out."

"He said that?" Luke asked. "Blue jacket?"

"Yeah. Why? Does that mean anything to you?"

"No, not at all. Odd thing to say, isn't it? I wonder what it means. Look, I'd better go. Got an editorial meeting I'm already late for. Let me know how your meeting with Deputy Weston goes, ok?"

"Sure," Matt said, and ended the call.

He looked back at the article he'd been reading before Luke had called, and drummed his fingers on the table.

Weston's military background was interesting, although he wasn't quite sure what to make of it yet. He'd seen enough of former military personnel who went on to be police officers to know that many made for brave, level-headed officers who could judge a situation carefully and use force wisely. But also that some carried scars and bore demons that weren't always obvious until the wrong combination of circumstances conspired against them. He made a note to see if he could get hold of Weston's psychiatric evaluation from the Sheriff's department, although he had a feeling that it wouldn't prove any easier than it had been to get hold of the video footage from his helmet cameras.

16

Josh's deception worked easily. First thing in the morning, he dropped into conversation with Jamie that he had to 'pop out at lunchtime for an appointment'. Jamie, who tended to go to the pub on Friday lunchtimes with the creative department and often stayed there, barely even registered the information. Josh picked up his jacket and tie from the locker room and got the tube a few stops to Hyde Park Corner, then walked down the road to the grand entrance of the Cavalry and Guards Club. As he went through the door, he was greeted by the porter.

"I'm here to meet Paul Tickner."

"Ah yes, sir. Colonel Tickner is waiting for you in the drawing room. You know where you're going?"

"Next to the bar?"

"That's right."

He walked through towards the bar, where he could hear a few voices, and turned right into a quiet sitting area with windows that looked onto the courtyard. Paul was sitting there, reading the paper. He was dressed in a formal military uniform. It looked to Josh a bit like a khaki suit, with medal ribbons on the chest and metal rank insignia on each shoulder. He looked up and smiled broadly as Josh entered, then folded his paper and stood, shaking Josh's hand and gesturing for him to sit down.

"Hello Josh. How on earth are you? It's very, very good to see you."

"You too. I'm sorry it's been so long."

"Oh don't apologise. You've got your life now, no reason you should be spending time with an old fogey like me."

Josh smiled awkwardly and mumbled, "oh, no, don't be silly."

"How's your mum doing?" Paul asked.

"She's ok. I think it's been hard though. She's starting to talk about coming back to the UK. What with the regiments being amalgamated, and the army leaving Germany, all the connection to my dad is gone, now. And that's what she stayed for in the first place. But then, it's been years really since there was anyone left there who she knew, or who'd known my dad, and she stopped feeling welcome there a long time ago…"

"I know. It changes so quickly. Hardly anyone left in the Battalion now who was on that tour with me and your dad. Honestly, barely any of them are even still in the army. Although, do you remember Tim Smith? Smudge?"

"I don't think so."

"No, well, no reason why you would of course. He was a rifleman, in your dad's and my platoon. He was there when it happened, gave first aid until the platoon medic got there, got the MEDEVAC request sent up." Paul tailed off, drifting back to being a 23-year-old watching his friend and mentor bleed to death propped against a compound wall in Rumalyah. He almost physically shook himself back to the present. "Well, between you and me of course, he did Selection a few years after we got back. Absolutely smashed it, by all accounts.

He's been at Hereford ever since." Josh was familiar enough with army terminology to know that the army's top-tier special forces units were rarely referred to by their real names but, more circumspectly, by the locations of their HQs; Poole or Hereford. Hereford almost invariably meant the legendary Special Air Service.

"Anyway," Paul went on. "I ran into him in Main Building not that long ago. He just got made a Squadron Sergeant Major. That's a serious accomplishment. But, what I'm getting round to, is, he asked after you. And your mum. Still thinks about you both, after all these years. I told him you're doing just fine!"

Josh smiled, blinking quickly and looking down for a second. "Thanks. Well that's kind of him."

"Yeah. He's a top bloke, he really is. Now, tell me about this BluJacket thing. I'm very curious to hear how you're involved in *that*."

Josh explained about BluJacket becoming a client, and the difficulty he was having in understanding what their product actually was, or how it worked.

"Interesting," Paul said, when he finished. His elbows were propped on his knees, hands steepled, with fingers pressed against his lips in thought. "So, I should tread a little carefully here, but, in broad terms, let me explain that as a rule the Ministry of Defence acquisition process for new technology and capabilities moves painfully slowly. But, there are some units in the armed forces that have the freedom to go more or less direct to market to buy things they want or need. Do you follow, so far?"

"I guess so. Special forces and so on?"

"Right. Now, I work down the corridor from a man who recently finished a two year posting to DSF, which is the headquarters that oversees these units. He's not badged, himself, but he worked a desk job investigating the latest things on the market that could be relevant for their specific role and, um, mission type."

'Badged', Josh knew, referred to a fully qualified special forces operator, entitled to wear the prestigious beret badge of the unit.

"Ok, I see. And he knows about BluJacket?"

"He does. From what I understand, BluJacket worked quite hard to sell it in to us, and DSF did a fair bit of testing to see if it worked for them."

"No way! They never mentioned *that*. Ok, so what is it? How does it work?"

Paul paused again, clearly weighing up how much to say.

"Have you seen about these new CCTV cameras they have at some railway stations and airports? They detect suspicious behaviour; people leaving bags unattended, holding weapons, that sort of thing."

"Yeah, I think I saw something about that."

"Ok, so, there's a real interest in the armed forces community about applying that operationally."

"As in, on bases? Or on drones?"

"Sure, yes, yes, yes, both of those, but that's not the real prize. The real prize would be what we would call a 'man-portable' capability. Something a soldier can carry."

Paul leaned in further as he went on with his explanation, and Josh could see the enthusiasm in his eyes, as though he'd never really stopped being a young infantry commander.

"Imagine," he said, "that I'm a rifleman, in a high-threat environment. Counter-insurgency operations maybe. I'm on patrol, walking down a busy street. Hundreds of people. I'm trying to look in all directions at once, scan every face for signs of tension, look out for weapons, wires, suspicious items, people with radios or phones, cars that look out of place. There are a million things to look for, I've only got two eyes, and if I miss something maybe I'm dead, or one of my section is dead. Now imagine I've got some kind of 360 degree camera, taking it all in, identifying the threats, and then alerting me. A heads-up-display in my goggles or something. Bit of recently-disturbed ground three metres ahead? Ping, I get an alert. Guy drawing an AK47 from under his jacket behind me? Ping, an alert. Chappy who matches the description of a known Taliban operative? Ping, an alert."

"Ok, yeah. That's pretty incredible. I see what you mean. So that's what BluJacket does?"

It made sense now. That fit with everything they claimed in their pitch and presentation, although Josh wondered why they weren't a bit more up-front about how it all worked. It was so much more impressive, Josh thought, when you understood the technology rather than when it was just a series of vague statements.

"That's what they claim to do." The brief pause and the emphasis on the word 'claim' made Paul's meaning clear.

"Claim? So it doesn't work?"

"Nothing works perfectly. That's to be expected. And it's still in trials. But I can tell you that after completing testing, our units passed on the technology, and it's not something the British Army is considering."

"But the Americans are?"

Paul looked a little uncomfortable.

"From what I hear, it's managed to get interest from some very senior individuals in the US military, and no doubt that's keeping the process moving."

"I'm not sure I love the idea of marketing something that doesn't work."

"I didn't say it *didn't* work, Josh. Take my advice, don't make waves with this. I told you what I found out because you wanted to know what the tech was, and now you know. This isn't for you to worry about. The product won't be used if it isn't safe."

"Like the army wouldn't use Snatch Land Rovers if they weren't safe, right?"

Paul looked as if he'd been slapped in the face, and Josh immediately regretted the comment.

"I understand how you feel, Josh," Paul said, his voice sounding tired. "But don't put yourself at risk. You're doing well, you've got a good job. Defence contracts are a big-money, nasty world. People don't take well to having awkward questions asked at the wrong time."

"Yeah. My mum found that one out, didn't she." Josh sighed. "It's fine, Paul, I won't do anything stupid. I appreciate you chatting to me about all this. I just wanted to understand how it all works."

"Yeah, ok. That's good. Well hey, enough about this, time is ticking on. Shall we go in for lunch?"

They took the stairs up to the dining room overlooking Hyde Park, and were shown to a rectangular table by one of the windows. Josh was relieved that Paul didn't order a bottle of wine, with the explanation that he was 'meeting the Secretary of State' later that afternoon, and Josh was able to stick to a glass of sparkling water with his potted shrimp and beef Wellington. For the remainder of the meal, conversation stayed away from BluJacket with so much ease that Josh suspected both he and Paul were each working equally hard to avoid the subject.

"How's the job going otherwise?" Paul asked, between bites of beef Wellington.

"It's… fine, the agency is cool."

"That's great. Marketing is the industry to be in. You made the right decision, you know."

"How do you mean?"

"Not joining the Army," Paul said, looking up at him.

"Well, it wasn't exactly my decision, was it?"

"No, well, I know, and that was the Army's loss. But

honestly it's for the best. It's not the career it used to be."

Josh shrugged, and concentrated on his beef. He was starting to wish he had ordered a glass of wine to go with it after all. He'd hardly be the only account manager coming back to the office on a Friday afternoon after a couple of units of alcohol.

"How, uh, how is all that, now?" Paul asked, after a second.

"The anxiety?"

"Yes. Sorry, tell me if I'm prying. But I know it was tough for you, and you had your heart set on Sandhurst."

"Better now, thanks." Josh said, firmly, and quickly filled his mouth with more beef Wellington in the hope of staving off more questions along this line. Paul was more than perceptive enough to take the hint.

"Ok, well. I hope you always feel you can talk to me. There's no shame in it, you know. I've had my own experience of that sort of thing. Lots of us have."

"I know, I'm sorry. But honestly, I'm doing great. How are your kids?"

Josh successfully shifted Paul to one of his favourite topics, and kept him there for most of the rest of the meal. When they were done, Josh made a wholly token and quickly-defeated attempt to split the bill, and then they both walked out into the chilly air of Piccadilly. Josh gestured that he was making his way to Hyde Park Corner, while Paul turned in the direction of St James's Park, declaring that he was going to walk to Horseguards. They shook hands and parted ways, and Josh watched Paul walk away, attracting a few interested glances from tourists noticing his uniform.

Josh checked his phone and, seeing a full inbox and a largely empty diary, decided against getting straight on the tube. Instead, he turned the corner into Old Park Lane and stepped into the Rose & Crown pub, a traditional boozer heaving with the post-lunch Friday drinkers crowd. It was the sort of place where Josh could comfortably stand at the bar alone, nursing the pint that he'd decided he needed after all, and trawling through his inbox. Feeling better and bolder after he'd finished his pint, he wrote an email to Abeke and quickly sent it before he could second-guess himself too much.

'Coffee yesterday was nice. Wine was even better! I don't suppose you fancy a drink over the weekend, do you?'

17

Bill made sure he was one of the first passengers off the plane, and moved quickly through the small airport to get to baggage reclaim as fast as possible. He ignored the conveyor belts; all his overnight gear was in the backpack he'd taken on the flight. Instead, he strode to the Southwest Airlines customer services desk, where he'd been told his one checked item would be waiting for collection.

There was a man in airline customer service staff uniform behind the desk as Bill arrived, and he raised his neatly shaped eyebrows and smiled thinly at him.

"How may I help you sir?"
"You should have a checked item of mine."
"Your flight number, sir?"
"WN 4658," Bill answered without hesitation.
"Your baggage will be arriving at carousel number 4."
"No." Bill kept his voice even. "I was told this item would be available from the customer service desk."
"And, what is the item, sir?"

Bill sighed inwardly. There was a point where trying to be discreet served only to attract more attention.

"It's a firearm."

"Oh I see." The tone was less one of surprise that anyone would be flying with a firearm, and more surprise that Bill hadn't simply said so to start with. "Special checked items will be coming off shortly. If you'll wait there, and please be ready with photographic ID."

Bill waited. He was keen to get moving. Time was tight, and he'd been given a clear deadline that left little scope for delay. Yet the ability to relinquish control and accept idle time of uncertain length was probably the single most useful skill he'd learnt from his time in the military. People talked about leadership, fitness, dedication, determination, and all that. Sure, those skills had played a part in his career at various times, but more than anything it was the ability to wait. If you could sit in a vehicle, knowing that it could move at any moment and take you into combat, but also that you could be there for another eight hours and then simply get off again, then dealing with the endless uncertainty of airline travel was nothing.

Eventually, a baggage handler came over with a small selection of packages, including at least one other that was pretty clearly a rifle case of some kind. Bill showed an ID card in the name that he'd used to book the flight, and was passed his own small box. It was barely larger than a hardback novel, with a handle and clips that could be – and were – locked with padlocks. He opened his rucksack, tucked the box inside, and strode out of the airport towards the taxi rank, pulling up the Lyft app and booking a car as he went. By the time he had crossed the terminal to the awkwardly-located ridesharing pick-up point, stopping for less than a minute at Starbucks to order a black filter coffee, the car had arrived.

He waved away the offer to open the trunk, and tossed his backpack into the rear seat. Then he glanced into the front window and noted the little camera on the dashboard that faced backwards to record the passenger. He pulled down the peak of the baseball cap he'd been wearing since he got off the plane and, as he climbed into the back seat next to his backpack, he made sure to look down at his phone and keep looking down.

"Evening, buddy." The driver looked down at the app open on his smartphone, and then up at the rear-view mirror, trying and failing to meet Bill's gaze. "Fort Pinebec, Laurel Drive North?"

"That's the one."

18

Matt took an Uber to the Brighton Beach Grill well before the meeting time. Late afternoon on a Friday, it was already starting to get busy, and there were no booths available when he arrived. He slipped the server a $10 bill in exchange for a promise to get the next one that came free, and sat at the bar waiting. To his relief, just before 5pm, another group left and he was able to take a booth in the very back of the bar. He sat himself facing the door and took his laptop out, more as a kind of signal than because he really had any work to do. Plenty of photographs were available of him online if Weston bothered to Google him, but the open laptop seemed like a good indicator that he was a journalist, in case he was difficult to identify in the gloom of the restaurant.

5pm came and went and Matt ordered some food. Initially, it just seemed the polite thing to do having insisted on taking up one of the popular booths. But, when the plate of grilled shrimp and bowl of fries arrived he realised how hungry he was. For a while, eating the fiddly shrimp distracted him from a growing irritation as time ticked on and there was no sign of Weston but, by 5:20, it was hard to pretend there wasn't some kind of problem. Matt realised he didn't even have the direct number for Weston, and he doubted that pulling the same trick he'd tried this morning was likely to work. He did, however, have Weston's home address, which Weston had unguardedly dropped into the conversation before changing his mind and asking to meet at the Grill.

So, finally, at 5:30, Matt paid the bill, left a large tip, and walked back out into the cold evening air. Streetlights had come on, and the windows of the bars and restaurants in the little row looked warm and inviting. Matt checked Google Maps and, sure enough, the Brighton Beach Grill was quite literally just around the corner from Weston's house. He walked the two minutes to 160 Laurel Drive East. A residential road, it had wide sidewalks lined with trees, and detached clapboard houses set back behind well-kept gardens.

Most of the properties were single-story and compact but 160 was a large, two-story building. Judging by the multiple front doors arranged along the front, it contained four apartments. For a second Matt wondered how he'd figure out which one was Weston's, then he noticed that each front door had a small black metal letterbox affixed to the wall next to it, and three of those had name-plates on. Since none of those showed Weston's name, Matt inferred that the sole blank one, for apartment C, was his. He wasn't entirely surprised that, even in this peaceful neighbourhood, a law enforcement officer might choose not to put his name on the front of his property.

The building was approximately an L-shape, with apartments A and B on one leg, their doors facing at right-angles to the street, while the doors to C and D were next to each other and faced directly towards the road. It wasn't completely clear which of the windows on the front of the building belonged to which apartment but, from the layout,

Matt was fairly sure the only window into apartment C was the one immediately to the left of its front door.

That window, at any rate, was dark, and had a curtain pulled across it making it impossible to see in. Matt went up to the door and pressed the buzzer. A bell rang inside the apartment, but he neither saw nor heard any movement. He pressed it once more, and then walked around the side of the building and to the back. It looked as if apartment C had a large window looking out over a communal garden, and sliding doors that gave access onto a little terrace area. The flagstones had weeds growing up between them, and there was nothing on the terrace except a pair of rusty metal garden chairs and a dusting of cigarette butts. Next door, Apartment D had an identical set-up, except that the terrace was bordered with pretty plant-pots containing flowers and miniature hedges, and there wasn't a weed in sight.

Matt looked in through the sliding door. The blinds behind it were pulled partly to one side, and he could see into a living space. A large L-shaped sofa surrounded a coffee table, and further back he could see a countertop that seemed to be part of an open-plan kitchen. A door led off the space to one side, but the rest was hard to make out. The apartment was all in darkness, and there was no movement at all. Without any expectation of a response, he knocked loudly on the window, and was startled when the door to Apartment D slid open and a worried-looking face surrounded by grey hair looked out.

"Are you the police? I called you half an hour ago."

The neighbour was a lady in her 70s, or perhaps early 80s. She was short, and made even shorter by her very rounded back, which pushed her head down so that she had to peer up at Matt to look him in the eyes. She used a wooden stick as she walked, though she didn't appear particularly unsteady on her feet.

"I told them I thought I heard a gunshot, but then they said, 'are you sure?' and 'just one shot?' and 'could it have been something falling over?' and I just don't know. With my hearing aids it's difficult sometimes."

Since she'd gone on talking without waiting for an answer to her question about whether Matt was a police officer, he simply ignored the question.

"I see. But you think you heard a shot? From inside Mr Weston's flat?"

"Yes. How do you know who lives here? Are you a detective?" She gave him a hard stare, and Matt took the view that his lightweight deception wasn't going to hold out long, so it was best to come clean.

"Actually, ma'am, I'm a journalist. I was supposed to meet Mr Weston but he never arrived so I'm a little worried. Did the police say they'd come?"

"They said they'd try to send a car, but I don't think they believed me about the gunshot."

Matt looked back towards Apartment C. The nagging worry that he'd been unable to shake since Weston missed their meeting was growing stronger.

"I don't suppose you have a key to Mr Weston's apartment, do you?"

"Oh, no, I'm sorry."

"That's ok. What's your name?"

"Lucia Knowles."

"Well, Ms Knowles. I'm concerned for Mr Weston's safety, so I'm going to break into his house."

Lucia Knowles raised her eyebrows in concern.

"Goodness me. You don't think… well, yes, I suppose that's the right thing to do. But really, the police should have come shouldn't they."

"They probably still will, but I'm not going to wait."

Something occurred to Matt, suddenly, thinking back to the first words Lucia had said to him. "What time did you hear the noise?"

"Well, I can just look here," she took an iPhone 12 Max out of the pocket of her cardigan. It looked absurdly large against her tiny frame, and she needed both hands to hold it and swipe at the screen. "Yes, I called the police at exactly seven minutes to five and that can't have been more than, oh, two minutes after? I went to Mr Weston's front door first, and knocked, you see, but then I called straight after."

"Thank you. That's helpful." The shot had been only a little before their intended meeting time. Matt wasn't sure what to read into that.

He looked at the window, and then at the sliding door. The frame was thin aluminium, and the wooden surround was flaking and peeling. He glanced around, thinking for a second, and then looked back towards Lucia's smart little terrace and the weed-free flagstones.

"Ms Knowles, do you have one of those little scrapers, for getting the weeds out?"

"Well, yes, why?"

"May I borrow it?"

It was kept in a box by Lucia's terrace door, so it took her only a second to get it and bring it out to Matt. He examined the frame of the sliding door again, and then inserted the flat, slightly hooked scraping tool into the gap between the door and the frame. He jiggled and twisted it to force the door back slightly on its runners and create space for the tool to go further in. Then, he got far enough to apply pressure to the little rotating hook that was the only thing keeping the door from sliding open. With one final movement, he popped the hook upwards, and levered the door open a couple more inches. After that, he could simply pull it the rest of the way. He handed the tool back to Lucia.

"Thank you, Ms Knowles."

"Goodness me. Do you do that often?"

"Oh no. It's been a very long time. Wait here please."

The apartment was silent as Matt entered. It smelt slightly of cigarette smoke and beer, and he saw open cans on the coffee table and the kitchen countertop. It was sparsely furnished, with little in the way of art, but the walls were scattered with photographs and memorabilia. Most of it was from Weston's service in the police, but there were older photos too; photos of a young man surrounded by other young men, all beaming smiles, high-and-tight haircuts, and desert camouflage. Some challenge coins and a little framed row of medals sat on one of the bookshelves.

Matt called out, "Deputy Weston?" There was no reply. He moved further into the apartment; there was the open-plan kitchen, a door into a small bathroom, and a flight of stairs near the front door, at the opposite end of the apartment. He tried the front door and was able to easily open it; the night latch was locked, which was what had kept him out before, but not the deadbolt. If Weston had gone out, Matt thought, surely he'd have locked the deadbolt. With an increasing feeling of dread, Matt climbed the stairs. At the top, there was a small landing; directly opposite was an open door into a bathroom, to the right an open door into what appeared to be an empty bedroom and, to the left, a closed door.

Telling himself it made sense to check out the open doorway first, but perhaps just putting off the inevitable, Matt gingerly stepped into the first bedroom. It looked like a rarely-used guest room; there was a bed with a bare mattress, pillows without covers, and no other decoration. Matt returned to the closed door, the door to what had to be the master bedroom, turned the knob, and opened it.

Although he'd more or less accepted what he was going to

find when he'd first heard about the gunshot, it didn't make it any less of a shock. Matt felt his hear rate soar as he took in the figure on the bed. Weston was dressed in sneakers, jeans and a sweatshirt. A pistol lay by his hip, where it had fallen, just after he'd put it in his mouth and pulled the trigger.

Matt didn't need to check the body, the amount of blood and other matter sprayed on the wall behind Weston's head made it very clear that he was far beyond any help Matt could give. He backed out of the room, treading quietly as if not to disturb the dead man. He went slowly downstairs and opened the front door to provide easier access to the emergency services that would presumably now, finally, show up. As he stepped outside and brought his phone out to call them, he saw a city police car pulling in at the front of the house. A heavyset man in a blue uniform climbed out of the car and began to walk down the short path.

"Are you Myles Weston?" He asked as he approached Matt.

"Afraid not. He's upstairs. It looks as if he's shot himself."

"Well, fuck," the officer said, hitching his belt up and looking towards the upstairs window as if he was somehow going to be able to see in. "Then who are you?"

"My name is Matt Ibarra. I'm a journalist. I was here to meet Mr Weston and when I heard about the gunshot I became concerned for his safety. so I, uh, broke in."

"Oh you did, huh? Ok, well, I'd better go take a look. You wait here."

"If it's ok with you, I'm going to speak to his neighbour. She was the one that called you, and she'll be concerned."

"Fine, but don't go far, and don't go back inside."

The police officer headed into the house. Matt went over to the front door to apartment D and rang the bell. When Lucia came to the door, he explained what he'd found.

"Oh, how terrible. How terrible. What a shock for you. Are you ok?"

"I'm ok, Ms Knowles, thank you. But what about you? Did you know Mr Weston well?"

"Not well really. He kept himself to himself. A nice man, but this, well, I don't think I'm completely surprised."

"What makes you say that?" Matt asked, resisting the temptation to take his notebook out.

"Oh, well, he never seemed a happy man. And a bit on edge, you might say? A bit jumpy. Do you know, I once saw him actually dive to the ground when some neighbourhood kids let off a firework one Saturday morning. He was so embarrassed, poor man."

"I see. You know about his background?"

"I know he was a deputy. Oh and I know he served, if that's what you mean. And, well, that's the trouble now isn't it. All these poor people, can't forget what happened to them over there, and they come back and years later, this… well, it's just very sad isn't it."

"It is. I should go out, the police are here, and they might want to speak to me."

"Yes, of course. I do hope you don't get in any trouble. You were right to break that door. You weren't to know that he wasn't up there dreadfully injured, were you?"

"Thank you. I am sure they'll see it that way."

By the time Matt got back outside, a second police unit had arrived along with an ambulance, as well as a green and brown police vehicle marked Sheriff's Department. The Sheriff's department had no particular jurisdiction here, but clearly someone had finally made the connection and worked out who the occupant of apartment C was, so Matt wasn't at all surprised they'd showed up. If anything, the only surprise was that there weren't a lot more of them. No doubt there soon would be.

The deputy spotted Matt as he came out of the house, and strode over, fists clenched, face red.

"What. The fuck. Are you doing here."

"I'm…"

"I know who you are. Leeches like you harassing people is exactly what makes things like this happen. Why couldn't you just leave him alone?" Matt could feel the deputy's breath on his face as he stood almost toe to toe with him. Matt took a step back.

"You've got it wrong, deputy. He asked me here, he wanted to speak to me."

"Bullshit. Wanted to speak to you so much that he blew his fucking brains out first?"

"I can't imagine the pressure he was under. But I don't think…"

"You know what, Ibarra. Get the fuck away from me. You've done enough damage."

"Perhaps I should stay until the local police say I can go."

"*I* say go. If they want you, they can find you." The deputy physically pointed Matt back in the direction of the street and gave him a little push. The encounter was humiliating but it did give Matt a neat excuse to leave. And the deputy was right, he was easy enough to find if they did want a statement, but the matter hardly looked like one that was going to need a whole lot of investigation.

Matt walked back in the direction of the Brighton Beach Grill, deciding he needed a drink before he went back to his hotel. As he retraced his steps back up the street, he couldn't shake the idea that there was something from the scene of Weston's suicide that didn't feel right.

19

Abeke had suggested that she and Josh meet on Sunday afternoon, and had picked a bar to meet at. It was behind an unmarked black door in Soho, and entry required ringing a bell and asking to be buzzed in. Inside, past a little coat-check and a red velvet curtain, the bar was dimly lit with flickering candles on each table and a low background track of swing music. When they sat down, Abeke in a red velvet armchair and Josh on a little satin sofa, a barman with a beard and manicured moustache crouched down next to them and asked them what sort of drinks they liked. Abeke ordered something specific by name, while Josh floundered and said he liked gin, and the barman promised to make him something he'd enjoy.

"Well this is… very cool. How on earth did you find out about this?"

"Well…" Abeke hesitated and then laughed.

"What?"

"For a second I thought I'd try and bluff that I just happen to know cool bars in every city in the world. But, to be honest, I might have called a friend who knows London well and asked them for some advice…"

"You have very different friends to me. Some of mine have lived in London all their lives, and if I asked them for a recommendation they'd still just say Wetherspoons."

"Wetherspoons?"

"I guess that's a British joke. It's a chain of pubs. If you want cheap beer and surprisingly ok food in a big, soulless room with sticky carpets, then it's the place to go."

Abeke laughed again.

"You crack me up, Josh."

Josh shrugged, smiling. He'd never really thought of himself as particularly funny, but the opportunity to riff on cultural differences – and the desire to make Abeke laugh – seemed to be working for him.

Their drinks came. Josh's was good; something like the gin and tonic that was about the closest thing to a cocktail he usually drank, but fruitier and richer and, he suspected, more alcoholic.

"How's your drink?" He asked.

"Oh, it's great. Want to try a bit? It's tequila, if you like that?"

"Oh, sure, thanks!" Josh took her cocktail and, ignoring the metal straw, drank from the side of the glass. It still felt pleasingly intimate. "Do you want to try a bit of mine?"

"Absolutely. Did he tell you what it was?"

"Not really. Something with lime and gin and berries I think. And maybe port? Is that weird?"

"Yes. It's good though."

They sipped their drinks and talked about work and comparisons between London and Palo Alto. Despite being a similar age and technically, both working in marketing, Josh couldn't help thinking how different their lives seemed. For one thing, Abeke had a close group of university friends who went round to each other's apartments and cooked dinners.

Josh had, well, Dan, who sometimes took responsibility for placing the Dominos order.

"So, I'm sorry, I can't believe I haven't asked. Where *did* you go to university?" Josh finally asked.

"Harvard. Did I not say? Sorry."

"Ah. That's impressive."

"Yeah. It's a good school."

"I thought understatement was supposed to be a British thing!"

"I apologise. Another drink?"

Josh agreed. This time he ordered the tequila-based drink Abeke had had.

"So, what was Harvard like? Is it what people think? Skull and Bones Club and... I dunno, geniuses in tweed jackets solving physics problems on chalkboards?"

Abeke laughed out loud.

"The Skull and Bones is at Yale. But, yes, everyone exclusively wears tweed except when they're rowing or playing lacrosse."

"And now you're doing sarcasm!" Josh said, mock-outraged. "At this rate I'll have nothing left!"

"Ok," Abeke said, smiling, "I'll stop, I'll stop. But to answer your question... it was great, of course. Sort of weird for me, in a way, though."

"Weird how?"

Abeke hesitated, eyes flicking upwards as if searching for the right words.

"Ok, well, I went to private school. And it sent a lot of people to the Ivy League. Like, a *lot*. So when I got there I already had some friends, and I was sort of in with the right crowd. So, I was lucky. But also... my private school wasn't exactly diverse, so Harvard was the first time I'd started making lots of other Black friends."

"Yeah I see what you mean. But, was that good? Being in a

different environment?"

"Oh definitely. I made loads more Black friends, went along to some events, even got involved in some campaigns. But then, some of the people there had this sense of identity that I've honestly never had. I kind of envied how certain they were of where they came from, what they were fighting for, even." She shrugged, looking slightly embarrassed by how much she was revealing. "Well, you know. Where I went to private school. My family. I'm not sure I'm exactly oppressed."

Josh thought how Abeke, for all her self-assurance and polish, must have felt stuck between two worlds, not totally fitting into either.

"I'm sure you've had your own things to contend with, though, right? I mean, it's not like oppression is a competition."

"Yeah," she sighed.

"Sorry, I didn't mean to pry."

"Oh, god, no. I'm just over-sharing. You didn't want to know all this."

"Of course I did. I asked, I'm interested."

Abeke looked as if she was hesitating for a second and then got up from her seat opposite Josh and came round to sit next to him on his sofa. They drank their cocktails in silence for a minute, and Josh could feel her leg resting softly on his.

The second cocktail led to three more, and a terrifying three figure bill that, despite Josh's protestations, Abeke snatched up and paid on her company card. "Supplier entertainment, right," she said. They walked, a little unsteadily, out into the freezing night air.

"How're you getting home?" He asked. She thought for a second.

"Walk to Piccadilly Circus, then straight run to Gloucester

Road. You could do the same, then change at Earl's Court, right?"

"Yeah, that works."

They walked together towards Piccadilly Circus tube station, chatting the enthusiastic nonsense of the happily drunk. Abeke swore a lot more when she was drunk, he noticed. It sounded incongruous in her bright Californian accent. As they chatted, though, Josh was thinking through possibilities, and possibilities that would probably be lost once they got on a tube train.

Finally, as they were approaching Piccadilly Circus, he stopped at the corner formed by one of the buttresses of the Piccadilly Institute.

"What's up?" She asked.

"Oh, it's just that once we get on the tube you'll have to jump off quickly at Gloucester Road and we won't be able to say goodbye properly."

"Say goodbye properly?" She said, with a little smile.

"Yeah," he said, and gently took her shoulder with his right hand, pulling her in for a kiss.

20

Matt knew the call from Luke was coming. He had been waiting for it all morning, after a sleepless night expecting the police to knock on his door, unable to shake images of Deputy Weston's dead body and brain-spattered bedroom wall, and unable to get rid of the sense that there was something important in those images that he was missing. Eventually his phone rang.

"Hi Luke," Matt said, resignation in his voice.

"Matt. How you doing? I hear you've had a tough time."

"It is what it is."

"You ok, though? We can help, if you want to talk to someone."

"I'm fine, Luke. Honestly." Matt wanted to move this along.

"Ok, well. Offer's always there. So, let's talk about your investigation. Where does this leave us?"

"There's definitely something here, Matt. Something's not quite right about it. I want to keep digging."

There was a long pause from the other end, then Luke sighed.

"Matt, honestly, from where I sit it's all looking pretty straightforward. The Sheriff's department have released a statement that makes it clear the blame is with deputy Weston. They've strongly implied undiagnosed PTSD from his military service."

"And that's it? He shoots a kid dead in broad daylight for no reason at all, and we're going to move on?"

"I'm not saying that. I'm saying, what's to investigate? Even the Defund the Police crowd are struggling to muster up much enthusiasm for protests when the only perpetrator has just killed himself."

"Come on Luke," Matt said, keeping his voice level. "You're smart enough to know he's not the only perpetrator. Things like this don't happen in isolation."

"That's a social studies thesis, not a Washington Record investigation. Do you have anything specific?"

"Not yet," Matt admitted.

"Right. Then look, you've got a decent story. This is a fucking tragedy; a young man's life cut short, a deputy with PTSD who shouldn't have been carrying a firearm, and a Sheriff's department that's rightly shouldering a lot of the blame. Write it up, send it in, and come back so you can move on to something else."

"What about the video footage?"

"What footage?" Luke asked, starting to sound impatient.

"The helmet camera footage from the deputies. Why won't the department release it?"

"God knows. Maybe it reveals the deputies were shit-talking the Governor. Does it matter? It's not like anyone's denying what happened. Ask them, then quote them in your story, when you send it in. Which will be today. By 10pm."

"That's it?"

"That's it. And come in to the office on your way back home, ok? We'll cover flights."

Luke hung up, leaving Matt looking at his phone, and at the partially-finished story on his laptop. Wearily, he began to add to it, including more detail about Weston's background, military and police service, and the hints at undiagnosed PTSD. He wrote dispassionately about the deputy's body being found at his home, without providing any information about the circumstances. He fleshed out the existing brief paragraph about the existence of the helmet cameras, adding in one of the screen-grabs he'd already taken from the video that showed them in best detail. Finally, he called the Sheriff's department media office for comment. He received, as he'd expected, a bland quote stating that the department was 'investigating whether any relevant footage had been captured'.

Finally, after one last proof-read, he emailed the story to Luke, and opened another tab to book his flights to Washington.

21

Josh levered his eyes open with considerable effort and peered at his phone. A wave of exhaustion and a dull ache in every joint in his body threatened to overwhelm him. He knew he done this to himself and now the day would be a write-off. Yet somehow, unlike the many previous occasions when he'd woken up filled with hangover and despair, he felt surprisingly cheerful.

As he walked to the tube station, he worked on a suitably breezy message to Abeke. *'Hey, yesterday was really fun — though feeling a little worse for wear this morning! Would be nice to do it again some time?'* Her response came back by the time he picked up signal again getting off the tube near his office; *'It was so nice! Me too - today's going to be a struggle. Definitely, are you free one day this week?'*

Josh glowed inwardly, and the hangover seemed to recede even further.

When he got to his desk and opened his laptop, there was an email from Pete Taylor. Josh had seen nothing of the BluJacket CTO since that initial meeting, and heard very little from him although he was occasionally CCd on emails. This email apologised, briefly, for the delay in supplying the technical documents and said that everything Josh needed was in two attached files.

Before Josh faced those, he replied to Abeke. He had no fixed plans all week, apart from a vague idea of doing something with Dan and Marco on Thursday. He let Abeke know he was free any other day, and her reply came back almost instantly.

'Great. Dinner? Tomorrow, if that's not too short notice? Do you know anywhere good?'

Josh thought for a second and then suggested a Tapas place he'd once been to in Fulham. He hoped it would strike the right balance of interesting but not overly formal. Abeke agreed enthusiastically, and he used OpenTable to make a booking.

Finally, he put his phone to one side and concentrated back on work. The documents from Pete were encrypted and passworded, which was promising somehow. But, when Josh opened them, they consisted of little more than a four-page PDF marketing leaflet and a short word document. The leaflet remained vague and prone to veiling simple facts in jargon – 'a 360 degree optical situational awareness system' in place of 'a camera' – but now that Josh knew from Paul how BluJacket worked he was able to read between the lines. The most notable thing about the leaflet, though, was that it actually showed a picture of the devices. Towards the bottom of the second page was a nicely staged and well-lit image of US soldiers moving into a compound. They were attractive and diverse with clean uniforms and shiny rifles, but what caught his eye was the little camera on the front of each helmet, and the unusually bulky, clear-lensed wraparound glasses that each soldier was wearing.

Josh scrolled to zoom in on the picture but it quickly became pixelated and didn't help to show much more detail.

He could see that each camera had a small black wire running down to the base of the helmet, where it wrapped around to the back. One of the soldiers was turning slightly away from the camera and Josh thought he could make out a camera on the back of his helmet as well. That made sense, from what Paul had told him about the system.

Josh closed the browser, went back to the encrypted folder that Pete had sent him, and opened the word document. This was far less glossy, and was described as a 'technical summary'. It certainly contained a lot of technical jargon; summaries of theoretical machine learning methodologies and links to white papers about existing technologies including the CCTV systems Paul had mentioned. In the final section, it listed a whole range of testing the system had undergone; in-house alpha and beta testing leading on to tests with the US Army and something described as a *'Live Pilot - Law Enforcement, Colorado'*. There was no mention of any testing at all with the British Army, but the US Government had apparently given BluJacket numerous stamps of approval including a gushing endorsement by a currently-serving three star General.

At the very end was a section labelled 'upcoming validation studies and pilots' and two items underneath it. The first, fairly innocuously, was *'Live Pilot - Consumer Use, Michigan'* but the second was far more eye-catching. *'Live Pilot - JSOC, Syria'*. JSOC was an acronym he recognised from movies and books; the Joint Special Operations Command of the US Army. Still heavily deployed in places such as Syria, and still taking casualties on a frequent basis. Giving them access to a tool like this, if it worked, could quite literally be a life-saver. But if it didn't work, or only partially worked – could it be dangerous or give them a false sense of confidence? As dangerous as going into combat in inadequately-armoured Land Rovers that the government insisted were fine? Maybe, maybe not. Maybe no one would know until the first casualties rolled in.

Josh forwarded the email on to Vijai and Rob with an accompanying note. *'Quite a bit more detail here about a) how the product works and b) that it does work. Hope this helps.'* Then he closed the folder, hoping that the documents convinced the creative team more successfully than they'd convinced him.

By the end of the day, Josh's failure to do any productive work was starting to eat away at his good mood. He was briefly relieved and felt a tiny sense of satisfaction at successfully resolving a small blocker in the project when Rob replied to his email. *'Well, if the US government have tested it, then who are we to question?! Vijai and I are getting on with the concepts. Catch up tomorrow?'*

He left the office on the dot of six. Not a single other person on his floor had left yet, and he knew he'd be noticed leaving before anyone else, but he wasn't sure he cared. He'd achieved nothing all day and he'd achieve nothing by spending another hour at his desk. All he wanted was to get home, crash on the sofa, and hope that Dan was sympathetic about his hangover.

As he was getting to the underground, though, his phone pinged with an email to his personal account. The sender's name showed as James McCormick, which wasn't a name he recognised. The email address itself was jamesmc@guerillamail.com, and that caught his attention as he knew Guerrilla Mail to be a free, anonymous, disposable email provider. Anyone could create any email address and send an email from it, but would be near-impossible to trace.

The subject line was 'Info'. He double-clicked the email, it contained just a link to a WeTransfer download, and three short sentences: *'I heard you're interested in BluJacket. This may be interesting. Be careful.'*

* * *

Josh, in spite of himself, waited until he got home to download the WeTransfer file, and even then did so on his personal laptop, not the mobile phone that his work paid for. He had no idea what to expect, but the cloak and dagger nature of the email made him wary.

The file downloaded quickly. It was just a PDF, and only a two-page one at that. It appeared to be a letter or memo, typed and printed but then scanned; there were signs of stapling at one corner, and large parts of it were blanked out by hand with black ink. It was laid out in the neat numbered-paragraph format that Josh faintly recognised as distinctive of military documents, but all of the identifying information at the top that might show the name of the sender or recipient had been redacted.

Josh scanned through it. Reading between the heavy redactions, it was evidently a brief summary of the results of the trials that had been conducted to test BluJacket. His pulse quickened as he read to the final two paragraphs:

7. More extensive testing in a wider range of settings demonstrated performance well below the promised functionality of the product, making it not viable for operational use for this or any other unit.

8. Furthermore, testing identified deceptive practices in the presentation and demonstration of the unit, and even into the initial testing phases, such that we could not recommend further engagement with this vendor.

I remain, sir, your obedient servant

The rest was redacted.

Josh looked at the document and read through it again. The clinical language of the author did not do much to disguise the blunt conclusions. Namely, the product didn't work, or at least hadn't worked when the unit had conducted proper tests on it. And, worse, they felt that BluJacket had been deceptive in some way. But how, exactly?

He looked back at the original email. The timing of its arrival and the words 'be careful' made him immediately assume that it had come from Paul. After all, who else had access to this sort of document and knew that Josh would be interested? And yet, why would Paul hide behind a pseudonym and say 'I hear you're looking into BluJacket' when Josh had directly asked him about it?

Not expecting to find anything, Josh nevertheless tried Googling 'James McCormick'. To his surprise, the name returned a huge number of results. Results that shed another worrying light on the information.

The top result for Josh's search was a BBC Article, *'James McCormick jailed for selling fake bomb detectors'*. Josh read the article; an almost unbelievable story about a man who had made millions selling bomb detectors to the Afghan Army. He'd successfully disguised, behind complex-sounding technology, the fact that they did not in fact work at all.

It seemed unlikely that the real James McCormick, only recently released from prison, had sent Josh the email. Equally, the idea of there being some other James McCormick who happened to be emailing Josh about malfunctioning military equipment seemed a coincidence too far. So, he had to assume it was the real sender making a point, and not a particularly subtle one.

He printed out the document from the email, folded it into a book shoved into the middle of his bookshelf, and then deleted the download, the email, and his internet history. He knew enough about computers to realise that wouldn't do nearly enough to erase the trail from someone with a bit of knowledge and determination, but he wasn't quite ready yet to embrace fully-fledged paranoia and take a circular saw to his hard drive.

Then he went into the living room to find Dan who,

fortunately, was entirely happy to commiserate over Josh's hangover. He'd had a similarly difficult day after a late night in an East London wine bar with Marco and was ready to share some misery, some takeaway curry, and some television. They both lay almost horizontal on their sofa and let episode after episode of *Below Decks* wash over them. After a bit, Josh turned his head very slightly towards his flatmate.

"Hey Dan."

"Hey buddy. What's up?"

"Give me some advice. Help me with something."

"Of course. As long as it doesn't require movement. Or doing the washing up."

"Neither of those. It's a work thing."

Dan sighed.

"Your work sucks. I can't help you."

"No it doesn't. Well, yeah, it does. Actually, right now it's kind of interesting but, that's not the thing. The thing is…" he hesitated. How to frame this? "We're advertising a product, and it might not work. And if it doesn't work, it might be dangerous. But the company says it's been tested, and it works."

"Oh, mate. I think I'm too hungover for this. What's the product? Why might it not work?"

"It's a sort of military gadget. And the British Army tested it and said they didn't want it, but the Americans tested it and seem to love it. So now I don't know if it's dangerous or not."

"Like chlorine chickens." Dan said, thoughtfully.

"What?"

"Like chickens, washed in chlorine. The British say it's dangerous, the Americans say it isn't. Which is it? Dangerous or not dangerous. Maybe we'll never know."

"No, not like that. Or, I dunno. Maybe it *is* like that, actually. I guess it *could* be just different safety standards."

"You sound as if you want proper advice." Dan said, looking over at him.

"I thought that's what I said."

"What you say and what you want are so often different, Joshie. It's hard to be sure."

"Well, yeah, proper advice."

"Ok," said Dan. "Well, do you actually have any evidence it doesn't work?"

Josh hesitated for so long that Dan actually levered himself up on one elbow and looked at him, a worried expression clouding his face.

"Have you got something you shouldn't have?"

"Let's say, I don't have what you'd call evidence. But I have… enough to be pretty sure there's an issue."

"Well, shit. If you're serious about this, here's my advice. Either back off completely, or go forward properly. You can put this to one side, forget about it, and live your life. No one would blame you. Or, if you can't live with that, then ok. Get some evidence, be a whistleblower, contact *The Guardian*, whatever it takes. The law protects whistleblowers. But whatever you're doing right now, it's worst of both worlds."

"Yeah."

"Yeah?"

"Yeah. I appreciate the advice, Dan. You're the best."

"Fucking right I am. 'Nother episode?" Dan asked, as Netflix cheerfully queued one up and gave them 20 seconds to summon the willpower to say no.

22

"Evening." Chris said, answering his ringing phone and letting his wireless headphones pick up his voice as he carried on with his bench presses.

"Evening. The Colorado situation is back under control then?"

"I told you I'd manage it."

"And I told you you'd fucking better, so I guess we were both right. No loose ends?"

"No loose ends." Chris answered, firmly, at the same time as he slammed the bar back onto the hooks and stood up, mopping his forehead with his towel.

"Are you sure, Chris? Are you quite sure? Because, let me tell you, I was reading the Washington Record with my toast and fucking orange juice this morning and the article by Matt Fucking Ibarra did not give me warm fuzzy feelings that this has all gone away."

"He's got nothing. He dug a bit, and found nothing, and now there's nothing *to* find. He's done."

"You'd better be right. The committee is meeting tomorrow and they're ready to move ahead, but if the chairman reads a load of idle speculation about BluJacket while he's taking his morning shit, then. Things. Will not. Go. Your. Way. Am I clear?"

Chris took a couple of deep breaths, and chucked another 5lbs on each end of the bar.

"You're clear. We're back on track now, trust me."

When he'd finished his final set of bench presses, Chris dialled Pete's number. It rang out the first time and he had to call back, before Pete finally answered on the fourth ring.

"What is it?" He sounded sleepy and irritated.

"Oh, I'm sorry, I didn't check the time difference…"

"Fuck me Chris, you run a transatlantic company. Maybe it's time to get a watch. It's four in the morning here."

"I'm sorry, dude. I really am," Chris said, hurriedly. "But look, we need to talk."

"Go on then."

"I think we've got this all wrapped up. We're clear to proceed with the Aleppo pilot."

"Fine. Anything else?" Pete said, voice tight with annoyance.

"I thought you'd want to know."

"I would. At, let's say, nine o'clock this morning? Now can I go back to sleep?"

"Wait. With Aleppo… we're going to have to carry on with the current approach. At least for now," Chris added hurriedly.

There was silence on the other end for just long enough that Chris wondered if his business partner had actually fallen asleep again.

"Why do we have to? Where's your faith in the tech?" Pete said eventually. He sounded more than usually petulant, and Chris had to calm himself before answering. It wouldn't do to piss off his partner. Not at this stage.

"It's not about faith. We've run out of time. The pilot will start any day now, and if we don't perform, it's game over. And I don't just mean the end of the company… serious people have staked their careers and personal fortunes on this. We cannot afford to disappoint them."

"Whatever," Pete said, still petulant. "If it gets me the time and the money to make this work, I suppose I don't care."

"Sure," Chris said, wondering silently how many times Pete had told him that he just needed a bit more time, and a bit more money. And Chris had secured both, doing whatever it took to keep the company alive and fed with a seemingly endless stream of investor capital, until that had become his only goal. Now, he reflected grimly, it was far too late to do anything other than maintain the illusion. By any means necessary.

"Well, I'll let you sleep." Chris said, and hung up.

23

Josh ran to the office the next day, delighting in simply not feeling hungover, and enjoying the burn in his legs as he pushed himself to try and achieve a new personal best for the route to work. It was always quicker on the way in, when the streets were less crowded, but his time was still somewhat at the mercy of traffic lights and pedestrians.

As he passed along the Battersea Embankment, he noticed a crowd of protestors in the road ahead of him, marshalled by a handful of police officers in yellow jackets. Some carried Black Lives Matter signs, or placards with the words 'I can't breathe' or 'Justice for Nate'. For a second he wondered what they were doing there, and then realised that he was running past the US Embassy, and made the connection to a story he'd seen on the news about a shooting in the USA. A young man had been shot dead by police and, as seemed to be the case in too many similar events, he had been Black, unarmed, and posing no threat at the time he was shot.

He kept on running, pushing his pace up and wondering why the shooting, despite being front-page news, had made so little impact on him until now. He thought about the gut-punch he still felt whenever he heard about British soldiers killed on operations, and a sick day he'd once taken to curl up in bed when a story focused a little too closely on young children left behind by those soldiers. Presumably those stories washed over most people, maybe a tut and a shake of the head at the futility of it all. Did that make them heartless? Did Josh's only faint awareness of the tragedy in Fort Pinebec make *him* heartless, or worse?

Maybe seeing some world events as nothing more than a sad bit of news, and others as devastatingly close to home was just part of being human. Perhaps, he thought, empathy had to work that way otherwise he and everyone else would spend every day of their lives curled up in bed in despair at the sheer amount of misery out there.

When he finally got to the office he looked at his message history with Abeke. They were now exchanging a few dozen messages a day, chatting about whatever was on their mind - with the exception of work, which was kept strictly to email. He started typing a question, wanting to ask her about her own thoughts on Nathan Adams, but not able to find words that didn't sound crass. In the end, he put his phone away and went down to the showers to get ready for work.

After he sat at his desk, trawled through emails, and made a coffee, he opened up the BBC news home page and found the latest update on the Nathan Adams story. It was no longer the top item, but was still prominently featured, although now the main headline was *'Deputy Implicated in Killing of Nathan Adams Dies in Suspected Suicide'*. He clicked into the story. Towards the top was a formal picture of Myles Weston in his Sheriff's Deputy's uniform, and further down was a picture of Nathan Adams taken from a recent half-marathon he'd completed. Josh looked at his expression, a combination of exhaustion, happiness and shy pride in his accomplishment that Josh recognised from some of his own post-race photos. That recognition, and the realisation that Nate had been killed when out on just the kind of early morning training run that Josh did several times a week, made the young man feel much more real.

At the bottom of the article was a grainy shot that looked like a still taken from a video, showing two men in body armour and helmets, one facing to left of frame but starting to turn round, while the other faced to right of frame and had his weapon raised to the aim. Something about the photo struck Josh as familiar, and he opened it in a tab of its own to look at it in more detail.

The image opened in the new tab at almost twice the size, and Josh peered at the SWAT officers. It was their helmets, specifically the little cameras on the front and back of each, with wires running around the base of the helmet, and the bulky clear-lensed glasses each was wearing. They looked identical to the ones he had seen in the marketing image of soldiers wearing BluJacket gear. Josh slowly re-opened the document Pete had sent him, with all of the details of testing done by BluJacket. Sure enough, almost at the bottom, *'Live Pilot - Law Enforcement, Colorado'*. By that point, Josh didn't need to check that Fort Pinebec was in Colorado, but he did so anyway. It was.

He went back to the article and read it again, then pressed Ctrl-F and searched for BluJacket, just to be sure he hadn't missed it. There was no mention of it anywhere in the article. He opened another tab and searched for *'Nathan Adams BluJacket'* but nothing containing all three terms came back. Then he tried just *'Nathan Adams helmet cameras'*. This time the top result was a long article from the Washington Record, and part-way down was a whole section about the fact that footage from the 'helmet cameras' had still not been released, but nothing to suggest the cameras were anything different to those regularly worn by police officers all over the US.

Josh sat back in his chair, stunned. Was it possible that no one else, or at least no one outside BluJacket, had made the connection? Even the author of the Washington Record piece seemed to be suspicious that footage was being withheld but not to have realised that the 'cameras' themselves were anything special. He scrolled back up to the top to see the byline, *Matt Ibarra*. It was underlined and, when he hovered over it, flashed up a little box saying 'Investigative Reporter' and showing his email address. Josh wrote it down on a piece of paper and put it in his jacket pocket. Then he closed all of the browser windows and stared at his laptop for a long time without doing anything.

24

Matt sat at the departure gate flicking through news coverage. His story was already buried well onto the second half of Washington Record's homepage, and similar stories about events in Fort Pinebec were no longer given top billing anywhere in other outlets. He sighed, closed his phone, and glanced up at the board above the gate. His flight to Washington DC left just after eleven, and would be boarding any minute. He stood and got into the queue, continuing to swipe through emails, news stories, back to emails, and occasionally Twitter as he waited for his row to be called.

Eventually, he was seated on the plane. He refreshed his email one more time, and saw a new email come in. The name, simply 'Josh' with no surname, didn't mean anything to him but the subject line *'BluJacket'* almost took his breath away. He'd spent the 48 hours since Myles Weston's death wondering what he could have meant by the phrase 'blue jacket' but unable to come up with anything relevant, and now it appeared to be staring him in the face. He quickly clicked on the email, and read its contents with fascination.

Dear Mr Ibarra,

I know you don't know me, but I read your article about the tragic shooting in Fort Pinebec. I am working, indirectly, for a company called BluJacket and I think they have a connection to the shooting that you may not be aware of. Is there a way we can speak? I am based in the United Kingdom but you can call me on my mobile, +44 7700 900195.

Thanks,

Josh

Matt swore under his breath. The engines were already starting up, there was no way off the plane now, and no point starting a call to Josh that he would be forced to end either by a vigilant flight attendant or simply by losing cell signal. The flight was nearly three and a half hours, a painful wait to access this tantalising information, but there was nothing that could be done. As quickly as he could, before he risked losing signal, Matt drafted a response.

Josh - this is extremely interesting to me. I am on a plane about to take off but I will call you in around 4 hours. Thank you for contacting me. Matt

Then he sat back in his chair and prayed for a quick takeoff and smooth flight.

When the plane landed, Matt quick set his watch to East Coast time and did a bit of math. It was only a little after 7pm in the UK, still surely a reasonable time to call the mysterious Josh. He got off the plane as quickly as he possibly could, found himself a quiet area of the terminal, and then dialled the number he'd been given in Josh's email.

It only rang a couple of times, and then was picked up. The voice at the other end was young, English, and sounded a little anxious.

"Hello?"

"Is this Josh? It's Matt Ibarra here, from the Washington Record. You emailed me."

"Oh, yes. Thanks for calling me back."

"You're welcome. So, I was really interested in what you said in your email. Is it ok to speak now?" Matt pulled out his notebook and a pen, and headed up a new page.

"Yes, sure. But, first off, can I ask for all this to be off the record?"

"Ok. So, that means I won't quote anything you say, or even suggest that it came from a source. Is that alright?"

"Yeah, that's what I want."

"Ok," Matt said. "Can you start by telling me who you are, and maybe how you're connected to this?"

"Yeah. Well, I work for a marketing agency. And recently we were employed by a company called BluJacket, which has a product – that's what I wanted to tell you about really. Because it looks from the photos I saw as if BluJacket was being used by the police officers who shot Nathan Adams."

Matt scribbled furiously, circling the word BluJacket with a mix of excitement and frustration that he'd had this crucial link in his grasp for several days and not been able to do anything with it.

"Ok, ok. That's great. You know what, give me a second, I want to plug my headphones in so I can look these guys up on my phone." Matt did so, and then Googled BluJacket. He quickly got their corporate website.

"Alright," Matt said, browsing through the site. "So they make some kind of self-defence tool? I'm struggling to figure out much from the site…"

The voice on the other end laughed, though it didn't sound particularly amused.

"It doesn't give much away, does it? What it actually is, is a camera, or two cameras really. You wear them facing forward and backwards. Then, those are linked to the BluJacket server, and that runs an artificial intelligence program. The program detects and highlights threats, and sends the information down to those goggles you could see the police officers wearing. Does that make sense?"

"I think so. Fuck me. Excuse my language, but... I think I'm seeing how this might have played out."

"How so?" Josh asked.

"Did you see the video?"

"I don't think so. There was a video?"

"Yeah. Uh, a lot of sites have taken it down but I think you can find it if you Google. Take a look." He waited, and after a minute or two, Josh's voice came back on the line. It sounded tense, angry, but maybe even a bit excited.

"He literally turned round and shot Nathan Adams without barely even looking at him. So you're thinking —"

"Yeah, what if he's got this BluJacket device turned on, so one of the cameras is looking backwards. Then for some reason it identifies the kid as a threat, Weston gets an alert from BluJacket, and he reacts without thinking."

Matt thought about Deputy Weston's experience in Iraq. The possible undiagnosed PTSD. And the words he'd said on the phone, 'I panicked. I should have waited. Should have checked'. Then he thought of something else. "Of course, that raises the question of why would the system have alerted?"

"Ok, so that's the other thing I wanted to tell you," said Josh, his voice quick with tension. "I have a friend in the British Army, and he got me some information. Apparently some special forces unit over here trialled it and it didn't work at all. They said it wasn't fit for use, *and* they even said they thought BluJacket might be intentionally trying to make it seem better than it was."

"Well. Fuck."

Matt stared at his notes. There was almost too much new information here. He tried to make sense of it and work out where to go next. Suddenly his phone buzzed, he had another incoming call – Luke. He ignored it.

"Do you think you can find out more?" Josh was asking. "I read an internal document that they're testing this with special forces units on operations, so if it's already failed like this, God knows what could happen…"

Matt's phone rang again. Luke again.

"Josh, hang on, please don't go away." Matt said quickly. "I need to take another call. I'll put you on hold." He hit 'hold and accept' on his phone. "Yes, Luke?"

"Matt, where are you? Our driver is waiting for you, he said you never come out of the terminal."

"I didn't know you'd sent someone."

"Well I did. Where are you?"

"I got delayed. I'll be there in a minute. I've got to go."

"Fine. Be quick." Luke hung up before Matt even had a chance. He reconnected with Josh.

"I'm back. Look, I've got to go. I can absolutely look into this, I think there's a story here. But we should talk more. Can I call you again tomorrow, first thing for me — around noon for you?"

"Uh, yeah, sure. Thanks."

"Thank *you*," Matt said, firmly.

Sure enough, the Washington Record had sent a car for Matt. He got into the back and immediately got his phone out, devouring everything he could online about BluJacket. Founded by an ex-US soldier, they appeared to have close links with the US Military and have signed some contracts with both the military and some small-town police forces. More recent press releases suggested a new focus on launching a product for the consumer market.

Trawling through their website, he found a press relations contact on a generic email address. He considered sending them an email but, instead, took a gamble and simply changed '*press@BluJacket.com*' to '*chris.adamson@BluJacket.com*' and put that into the to field instead. He thought for a second and then, having a bit of experience with how start-ups tended to operate, also added just '*chris@BluJacket.com*'.

He considered appealing to the founder's vanity and approaching him as if he were working on a puff piece, but he knew that a second's Googling would expose Matt's recent stories from Fort Pinebec. Besides, he was in a rush and thought there was a chance that fear might work faster than vanity. He drafted a quick email saying that he was 'looking into the role of BluJacket products in the recent tragedy in Colorado' and 'would be grateful for a clarifying interview with a senior representative from BluJacket before imminent publication of a major story'. He hoped that would do the job.

Then he settled back into the taxi and watched Washington roll slowly by outside until he arrived at his newspaper's headquarters. It had been almost six months since he was last here. Working remotely from New York and spending a lot of time on the road pursuing stories left him with few reasons to come in to the newsroom, and increasingly he felt less energised by the buzz of it and more depressed by the fact that all that buzz was generated by people younger and more ambitious than he.

Matt found Luke in one of the building's coffee areas, reading what looked like an early mockup of tomorrow's paper. He looked as if he'd aged a lot more than half a year since Matt had last spoken to him in person. His hair was thinner and greyer and his eyes looked sunken. Matt placed himself in a chair opposite him and raised his eyebrows expectantly.

"You summoned me, master."

"Don't do that, Matt. You need to come into the office occasionally."

"I'm working on a story."

"No you're not. You've finished a story. And by the sound

of things you've had a hard time. What about taking a break?" Luke smoothed the pages of the newspaper mockup. It looked odd with all the white spaces where adverts and, in some cases, final stories would go.

"I don't need a break. And I'm still working on the Nathan Adams story. I've got new information."

Luke's eyes narrowed.

"Oh?" he said.

Matt explained the latest information he'd got from Josh. Luke listened, leaning in closer and closer as Matt unraveled more details. Finally, when Matt was done, he laid both hands flat on the table and looked up at the ceiling, deep in thought.

"Ok," he said, eventually.

"Ok?"

"Ok. I have to tell you, Matt, you're on thin ice with some of the staff here. But, *if* this pans out, it's an absolute beast of a story. So, yes, fine. You win. Pursue it."

"That's it? You brought me all the way to DC for that?"

"No, obviously not. I brought you all the way to DC to tell you to get your shit together and work on some proper investigations or you won't be on this staff for much longer. Yet here we are. So go and finish the story."

Matt went back out into the newsroom and found a spare hot desk to work at. The first thing he did was pull up his email and see if he'd had a response. There was no reply, but the chris.adamson email had bounced back as undeliverable. That was, in fact, a good sign. The 'chris' address *hadn't* bounced so presumably was a working email. Matt wondered how long it would take to get a reaction from BluJacket.

25

"Sorry about that," Josh said, hanging up his phone call with Matt. The journalist had called while Josh had been waiting outside the restaurant where he'd agreed to meet Abeke, who had appeared just as he was finishing the conversation.

He leant hesitantly towards Abeke and, to his relief, she gave him a long kiss. She looked amazing; dressed with an elegance that made Josh feel scruffy and awkward, despite the time he'd spent picking out and ironing a shirt.

"That was a work thing," Josh explained. "They called just a few minutes before we were supposed to meet and I thought they'd be done by the time you got here."

"That's ok. Anything important?"

"Oh, no, not really. So, shall we go in?"

"Absolutely," she said, following him into the tapas restaurant.

As they sat at the table and began looking through the menu, she began cheerfully asking him about his day. After a few questions, though, she obviously noticed something was up.

"Hey, Josh, is everything ok? You seem distracted."

"Oh, yeah, sorry. Just work stuff." He answered quickly, and tried to snap himself back to the enthusiasm that he'd felt for the date when Abeke had first suggested it. Before he'd realised BluJacket's role in the death of a young man in America, and before he'd learnt that potentially broken technology was about to be deployed to special forces units in Syria. He slid his hand across the table for Abeke's. She took it and interlaced her fingers with his.

"You always dress this nicely?" He asked. "I feel bad, I look a complete scruff-ball."

"You look cute!" She said, and squeezed his hand. "But yeah, I do. That's a me thing though, I'll tell you about it some time."

Josh laughed. "Oh ok then. Well, I'll just continue to let the side down as long as it's cute."

She smiled at him, and for a while Josh was able to push all his concerns out of his mind and enjoy the conversation and the food. As they finally polished off all the gambas and pulpo and patatas bravas they could manage, though, Josh kept thinking back to his conversation with Dan. Back off or move forward, Dan had said, but you can't just wait and worry and do nothing. He also couldn't shake the image of Nate Adams happily holding his half marathon medal, the anger he'd felt at the senselessness of his death, and the desire to *do something* about it.

"By the way," Josh finally said, sipping some wine to hide his nerves. "Thanks for that information Pete sent over. I passed it on to Vijai and Rob and I think they're happy so, full steam ahead on the concepts and we should have a first pass for you by the end of this week."

"That's great."

Josh hesitated for a second, put the glass down, and went for it. "I was interested to see all the testing done in America. You haven't thought of trying it with the British Army?"

Abeke's expression didn't change; if there was anything uncomfortable about the question, or she had any suspicion that he had an ulterior reason for asking it, she gave nothing away.

"No, not yet. From what I hear Chris is focusing on the US first. That's his background of course, even though the technology was developed here."

"Oh, yeah. Well, that makes sense. And it all works, right, the tech?"

"Of course it works. Why're you asking? Is someone saying it *doesn't* work? Is that why you've been off all night?"

Josh, surprised by the genuinely hurt expression on her face, quickly tried to recover the situation.

"Oh, no, not at all. It's just the creatives. Vijai and Rob. They're conspiracists, honestly, they're always giving me shit about how customer claims are too good to be true. I'm sorry, I just wanted to set them straight."

"Trust me, I believe in Chris and if he says it works then it works. But, let's not talk about work?"

"Yeah, of course. Sorry."

Josh covered the awkwardness by looking round for a waiter and summoning the bill. As they paid and gathered their coats, Josh asked, "so, do you want to go on somewhere for another drink?"

"Yeah, although... I'm not gonna lie, I'm kinda tapped out budget-wise," Abeke said, laughing. "We're not far from my place. It's an AirBnB but it's pretty nice – we could swing by a liquor store, get a bottle of something, then head back there?"

"Sure," said Josh, as if the suggestion had no implications beyond the convenience of a cheap drink. "Let's find a 'liquor store' then. Pretty sure there's a Tesco on the corner just around here."

Abeke's AirBnB *was* surprisingly nice. A mews house a few minutes walk from Gloucester Road, it had been clumsily divided up into glossily generic apartments, clearly with AirBnB and business travellers in mind. Abeke's was a studio with the bed tucked into a curtained alcove, and one corner kitted out as a kitchen. A soft seating area was clustered around a modern-looking gas fireplace set into an exposed brick wall.

"This place is pretty great. The only time I travelled for work I ended up in a Holiday Inn."

"It's nice, but honestly it works out cheaper than a hotel for the length of time I'm here. And having a kitchen means I don't have to be eating out all the time, so the company actually prefers it."

At that moment, Josh's phone buzzed in his pocket. He glanced at his wrist, where the first line of the notification appeared on his Garmin watch, and his pulse quickened when he saw it was another email from the mysterious 'James McCormick'. Discreetly, while Abeke went over to the kitchen to find a corkscrew for the bottle of wine they'd bought, he clicked the 'down' button on his watch a couple of times to read slightly more of the limited preview available.

From: James McCormick <james.mccormick@guerillamail.com>
Subject: Mickey Cook
You should look into a YouTuber called Mickey Cook. He supposedly 'killed himself' but I'm pretty sure that's not true.

Josh froze. Mickey Cook was the cheerful, if pompous, YouTuber whose videos about AI Josh had watched when he first started working on BluJacket. How on earth, Josh wondered, was Cook connected with whoever was emailing him? He stared at the message on his watch for a second, then reached for his phone, just as Abeke came over with two glasses of wine.

"Everything ok?" She asked.

"Oh yes, sorry." He put the phone back in his pocket and took the glass of wine. "Just, um, checking something."

He was more sure than ever that 'James McCormick' wasn't Paul. The dignified colonel and self-appointed Godfather to Paul was hardly the type to be sending cryptic messages about the death of obscure YouTubers. But that only raised more questions. Who was sending the emails? Why were they interested in Mickey Cook? And what did Mickey Cook's supposed suicide have to do with anything?

They took the glasses of wine over to the seating area and, despite the great lengths of plush grey sofa, sat close to each other. Abeke leant into Josh, and he sat with one arm along the back of the sofa so it draped softly over her shoulder. As they chatted and drew closer, and eventually abandoned the last quarter of the wine and went up to Abeke's bedroom, there remained an insistent, distracting voice in the back of Josh's head. A voice that asked; was he being lied to and, if so, who by?

26

Matt itched to have another conversation with Josh, but he knew it would have to wait. By now the young Brit would probably be in bed asleep and, by the time he woke up, Matt would be asleep himself. He pledged to call him first thing in the morning. In the meantime, he looked at his scribbled notes and debated what from the mass of information from their first call he could usefully follow up on. The use of BluJacket by Special Operations was worth trying to get a quote on, even though it would be likely be a flat denial or refusal to comment on classified new technology. He stood up and looked across the newsroom, checking that his colleague Simon was at his desk before making the journey over. He was there, and Matt walked across to him.

"Hey Simon."

"Hey Matt," Simon exclaimed with genuine enthusiasm. "Haven't seen you in the office in a while. What gives?"

"Oh, just came in to get torn a new asshole by Luke. The usual. Hey, listen, you ever heard of anything called BluJacket?"

Simon was one of the Record's National Security

Correspondents, with a special focus on the US Military. He was well-connected and well-liked at the Pentagon, and had an inside track that often enabled him to get off-the-record comments even on some of the most sensitive topics.

"I have actually. Why, what's your interest?" Simon spun his chair round to face Matt, and gestured to a little stool that he kept by his desk for visitors. Matt took a seat.

"It's come up in a story I'm working on. What can you tell me about it?"

"Defence-tech start-up. Founder is a guy called Chris Adamson. Former Green Beret and well connected in the SpecOps community. He's hired a buncha guys from tier one units, too, so he's got all the right links. On the tech side, you've got some Brit with a funny accent and an IQ that looks like a zip code, talking about artificial intelligence and machine learning until investors get so turned on they're just throwing money at it."

"Ok." Matt scribbled some notes down, there wasn't a lot here he hadn't figured out himself. "And it's this, like, magic camera technology?"

Simon laughed. "Sure, you could say that. The hardware is nothing, honestly you could pick that shit up from Walmart. But, this Brit, he's developed something he calls The Mind. Started it off for his PhD. And now he's spending 200 million dollars in VC money on the Bay Area's best and brightest engineers, and he's got some all-singing, all-dancing, artificial intelligence. The cameras just send footage to it, then The Mind analyses it all in ten millionths of a second and sends back alerts. You know 'look closer at this wire' or 'that dude has a gun' or whatever. Incredible stuff, honestly."

"No shit. And he's selling it to the Pentagon?"

"From what I heard, the Pentagon is *begging* for it. Apparently, when a bunch of generals saw the tests, they threw themselves at Adamson like sixteen year old girls at a

Justin Bieber concert."

"The tests went well?" Matt asked, trying to keep the surprise out of his voice.

"That's what I heard. So, you're working on this shooting in Colorado?"

"Yeah." Matt knew he was going to have to give something away here. The quid pro quo was implicit. "Keep this to yourself for now, please, Simon. But it seems like the cop who shot Nathan Adams might have been wearing a BluJacket device."

Simon's eyebrows raised. "No shit. That would be… well, could be pretty huge."

"Could be," Matt agreed. "But there's a lot we still don't know. Look, where did you hear about these tests, I'd love to hear more about that?"

Simon twiddled his pen in his fingers.

"I have a contact. Senior Army dude, works in procurement so he was there at one of the demonstrations, but… this is a close-knit world. I'll vouch for you but I can't promise he's going to talk to you."

"I get it. See what you can do, though? Please, it's important."

"I'll do my best," Simon said, and Matt left him to his work.

Matt checked his email one more time. There was still no reply to his email to Chris Adamson, whom he was more anxious than ever to speak to. Finally, he made a decision. A decision to keep the momentum up and gamble that, if he flew back out to the West Coast, he'd be able to get the interview. He walked over to the little cluster of desks that was home to the Washington Record's few remaining personal assistants, team assistants, and travel bookers. He didn't recognise a single one of them from last time he'd been in; all were young, most in their early twenties and some looked as if they were barely out off their teens. He stood awkwardly near the cluster and, trying to force a winning smile, addressed them generally.

"Hi. Would one of you be the right person to help me out with a flight booking?"

"Oh sure," said one cheerfully, to Matt's relief. He walked over to her desk and asked if she could sort him out with the next available flight to San Francisco.

"Last flight tonight leaves at 17:55 I'm afraid. No chance of making that. How about first thing in the morning? I can have you landing at 09:50?"

It would have to do.

"Sure. Let's do it."

"Okie doke. Who's the authorising editor? We're cutting it fine, so if you can have him email me straight away, I can get this done."

"Ok," said Matt, wondering if there was even the slightest chance of Luke approving him to fly across the country just so he'd be well-situated to take advantage of an interview that hadn't yet been arranged and might never happen. "You just hang there with your finger over the 'book' button, and I'll get you an email any minute."

"Sure thing," said the assistant, almost immediately tabbing back to whatever she'd been doing before he came over. Matt ignored it, and went in search of Luke. He found him in his office with the blinds drawn, sitting on his sofa with half a dozen of the younger writers on the team. Matt poked his head in and caught his eye.

"What is it?"

"I need you to sign off on some travel."

"I'm busy. Send me an email and I'll take a look."

"It's urgent." Said Matt, embarrassed at having to beg for permission in front of these junior reporters. "Can you just send an email to… whoever that blonde girl is downstairs."

"Where are you going?"

"San Francisco. I have…" he hesitated, and chose his words carefully. "I'm getting an interview with the guy. The CEO. Of the thing." He flicked his eyes meaningfully at the other people in the room and hoped Luke would just send the email, simply for the sake of discretion.

"Fine. I'm sending it. So you'll be gone tomorrow will you? See you in six months I guess."

Matt almost jogged back to the assistants' desks, giving a thumbs up to the lady who'd helped him.

"Got it," she said. "I'll email you all the booking details. Have a good trip."

Matt gathered up his laptop and notepads and started to head out the door, when he saw Simon beckoning him over.

"Ok. My guy will speak to you."

"That was quick work. Thanks Simon, I really appreciate that."

"You're welcome. So, he'll call you. We have a standing off-the-record agreement, so don't even try to change that. Don't ask his name, or where he works, or who he is. Just take my word for it that his intel is good. And don't fuck with him. I'll just end you professionally, but he'll probably kill you."

"I've got it. I know how to handle a source, Simon." Matt said, a little more sharply than was really necessary.

"I know, I know. Just, he's sensitive. Ok, well, good luck. You in tomorrow?"

"Nah, I'm off to the West Coast. Going to try and meet this Adamson guy."

Simon pursed his lips.

"Ok. Well, Matt. Be careful, ok?"

"What do you mean?"

Simon hesitated for a second.

"Just, I've heard one or two rumours about some of the ex-military guys he works with. Some of them, they're not necessarily who you'd choose if you were just looking for consultancy, ok."

Matt stared at him. A prickle of an idea, of something he'd missed, made the hairs on the back of his neck stand up. He couldn't pin it down, but somehow Simon's warning tied in with a nasty feeling he'd been getting about the events of the last few days.

"Yeah, I'll be careful."

The Washington Record hadn't bothered to book Matt a hotel for the night. Luke knew him well enough to know that he'd be staying with Lori Woodward, an old university friend who lived in Georgetown, just as he did every time he came to town. Matt walked there, it was only about 45 minutes and he loved DC in the fall, especially at this time of the day, as the streetlights were starting to come on and the various monuments and historic buildings were lit up. New York was home, would always be home, but a part of his heart was in the nation's capital, surrounded by decision-makers and power-brokers, front-men and string-pullers, and of course history layered upon history.

He was just crossing over Rock Creek when his phone rang; 'No Caller ID' showed on the screen. So hurriedly that he almost dropped the phone, Matt plugged in his headphones, grabbed a notebook, and answered the call.

"Hello?"

"Matt Ibarra?" A man's voice, deep, almost husky.

"Yes. Is this… Simon's friend?"

"Yeah. Let's go with that. He said I could help you." The voice sounded amused, maybe pleased to be sought-after. Matt imagined a bitter staff officer, overlooked for promotion one too many times. Or perhaps a former special forces operator, bored and looking for something to give life some excitement. If there was one thing he'd discovered about sources it was that they all had their own reasons for talking to journalists, often ones they wouldn't even admit to themselves.

"That's right. I'm told you have some insight into the trials that were conducted of BluJacket's technology?"

"Insight?" He laughed softly. "Maybe. I can tell you I observed them. Well, some of them. They've been running around showing that stuff to everybody with a discretionary budget. But I saw one of the big ones. A full trial. A squad of these former tier one guys from BluJacket, rigged up with the cameras and goggles, going force-on-force with simunition against Navy Seals. Who didn't have the kit, of course."

Matt was scribbling in his notebook. He underlined some of the terms he didn't fully understand and then, since the voice had paused, he asked; "Force-on-force, as in what, two units just going at each other?"

"Something like that. I mean, both units using their own tactics and doing their best to win. A fair test. And with simunition. Think, paint-balling on crack. Real cartridges, fired from real guns, but non-lethal, with chalk marking."

"Ok, I get it. So, BluJacket performed well?"

"It performed brilliantly. Their guys… it was like they had eyes in the backs of their heads. They noticed tiny movements, even out of their direct view. They reacted faster to threats, differentiated more quickly between hostiles and non-combatants, shared information faster between them. This lot were already switched on, former professional shooters, of course. But the gear made them into… ninjas or something. Even our top operators struggled to compete."

Matt sighed and scribbled more notes. None of this tallied with what Josh had told him. Maybe the Brits had just got it wrong. Maybe Myles Weston was just a jumpy, trigger-happy cop. Maybe Matt had reacted too enthusiastically when he saw a way to turn his story into the sort of investigation his paper would be interested in.

"Ok. That helps. So what other testing has been done?"

"Not a whole lot," the voice said, elongating the word 'whole' for emphasis. "BluJacket are pretty protective about handing the kits out. They like having their people on site, demo-ing using their own operators when possible. I know they've been doing a pilot with a Sheriff's department, and they're gearing up for a big pilot with one of our units in Syria."

"One more question, if I may?"

"Ok. But make it quick. We're nearly done here."

"Did you have any idea that the British Army had tested this too?"

"Oh yeah, I heard that. There's usually a lot of sharing between us and the Limeys. Especially in the spec-ops world. So, their report made its way over."

"And?"

"Well, I never saw it. It got classified. Top Secret, codeword clearance, eyes-only."

"Is that normal?"

There was a pause on the other end.

"It's... unusual, I guess. That kind of sensitivity is normally reserved for, you know, nuclear secrets and human intelligence source details. But then, the tech was groundbreaking stuff, so I just assumed someone was playing it safe. I heard the Brits weren't particularly happy about it, but then their hands were kind of tied. Once we'd given the report that classification, it would have been pretty awkward for them to try circulating the same document again, so it just went quiet."

"So you assumed the report was positive?"

"Of course. Wasn't it?"

"From what I heard, quite the opposite. The Brits thought

BluJacket not only didn't work, but was actively lying to them."

There was a much longer pause this time. So long that Matt almost broke the silence to follow up, but then the voice answered. For the first time, it sounded a lot less sure of itself.

"How do you know that?"

"I can't say. But I've seen a copy of the original report."

"And you're actively investigating this?"

"Yes. It's linked to a death that I'm looking into."

"Listen, Ibarra, I need you to keep me informed about your investigation. Give me updates on what you find." An edge of worry had replaced the earlier confidence in the voice on the other end.

"Why would I do that?"

"Because if you're right, then this company is actively trying to defraud the US Government. So I want to know what you know, and what you find out."

Matt thought for a moment before answering.

"It's not my job to investigate for the US Government. And I'm not giving you a play-by-play on everything I discover. But – hang on," Matt carried on over the objections from the other end. "But, we can talk. A fair exchange of information. As long as I get your side, the view from inside the Army. You can stay anonymous, as long as I can quote you as a military source. Deal?"

There was a sigh from the other end.

"Deal. I'll call you back tomorrow and we'll talk."

Before Matt could say anything else, the phone went dead. Matt unplugged his headphones and put his notebook away in his backpack. He carried on walking the rest of the way to Lori's house, deep in thought, and full of questions to ask of Josh when he finally got to speak to him next.

The evening with Lori was, as he'd known it would be, full of great wine and decent food and sparkling conversation.

Lori was excited about a long trip she was taking to Europe, leaving in just two days' time and spending four weeks travelling, solo, around cities she'd only seen in movies and dreams. Paris, Venice, Rome, Madrid, London, Oxford. Her enthusiasm and excitement was contagious and briefly helped to mute the questions and thoughts that were bouncing around Matt's mind about BluJacket, Weston, Josh, and everything else he'd discovered in the last few days.

Matt managed to avoid checking his phone until long after the wine was finished and the kitchen was cleared away, and he was ready to make his way to bed. Wondering if he was about to set off on a completely pointless trip across the country, he looked at his email one last time and, to his enormous relief, sitting at the top of his inbox was a message from Chris Adamson. The interview was on.

27

The call from Matt Ibarra came, conveniently, as Josh was out at lunch. He was sitting in a Pret a Manger near the office, finishing an egg sandwich when caller ID flashed up 'Matt' — the only name he'd entered into his contacts for the journalist. His gut lurched when he saw it. For just a moment, he was tempted not to pick it up, to follow the other course Dan had offered. Back down, drop it all, live his life, embrace his burgeoning relationship with Abeke without question, and trust to other people to deal with whatever was going on with BluJacket.

He picked up the phone. "Hi Matt."

"Hi Josh. I'm glad to speak to you again."

"Yeah," Josh said, not yet quite sure about his decision to pick up the call.

"I'm getting a flight to San Francisco soon. I'm going to speak to Chris Adamson."

"He agreed to a meeting?" Josh asked, a little surprised.

"Sure did. Got back to me late last night, we've got an hour scheduled at his office later this afternoon. But, I've got a million questions for you."

"Honestly, Matt, I doubt I've got answers. But, look, I'll do what I can."

Matt recounted the gist of his conversation last night with the Pentagon source, and then moved on to the favour he wanted to ask.

"You have contacts in the British Army, right?"

"I wouldn't go that far. I have a friend."

"I have to understand what your guys saw that made them not progress with BluJacket. Otherwise all I've got is a source telling me it works great. That pretty much undermines our whole story."

Josh sighed.

"Matt, these aren't 'my guys'. These are special forces units. Honestly, you'd have as much luck just coming to Hereford and asking people nicely on the street as you would expecting me to find anything out."

"Ok. Ok," Matt conceded. "But, you can ask your army friend, right?"

"I'll try," Josh said, not sure even as he said it whether he was lying or not. He doubted Paul was either willing or able to do any more digging, but maybe he had a better idea. Maybe he'd just try emailing back the mysterious 'James McCormick' and ask them.

"Thanks. I hate to pressure you, but it's key information and I really need an insider. Right now, you're the closest thing I've got."

"Yes, ok. I said I'd try. But since I'm doing this for you, I have a favour to ask you too."

"Ok, go on."

Josh told Matt about Mickey Cook, the blogger. He explained about the videos, and then the cryptic email he'd received from whoever James McCormick was.

"I tried contacting him through YouTube, and I found his Twitter and messaged him there too, but I've not had any reply," Josh went on. "Anyway, it looks as if he lives in San Francisco. If you're going out there anyway, is there anything you can do to look into it? Just find out if he's ok, or what happened?"

He realised how thin it all sounded, and half expected Matt to simply laugh at him. Matt didn't laugh, but his tone was skeptical.

"Are you sure this is worth pursuing? Do we have any evidence that this Mickey Cook was even looking at BluJacket?"

"No, that's what we need to find. Well, what you need to find. But whoever is emailing me has already sent through one piece of seriously classified information, so this isn't just a wind-up. If they're asking about Mickey, we owe it to them to look into it, surely?"

Matt thought for a second.

"Alright, well, I'll have a few hours to spare after I land. I'm not going to have much time, but I can make a quick stop and at least find out if he's alive."

"Thanks Matt. I appreciate it. And I'll do everything I can to find out what happened with the testing in the UK, alright?"

"Great, thanks Josh."

Josh hesitated for a second, and Matt must have somehow picked up on the silence as he stayed on the line instead of just ending the call.

"Josh, anything else?"

"Ah, probably a stupid question…"

"Go on."

"If BluJacket is some kind of scam. Or fraud, or whatever. Do you think everyone there knows it?"

"What, all the employees?" Matt sounded puzzled.

"Yeah."

Matt sighed.

"Honestly, I just don't know enough at this stage. I can't even be completely sure if Chris knows about the issues. Why do you ask?"

"Just… wondering. I mean, I'm working with some of them, so… yeah. Just curious to know if they're lying to us." One of them in particular, though of course Josh wasn't about to admit that to Matt.

"For what it's worth, I doubt it. You look at Enron, Theranos, places like that – a lot of the employees honestly had no idea. But, I guess that's what I've got to figure out."

"Yeah. Ok, thanks Matt."

When Matt had hung up, Josh sat for a moment, looking at the second half of his sandwich. It didn't appeal anymore, and he threw it away on the way out of the cafe. He ignored Matt's request until he got back to the office, then he sat at his desk for a while, trying to strategise his way through the whirl of competing thoughts going round his head. To be asked by a Washington Record journalist to help on a story that he clearly thought was important was flattering, and exciting, and of course intimidating. It made trying to focus on writing an agenda for a creative workshop about branding a new life insurance product almost impossible.

Josh decided he wasn't going to bother Paul again, at least not directly. Instead, he emailed back to the James McCormick address.

Can you give me more? Why did the British Army think that BluJacket doesn't work? And what do you know about Mickey Cook?

He wasn't at all sure it was going to work. In fact, he wasn't even sure that the address would be monitored. And, it occurred to him, maybe there was another way to get the same information. He just didn't particularly like the road it would take him down.

Telling himself that he hadn't made any decisions yet, and he was just arranging a date, Josh re-opened his WhatsApp conversation with Abeke.

'What're you up to this evening? Fancy dinner or a drink?'

28

Once Matt was settled in the airport lounge, he opened YouTube and found the Mickey Cook profile, then scrolled through videos at random, trying to find one that looked as if it might have been filmed outdoors, and so give him any idea of where Cook lived. All of them, from what he could see, were filmed in the same indoor space. The channel homepage was no more helpful, and the location on the 'about' tab just said United States.

As Matt's Uber arrived, he switched to Twitter instead, and was immediately more lucky. As Josh had said, the location on Cook's twitter profile was 'San Francisco, CA'. It wasn't guaranteed to be correct, of course, but there was no particular reason to think it wasn't. And it was a perfectly plausible place for an expert in Artificial Intelligence to live, after all.

Matt pressed the 'media' tab on Cook's profile and scrolled down the list of photos. Unlike the YouTube account, the Twitter feed was a much more personal and candid social media presence and there were plenty of photos of Cook outdoors or visiting bars. Matt stopped on a tweet that read 'exploring the new neighbourhood', accompanied by a photo of Cook standing in front of what looked like a bar or restaurant with a vibrant green-painted frontage. For a second it didn't seem to have a sign or logo of any kind, and then Matt noticed a chalkboard in the window with the name Philz Coffee. A quick Google confirmed that it was a San Francisco-based chain, although one with more than a dozen locations in the city. Matt began checking each one, looking at the images provided on Google Streetview. Most looked blandly corporate, but on the fourth try he found one with a distinctive green frontage that clearly matched Cook's photo.

That was confirmation enough that Cook lived in San Francisco, and might even narrow him down to a square mile or so of the city, but that was still a long way from having any kind of lead on what had happened to him or how he was tied up with BluJacket.

As Matt's flight was called and he boarded the plane, he decided to break the habit of a lifetime and pay for the pricey onboard Wifi. He'd have to keep researching Cook while he was in the air so that he had some idea of where he was going when he landed, otherwise he'd quickly run out of time.

On board the plane, he began systematically searching through Cook's tweets, hunting for anything that could narrow down his address and bit further. He'd gone back almost a year, several months earlier than the tweet with the Philz Coffee picture, when he started to see a series of tweets that clearly indicated Cook was moving into a new house. Surely, he thought, he'd give something away there.

There were several pictures of the interior of the property, as Cook carried out various bits of DIY and furniture-arrangement. It was spacious and bright, if fairly generic-looking, with large windows that looked out onto a bit of greenery, blue sky, and a sliver of other houses, but gave little away about the location. Scrolling further back in time, a delighted tweet announcing his move was accompanied by a picture of him putting a key into a door; presumably the front door of the house. It was too closely cropped to see much, but off to the left a stretch of pale blue clapboard was visible along with the numbers '1123'.

Matt opened up Google Maps on his laptop and looked at the streets around the coffee shop. Alternately numbered and named streets ran east-west through the area, intersecting named cross streets running north-south. He picked one of the numbered streets at random and found the property at 1123. It was more than three miles away - not outside the realm of possibility, but certainly not 'in the neighbourhood'. He tried one of the cross streets next. 1123 was just a couple of blocks away. The same number was similarly close on the next cross street, and the next one.

There was, he thought, nothing for it but to try every 1123 on every cross street in, say, a fifteen block radius of Philz Coffee. He did so, looking at Google Street View until he spotted the blue clapboard and grey-painted door from Mickey's photo.

While tedious, the task didn't in fact take that long, and within a few minute's he'd found what was clearly the right building. Just a five minute walk away from Philz Coffee, a single-storey blue clapboard building with a garage and a small balcony. There was something slightly eerie about recognising details from Cook's twitter photos on Google, and how easily Matt had managed to track down the exact building. With a shudder, he realised that if he could do so, then so could anyone else.

Matt wondered again at the coincidence of two suicides in quick succession seemingly with some connection to BluJacket. He thought back to Deputy Myles Weston's bedroom, and outstretched body, trying to remember what it was that had been gnawing at his mind ever since. The gun, an issue police pistol, next to his outstretched hand.

Matt tried to visualise it. It wasn't hard, the image had been burnt into his memory, and he could still picture every detail.

What was it about it that was bothering him?

Then it came to him. A tiny detail; so small that for a moment he doubted whether he was even remembering it right. But he had to be, he'd even noticed it at the time because of how apt it seemed – a detail stored away in the back of his mind to add texture if he ever wrote the news story. The hammer on the pistol had been forward, as though to emphasise that it had just landed on the firing pin and triggered the fatal shot.

Except, he finally realised, that wasn't how semi-automatic pistols work. When you fire a shot, the slide cycles and the hammer is reset to the cocked position. So how does someone fire a shot into their head, that surely kills them instantly, and yet the pistol is de-cocked? Unless, of course, someone else fired the shot. Perhaps someone with years of military training handling firearms. Years of muscle memory that would cause them to de-cock the weapon when they were done using it, and not think to re-cock it again after placing it next to their victim's outstretched hand.

By the time Matt landed and got to Mickey Cook's apartment, it was almost eleven in the morning. He wouldn't have much time, but he was reluctant to delay another day on what was already a speculative side-venture.

He had the Uber stop on the street corner, and then walked down to number 1123.

It was odd seeing the neighbourhood in person after spending so much time looking at it on Google, but it was all just as the Street View images had shown it. And there was the little blue clapboard house. A light was on behind one of the front windows – did that mean Cook was alive, and at home, or did someone else live there? There was only one way to find out. He stepped up to the front door and rang the bell.

The door was answered by a skinny young man with a shaved head and extensive tattoos on his arms and, from what Matt could see poking up over the top of his v-neck t shirt, his chest.

"Yes?" He said, looking Matt up and down.

"Ah, hello. I'm looking for Michael Cook."

The man's expression hardly changed.

"Are you the police?" He asked.

"No, were you expected the police?"

"Yes. Because Mickey's dead. And because I've been telling the police for days that I don't think he killed himself like they say he did."

"Well, that's why I'm here actually. I'm a journalist, my name's Matt Ibarra and I'm wondering if Mickey might have been working on something that put him in danger. How did you know him? Do you live here?"

"Yes, I'm his lodger. My name's Ronnie. Why don't you come in."

Matt followed him in. The house was familiar from Mickey's photos and videos; it was tidy and attractively-decorated in a faintly mid-century style, dominated by light wood and green plants.

"Please do take a seat Mr Ibarra. Would you like a coffee? I've just made a fresh pot. I can only offer oat milk I'm afraid, though. Mickey used to always have regular milk but of course there's no need to keep it in the apartment anymore."

"Ah, yes, coffee sounds great. Oat milk is fine."

"That's good. I'll make us both a cup. I'm very pleased that you came actually, I've spoken to the local police force several times about what happened to Mickey but they've been conspicuously unhelpful in following up any of my investigative leads. I hope that even though you're only a journalist and not a police officer you might be able to help. I would be very unhappy to think that someone killed Mickey and simply got away with it, you understand."

There was something stilted and formal about Ronnie's speaking style, Matt noticed.

"Of course, I completely understand. So how did you know Mickey?"

Ronnie handed Matt a mug of coffee. "We actually met at a coding conference in the city four and a half years ago and although Mickey worked more in artificial intelligence than coding, and I am personally a mobile application developer, there is quite a lot of overlap in our work. We got on extremely well so about a year ago when he rented this place he needed a new flatmate. I had just ended a relationship and needed somewhere to live so I moved in here."

Matt took a sip of the coffee. It was, slightly to his surprise, absolutely excellent.

Ronnie's precision, memory and grasp of details were a journalist's dream. His loquaciousness and tendency to clarify even irrelevant details were less so, particularly when Matt was desperate to get to the point. Nevertheless, Matt allowed Ronnie to talk freely, confident that he would eventually get around to the information that Matt was interested in. And, sure enough, he was soon explaining exactly why he didn't believe Mickey could, or would, have killed himself.

"We were close friends, we talked all the time. I am quite certain I would have known if he was unhappy, and he wasn't. Quite the opposite, he loved his work and was proud of the success of his YouTube channel. Just the night before he died, we sat up late talking about it, and we'd made plans for that weekend. Then I went out to work and when I came home…"

Ronnie tailed off, his calm, unemotive facade finally cracking a little. Then he steeled himself and carried on.

"A drug overdose, apparently. The police said it was deliberate."

"And you don't think it was?"

"I know it wasn't. For one thing, unlike the police, I took the simple step of asking at Angel's Market if Mickey had bought the pills there. Angel's is the only place we shopped; there's a Whole Foods on 24th Street but Mickey wouldn't set foot in the place. He said now it was owned by Amazon he didn't want them recording all his shopping data. Anyway, we know the staff in Angel's and they said Mickey had been in that day for some groceries but he hadn't bought any pills. Not then, not any time that week."

"Could he have gone somewhere else? Perhaps he just didn't want to buy a large quantity of painkillers somewhere that knew him?"

"Perhaps." Ronnie looked unconvinced. "But anyway the note is conclusive proof."

"The suicide note? Why?"

Ronnie picked up a blue cardboard folder from the kitchen countertop, opened it, and took out a single sheet of paper. He handed it to Matt. It was a print-out of a photograph of the original note, which was written in neat handwriting on a piece of lined notepaper.

"This is his handwriting?"

"Yes, but that's not the point. The point is what it says. Read it."

Ronnie, my friend. I'm sorry to do this to you, but I think I've finally reached the finish line. I wish I could have been a better friend and a better person, and in another life perhaps I might have been. Farewell old buddy.

"It's… sad. I'm really sorry about your friend. What do

you think he meant?"

"I know it's sad," Ronnie said impatiently. "But I know exactly what he meant. 'The Finish Line', 'Another Life', and 'The Farewell'. Those are all the names of missions from a game we both played. He knew I'd recognise them. It was his last chance to send me some kind of message, but the police don't believe me. Or aren't interested."

"What game?"

"*Hitman*. It's about an assassin. He goes around killing targets and making it look like an accident."

29

"This place is nice," Abeke said, looking around at Josh and Dan's living room.

"Thanks. I mean, it's not great, but it'll do."

"It's your flatmate's?"

"Well, we both rent it. He pretty much picked it and I moved in. Back then I still thought I'd be joining the army, so it was going to be temporary, but it's a good set-up."

Abeke handed him the bottle of wine she'd brought with her.

"We don't have to have this now," she said. "But, just thought I should bring something…"

"Ah, thank you! I feel bad now, I was just going to order curry. Sorry, it's just that some people find my 'spaghetti with Lloyd Grossman sauce' so delicious that they can never enjoy any other food again, and I wouldn't want to do that to you…"

Abeke laughed. "I don't mind at all. Curry's great. I've been making a lot of boring meals for one, so it's nice to have a break from that."

Josh opened the wine and took a couple of glasses through

to the living room. Once he'd found out that Dan planned to be staying at Marco's that night, he'd suggested Abeke come round to his for dinner, and then had immediately dashed home from work to tidy up a bit. He was glad he'd cleared away the clothes horse of laundry, but the small room and battered Ikea furniture didn't seem quite as cosy and comfortable as he'd always thought, now that he looked at them through Abeke's eyes. Instead they seemed bleak and depressing compared to her fancy AirBnB in London and the life he imagined she had back in California.

Abeke didn't seem at all bothered though. She took her glass of wine and sat cross-legged on the sofa, flicking through movies and TV shows on Prime, and occasionally commenting on them.

"Terrible. Terrible. Hmm, that could be fun, oh it's not free. That one's awful. How about this?"

She'd highlighted a recent Oscar-winning movie with Frances McDormand. It didn't look like the sort of thing Josh would normally watch – mostly over-complex detective dramas that demanded closer attention to the plot than he typically paid – but that was ok.

"Sure, looks great."

They turned to the movie. Josh sipped his wine again, feeling the butterflies returning to his stomach. He could keep putting this off, he could just get back to Matt and say it hadn't been possible. Matt would never know, and wouldn't blame him anyway. Josh wasn't a journalist. He could, and probably should, just return to focusing on his clients and their needs. But none of that felt possible. He knew he wouldn't be able to relax until he'd at least tried to find out the truth.

"Hey, Abeke. You must have seen about this shooting in Colorado, right?"

"Of course! Yet another Black kid." She didn't look at him

though and, was it his imagination or did the outrage in her voice sound a little forced?

"Yeah. It's absolutely horrendous. But… ok, stop me if I'm completely out of line here. It's not possible, is it, that the cop who shot him was wearing your kit? BluJacket cameras, I mean?"

He had her full attention now. She put her glass of wine down and arched away from him as if trying to get a better angle to look him up and down.

"Where would you get that idea? What's this about?"

Josh could feel his palms sweating.

"I saw a picture," he said. "Of the cop. The deputy. And it looked as if he was wearing BluJacket cameras."

"We are doing some pilots with police forces in the US," Abeke replied, with a an air of firmness and finality that made it sound as if she was quoting from PR talking points. "It's not my area. What's your point, though?"

Josh took a deep breath. He felt a muscle at the side of his neck twitch with tension and he was worried he was visibly trembling.

"Would you not want to know, if maybe there was a bug or an error in the programme, and that led to someone being killed?"

"There isn't, though. It's been thoroughly tested. Literally months and months of testing by us, and then tests by the US army. They don't take kit that doesn't work."

"People keep telling me that. I wish I had your confidence. But, couldn't you just look into it? Maybe double-check that the testing really was as thorough as they're claiming? For peace of mind?"

"Not really, no." Her harsh tone surprised Josh. He wasn't sure what he'd expected, but this was going even worse than he had feared. "Why would I expose something that would put the company at risk?"

"But, if it caused —" Josh started.

"It didn't cause anything. BluJacket just provides guidance. Information. The action the user takes is on them. It's the deputy that pulled the trigger. It's *his* fault if he didn't think first."

Josh hesitated and looked down. She sounded so certain, it took him a second to try to reassure himself of the righteousness of his own cause.

"You know…" he said, eventually, "you told me that BluJacket had never tried to sell to the British Army. But I know that's not true. You *did* try to sell it over here, only it didn't work properly. And somehow now it's out there in the hands of cops."

Abeke looked at Josh for a long time, as if studying him and, worse, as if seeing something for the first time that she didn't entirely like.

"How the hell do you know that? Are you *investigating* us?"

"No! I'm *trying* to run an advertising campaign for you. But I can't advertise something that doesn't work."

Abeke took a deep breath.

"You know how I got this job, Josh?"

"No," said Josh, confused.

"I applied for… I don't know, a hundred other ones first. Maybe more than a hundred. I have a first class honours degree from Harvard, I have four years of graduate experience. Girls from my school with half the ability but names like Grace and Abigail and Cassidy - they walk straight into jobs. Some of them get given jobs without even applying. But me, I'm not even getting replies to my applications. I wonder why that is?"

"I don't see —"

"And then Chris Adamson, war hero and tech entrepreneur, finally gives me a job. In his Silicon Valley start-up. I'm basically heading up marketing. He pays me the same as my white male colleagues, he listens to me when I talk in meetings, he doesn't wheel me out to show off how diverse his company is, oh and he doesn't try to touch my fucking hair. So, excuse me if I don't want to burn the whole thing to the ground because some dumb, racist cop can't take a second to think about what he's doing before he pulls the trigger."

"I'm sorry." Josh said. His hands felt cold, his vision had narrowed, and his legs were numb, as if all the blood in his body was being pulled to his heart just trying to keep it pumping.

"Sure," she said, dismissively. "Well, and now I'm wondering whether the guy I've been dating is investigating me."

There was silence for a minute. Abeke swept her phone off the table and put it in her pocket, looking as if she was about to get up and go.

"Abeke," Josh said. "Honestly, I'm not trying to undermine the company. But I know what happens when soldiers get sent to war with kit that's not up to scratch. I just don't want that to happen."

"That's not your job, Josh. You're an account manager. So, manage. Our. Account."

Now she actually did get up, and walked out of the flat. Josh didn't try to chase her. He sunk into the sofa and just lay there for a long time.

It was only much later that evening when Josh could finally drag himself out of his deep well of depression long enough to consider composing some kind of apology to Abeke. He stared at his phone for a long time, trying to muster up words and the energy to string them together, but finally sent a brief but profuse apology and a request to talk again properly. It was as he was doing so that he noticed that a new email had come in to his inbox in the last couple of hours. From James McCormick, it simply said.

Ok, let's meet. Can you be at St James's Park, on the bridge over the lake. 5pm tomorrow?

Josh looked at it for a second and then simply deleted it. Whether Abeke was right or not, Josh knew he'd had enough of this.

30

Matt glanced at his watch. He didn't want to rush, but time was getting tight to get to BluJacket in time for his interview with Chris Adamson.

"Mickey made videos about Artificial Intelligence companies, didn't he? Was he working on anything specific when he died?

"Oh yes, well, I'm afraid Mickey didn't usually talk a lot about his videos while he was working on them so I can't tell you exactly what he was covering. But I can tell you that he was extremely excited about it. He always published on a Saturday and he died on the Friday so by then the video would have been finished. That's why, as I told the police, I find it a highly suspicious fact that Mickey's laptop was wiped. Why would he want to remove his last piece of work?"

"Perhaps he didn't want it published after his death?" Matt suggested.

"I can't say that I find that very credible. Mickey was proud of his work and I think he would very much have wanted a video published that he said was the best he'd ever made. But anyway that is a moot question if he *didn't* kill himself."

"That's true. So there's no way to get his video back?"

"I'm afraid I'm not an expert on data retrieval but of course I tried the obvious steps such as checking deleted items and back-ups and they have all been cleared out. His equipment is all still on his desk over there if you want to try, though." Ronnie gestured to a desk in the corner of the living room. It looked largely un-touched, still with a large screen and a laptop on a stand, an iPad and a notepad to one side, a ring light and microphone for vlogging, and even an unopened can of Pepsi.

Matt thought for a second and then had an idea, based on his own experience of using Adobe Premier Rush for simple edits.

"What software did he use for editing?" He asked Ronnie.

"Adobe Premier. Why do you ask?"

Matt shrugged, unwilling to show too much excitement about what seemed like a long shot. "Adobe tends to sync projects to the cloud. If you're right that someone killed him, and if they cleared off his laptop, they might not have realised there would be a copy in his Adobe Cloud account. I don't suppose you know his password?"

"I'm afraid he didn't share login details with me, and I do know that he was a proponent of highly secure passwords so I would be rather surprised if it was something you could guess either."

Matt was stumped for a moment. His eyes went back to the stack of equipment on Mickey's desk, and then he had an idea.

"Is that Mickey's iPad?" Matt asked. Ronnie confirmed that it was.

Matt took it from the stack of items. It was a couple of years old and still had the fingerprint-enabled home key, which he pressed to bring the screen to life. It came on straight away, showing a small amount of charge on the battery icon, but also showing a padlock and keypad indicating that the device was locked and required either a pin or Mickey's fingerprint to unlock it. Matt turned to Ronnie.

"You don't have the PIN for this, do you?"

"I don't, I'm afraid."

Matt looked back at the desk. He had an idea, just the germ of an idea, based on a video he'd seen on YouTube that he had been fairly certain was fake. He looked at the can of Pepsi. Maybe it was worth a try anyway.

"That Pepsi was left there by Mickey was it? Have you touched it?"

"It was, and I haven't. Honestly, I didn't want to disturb this as I still believe it is a crime scene and I hope that one day the police might decide they want to investigate. But of course I still have to live here so I suppose it can't be maintained forever."

"Ok. Well, that's good that you did. Do you have some sellotape, and maybe some talcum powder, or some chalk and a knife?"

"Talcum powder is carcinogenic, Mr Ibarra. But I do have some sticks of chalk; we have a chalkboard in the kitchen for shopping lists."

Ronnie brought the chalk, sellotape and a kitchen knife to Matt, who used the knife to shave a little chalk dust onto a plate. Then he carefully picked up the can, holding it only at the top and bottom rim, and gently sprinkled some chalk dust over it, turning it in the light to try and see if any of the dust adhered to existing fingerprints. He detected a pattern of fingers where, he assumed, Mickey had held the can to take it out of the fridge. Matt carefully sprinkled a little more chalk dust on then blew it to spread it around and remove the excess.

Next he took the sellotape and delicately lifted what seemed to be the forefinger print, and then the thumb print. He stuck another piece of sellotape to each print, sticky side to sticky side, locking the print between the two layers. Finally, trying the forefinger print first, he laid it over the fingerprint sensor and then put his own finger on top, pressing down gently, and rolling his finger around slightly to try and get a good read. For a fraction of a second, nothing happened. As he'd suspected, either whatever video he'd seen had been fake, or the security flaw had long-since been patched. Then, as he began to lift his finger off, the movement seemed to finally trigger something and, with a satisfying little flicker of the screen, the iPad unlocked.

"We're in. Ok, let's see… doesn't look as if he has Premier installed here, but he's got his email, so…"

Matt opened Mickey's email, checked what his email address was, then went to the Adobe Creative Cloud website and did a password reset to that address. Finally he went back to the inbox to pick up the resulting email and set a new password. A moment later, he was in to Mickey's account. Sure enough, it was full of raw footage as well as dozens of complete videos. One, dated just a day before his death, almost made Matt's heart stand still. The title, in Mickey's usual bold and hyperbolic style was *'BluJacket Debunked! When AI isn't just BAD but DANGEROUS'*.

The video was much like the other videos by Mickey Cook that Matt had watched while researching him. Same intro, the same desk and lighting set-up that, a little bizarrely, now sat across the room from where he was watching the video. And the same figure talking straight into the camera. It was both poignant and a little creepy knowing that he had died only a short time after completing the video, and that he was talking about a company that had come to dominate so much of Matt's time and thoughts.

"Ladies and gents," Mickey began. "This week I have a really extra-fucking-special video for you. You may recall that in August's roundup I talked about a little company called BluJacket that is claiming to do some frankly incredibly things with artificial intelligence. And you may recall that I said 'that is bullshit because there is no way that they can do this in real time, at a distance, with sufficient accuracy to be useful *and* avoid any potentially dangerous error.' And, well, some people didn't agree with me." At this point the screen filled with a collage of screenshots of YouTube comments. They appeared too fast to read most of them, but the ones Matt saw appeared to be vehemently taking issue with Mickey's analysis.

"Well, DiscoFox876 and 9MilFreedomFry, you can eat your words because two days ago I received some very, very, very interesting leaked files *directly* from someone who has, let's say, first-hand knowledge of BluJacket. And let me tell you they do *not* paint a pretty picture. But first, let me talk about one of my sponsors today…"

After Mickey had introduced one of his sponsors, he came back to BluJacket. Matt leaned forward without even realising it.

"So, as you know, I maintain a file drop where anyone can place anonymous tip-offs. And last month I discovered a file there. Hundreds of gigabytes of data and videos, which turn out to be from about six months of testing by BluJacket."

Here the screen changed to show a whole series of clips a few seconds long. Each appeared to be from shaky helmet or body cameras. Most were moving around what at first looked like Middle Eastern towns, but the blank, generic shop-fronts and occasional glimpse of a two-dimensional facade of a building suggested that these were little more than sets.

Overlaid on the clips were red, yellow or green boxes that appeared and highlighted items or people. All people got boxes around them; mostly green, but sometimes yellow or red, while items in the streets were sometimes highlighted and sometimes not.

As each clip flashed up, a clear pattern began to emerge. A football gently kicked along the street by a small boy was highlighted in red with the text 'danger – IED' flashing above it. A man with a bomb strapped to his chest strolled cheerfully towards the camera without the colour of the box surrounding him ever changing from a warm green. A flock of birds passing overhead received another red box, and the words 'air strike air strike air strike' flashed on the screen. A sniper silhouetted on a rooftop didn't even get a box until a disembodied hand came into view and readjusted the camera to point right at him. Then a second passed, and finally a yellow box appeared around him.

And so it went on, for almost two minutes, a sort of dark slapstick comedy taking place in a clunky film-set version of the Global War on Terror. Eventually Mickey reappeared, smiling broadly.

"As you can see, their testing has been going about as well as I'd anticipated. But, folks, this has a serious side because this company has just raised another hundred million dollars in venture capital funding, on top of around four hundred million dollars raised in previous rounds. And yes, I hear what you're thinking, Mr DiscoFox876 – you're thinking 'gosh Mickey, why are you hating on people who are just trying to invent something? Didn't Edison try and fail 1,000 times to create a lightbulb before it worked?' And I say to you, yes but Edison wasn't out there selling lightbulbs to the army, claiming they worked, when actually they'd burn your house down. You see, a man in the know tells me that BluJacket is currently going through secret hearings in congress to be approved for use in a war zone. That's right folks…"

One of the clips reappeared. It showed a squad of almost cartoon-like terrorists, all white robes and AK-47s, advancing down the street. After several seconds, they began to be covered in dozens of red and amber boxes. The boxes kept multiplying until the footage underneath was barely even visible anymore. Mickey let that image linger for a second, and then swapped to a sarcastic clip of a stiff-armed cat playing a series of upbeat chords on an electronic keyboard.

The video went on, Mickey explaining the difficulties in conducting real-time analysis of complex video footage using processing power, software and algorithms located hundreds or thousands of miles away and connected solely by unreliable wireless communication networks. Matt watched to the end, but didn't take much more of it in. The image of those absurd clips stuck with him. Presumably Mickey had selected them for their comic effect, but if they were representative of how well the product worked… and if BluJacket knew that, which surely they must, then allowing it to be used on the streets of America or on operations in Syria, or sold to the public as a safety product, was unconscionable.

31

Matt only barely made it to the BluJacket office in time for his meeting. He and Ronnie had watched Mickey Cook's BluJacket video together, and Matt would happily have watched it another half dozen times if he'd been able to. Instead, he'd had to make do with copying it to a USB stick and hurrying off, leaving Ronnie with promises to expose what had happened to his friend.

BluJacket's headquarters was a squat building made of glass that reflected the cloudless blue sky. It was on the very edge of Palo Alto, in the hills where tree-lined roads rolled between the campuses of tech companies. Unlike its neighbours, though, BluJacket had armed security guards on the entrance to the parking lot, and again at the front door. Matt reassured them that he had an appointment with the CEO and, after a brief radio conversation, he was allowed through and into the lobby.

The lobby acted as an atrium for the whole five-story building, and at the back a huge flight of stairs reached up and offered glimpses of each level. Matt walked across the BluJacket logo set into the dark marble floor, towards a reception desk, behind which sat attractive twenty-somethings in BluJacket-branded polo shirts.

Matt introduced himself for the third time since pulling into the parking lot, and was directed to sit at one of the clusters of sofas that broke up the otherwise-empty space. He stood, instead, and waited. He more than half-expected to be kept waiting long past the agreed meeting time, in the sort of classic power-move that every journalist experiences dozens of times in their career. To his surprise, though, at the exact second that his watch ticked to 15:00, a voice called his name from the stairs at the back of the lobby. Maybe precise adherence to timings was a different kind of power move. A reminder that Matt was meeting with a military man, a man who had once directed close air support in to-the-second missions. A man who did things properly.

The man himself was waiting in a conference room on the second floor, to which Josh was taken by an assistant. One glass wall looked out over the lobby, and another looked into an open plan office space in which casually-dressed young men and women, but mostly men, were working away at computer terminals.

"I'm Chris Adamson. Come in." He said, gesturing to a chair. "Can I get you anything? Water, coffee, kombucha?"

"Water is fine, thank you," Matt said, taking a seat and opening his notebook. The assistant nodded and disappeared.

"So, I'd say we're both busy people, Matt - is it ok if I call you Matt? - maybe we can cut to the chase a bit here?"

"That works for me. Do you mind if I record this conversation?" Matt asked, placing his iPhone on the table.

"Oh, be my guest," Adamson replied. "You're looking into this shooting in Colorado, you said?"

"That's right." Matt answered, noncommittally. He was eager to see how far Chris really planned to 'cut to the chase'.

"And how do you think I can help you with that?"

Not that far, apparently.

"Can you confirm that the deputies involved in that incident were using equipment manufactured by your company?"

"Yes."

Matt tried not to look surprised. Ok then.

"At the time of the incident, was the equipment enabled?"

"To my knowledge – yes," Chris answered, voice completely casual.

Matt was taken aback at the easy admission. He looked down at his notes, taking a moment to gather his thoughts.

"So did your system tell deputy Weston to shoot Nathan Adams?"

Adamson sat back in his chair, wheeling back slightly from the table and crossing his legs at the ankle.

"Absolutely not. Matt, our artificial intelligence system, what we call The Mind, doesn't tell anyone to do anything. It simply provides advice and information. It is for highly trained law enforcement officers to act on that information correctly. If they failed to do so, then that is certainly tragic but cannot be laid at our door."

"Ok. And would you be willing to release the footage and any analysis from the, uh, 'Mind' to the public, or to me?"

As he answered, Chris gave a little laugh that very nearly sounded authentic.

"Oh, I don't think so. Please understand, we are a private company developing revolutionary products in a highly competitive market, and I am in the process of attracting new investors. We cannot and will not release anything that could expose our product to intellectual property theft."

"That's your concern? Are you sure? Because, an unbiased observer is going to assume you have something you want to hide."

"They can assume what they like," Chris answered,

opening his hands, palms upwards, in a gesture that was part 'I have nothing to hide' and part 'I just don't care'. "This company's product has been rigorously tested and any attempt to undermine it will, I must warn you, be met with the strongest possible legal consequences."

"There's no need for that," Matt said. "But, since you mention it, maybe we should talk more about the testing. What testing *has* your product undergone?"

"Theoretical assessment, extensive code review, testing under field conditions, and of course trials and limited proof-of-concept deployments with our customers." Chris reeled the list off breezily.

"Ah yes. And *all* your customers were equally satisfied? Could you comment on allegations that BluJacket failed testing with the British Army?"

For the first time, Matt felt as if a shot had landed. Chris's eyes flicked down in surprise, and then came back to Matt with the same steady, half-smiling gaze as before.

"I can't possibly comment on the affairs of another nation's military. Any discussions with them would be highly confidential as you well know. Now, do you actually have anything beyond supposition and conspiracy?"

"I'm just following up on a lead. Had to ask the question, and now I have my answer. So thanks," Matt replied, evenly. Adamson narrowed his gaze and studied Matt, as if trying to work out which of them had won that exchange. Finally he spoke.

"Of course. Well, anything else I can help with?"

Matt thought for a moment about the right question to ask. He ran his mind back through the video he had found and watched at Mickey Cook's, barely an hour earlier.

"What safeguards are there against BluJacket mis-identifying a target?"

"BluJacket doesn't identify *targets*, Matt. That's the job of a human operator with a firearm, if appropriate. BluJacket identifies potential *threats*. Will every potential threat be an actual threat? Of course not. And should every threat be met with lethal force? Again, no. That's what the human operator is there to determine."

"That's a lot of reliance you place on people to do the right thing. You're expanding into the consumer market, I understand. So do you not have any concerns about the safety of your product if it starts being used widely be untrained consumers?"

"I'm absolutely confident in our testing process and we will, of course, comply fully with consumer protection laws and maintain the highest possible safety standards."

"And yet despite all that, a young man has recently died because of one of your products."

"Not *because of*," said Chris quickly, betraying a hint of irritation. "Do you need me to tell you how many people are killed every year by vending machines? In fact, we are confident BluJacket can *reduce* use of lethal force by both police and civilians. That has to be a good thing."

"Ok. Well then, one final question. Some people will naturally be concerned about the race element in this incident. How do you ensure that your artificial intelligence isn't programmed with the same biases held by many police officers?"

"Quite simply, because it isn't programmed in that way at all. The Mind learns and develops, and that is what keeps it free from exactly those biases. Now, you did say that was your final question, so if there's nothing else…"

Without waiting for a reply, Chris walked over to the door and called to someone. The assistant, who never had brought Matt's water, reappeared.

"I think Mr Ibarra is about ready to leave," Chris said. "Would you mind showing him out?"

He turned, gave Matt a warm handshake and a cold stare, then walked away into the open-plan office area without looking back.

Back outside in the warm Californian sun, Matt paced irritably as he waited for an Uber. He was more certain than ever that BluJacket was hiding something about their product. But without hard evidence, there was no way to crack the polished Silicon Valley facade, and no chance of publishing a story if all he had was hunches and insinuation.

As the Uber arrived, Matt felt his phone buzzing. It was a cellphone number that he didn't recognise, but as soon as the caller spoke, he recognised the husky voice of his military source from the day before.

"So," the voice said, "are you going to tell me what you know about BluJacket?"

"That's not what I said," Matt replied. "An exchange of information. First, tell me who you are."

There was a hesitation, and then a little snort of laughter.

"I guess I'd better just hope the Washington Record maintains its reputation for protecting sources."

"We will, trust me."

"I don't. But fine. Brian Rogers. I'm in Defence Innovation. We assess and acquire novel technological capabilities in support of defence objectives."

"Hence why you're involved with BluJacket?"

Another snort of laughter.

"'Involved with'? I'm leading the fucking project. Why do you think I'm so keen to find out if I've been taken for a ride. Preferably without alerting the rest of the team yet. Ok, my turn. What's this death you're investigating?"

"A kid shot by police in Colorado. Looks like the cops were wearing BluJacket gear."

"Yeah, I knew they were doing pilots with law

enforcement. But you're saying the gear malfunctioned?"

"I don't know that yet. BluJacket says not. So how close are BluJacket to securing a deal with the military, then?"

"Oh they've already got a deal. We've shelled out millions of dollars for the trial stages and a pilot with some operational units. What they want now is sign-off from congress for a full rollout and a multi-year programme."

"And that's a lot of money?"

"Billions," Rogers said. "Spread over a few years but still, billions of dollars."

People would do a lot for that kind of money, Matt thought. They'd certainly kill for it.

Rogers spoke again, getting his question in before Matt had a chance to ask a follow-up.

"So how sure are you that BluJacket's lying to us? You got any evidence for that?"

"Not directly," Matt admitted. "But I know they lied to the Brits. Somehow making it seem like the product was working when it wasn't."

"Maybe they've improved it since then."

"Maybe."

Rogers sighed.

"Look, this project is a fucking freight train. I honestly don't know if I could stop it even if I wanted to. It's gone too far and too many senior people have bet their reputations on it. But if I'm to have even the slightest chance, you've got to get some proper evidence."

"That's what I'm trying to do."

"Well, keep trying. And when you've got it, I want to be the first to know, alright? You can call me on this number any time."

"I'll keep you informed," said Matt, deliberately not making the promise Rogers wanted. It seemed to be good enough for now, though. As before, Rogers hung up without another word, leaving Matt looking at his phone and wondering which of them was getting the better end of the deal they'd made.

32

When Josh woke up, the first thing he did was look at his phone, hoping that Abeke might have messaged him. When he saw that she hadn't, he dropped the phone back on his bedside table. He noticed he had two missed calls from Matt Ibarra, but had no interest in returning them. It took a physical effort to force himself out of bed, into the shower, and into some clothes and, when he got out of the flat into the still dark London morning he nearly gave up and went back to bed again. From somewhere he found the will to get on the tube and into the office, though not to make conversation with colleagues. He put a pair of headphones on and, even though he couldn't actually be bothered to listen to music, left them on all morning in the hope that it would indicate that he didn't want to be disturbed.

By the end of the day, Matt had called twice more, and Josh had ignored him both times. Abeke, on the other hand, hadn't communicated with him at all, either by text or by email. Within a day or two he was going to need to send the first creative drafts to her and probably set up a meeting for Vijai and Rob to present. At the moment he couldn't imagine anything more awkward. The prospect of his relationship with Abeke becoming professional and, inevitably, cold and awkward, sat heavily around his shoulders. As he left, he messaged Dan, simply *'Feeling shit. You about this evening?'*. A reply came back promptly; Marco was over, but the two of them were cooking dinner and they'd make enough for Josh, then he could join them for their movie night.

Dan's quick and warm reply cheered Josh up slightly. Dan had been there at university when the depression and anxiety that had probably been nipping at Josh's heels since childhood finally caught up with him and sent him into a downward spiral that ended up with him missing a term. When other friends' initial sympathy had eventually waned into boredom and occasionally even irritation with Josh's struggle, Dan had never wavered in his willingness to offer support when it was needed, and encouragement when it was called for. The idea of joining him and Marco for dinner was exactly what Josh needed, and that, combined with a painfully fast run home from the office left Josh feeling in slightly better spirits, despite an email from Matt Ibarra.

Josh - hope you're ok. We need to speak. You were right I'm afraid, Mickey Cook is dead. Suicide, maybe, but I think your contact is right there's something sketchy. For one thing, I found what Mickey was working on - watch this.

It was followed by a link to a video on Vimeo, and a password to access it. This time, Josh didn't delete the email, but he didn't click the link. Instead, he showered and changed into tracksuit bottoms and a t-shirt, and joined Dan and Marco in the living room.

"Hey Josh," said Marco, warmly. "Nice to see you again."

Josh wondered if Marco had been specifically briefed by Dan to be friendly. He didn't really care.

"Hey Marco. You too. You guys ordering curry? I'm starving."

"Well," Dan said, throwing him a menu from a local takeaway, "if you will run home, you're going to end up starving. There's crisps if you can't wait for food to come."

They put a movie on in the background, ate crisps, drank beer, and eventually ordered and ate a curry.

"So, Josh," Dan said casually as they waited for the curry to arrive. "Anything particular making you feel down?"

"Ahhhh, it's stupid really." Josh was already feeling a little embarrassed at the message he'd sent earlier. This, he had discovered, was a recurrent problem. He'd feel terrible, and eventually reach out to someone about it. Either with or without their help he'd feel better, and then be embarrassed that he'd said anything. And would often then avoid everyone for a few days.

"Is it that girl you went on a date with?"

"Yeah. I fucked it up, to be honest. I shouldn't have dated someone from work."

"Yup," said Marco, grinning at Dan, "stick to the apps. That's the way forward."

Josh smiled faintly, and took the opportunity to deflect attention away from himself.

"So, Marco. I hear you're an expert in penetration. That sounds… very interesting."

"Oh fuck you Josh." He said it with a smile, and the swearword sounded somehow funnier in Marco's soft Italian accent. "It actually is extremely interesting thank you."

"Ok. I'm sorry. I'm a child. So, you just spend all day breaking into buildings?"

"I wish. I spend one day breaking in and ten days writing a report about *how* I break in, and I tell you how to fix it and make sure no one breaks in next time. And I send you a bill. And then sometimes a year later I come back and I break in again and I write another report saying, 'hey, why you not fix that' but I get to bill you again so…" he shrugged expansively. Josh and Dan both laughed.

"Well, it sounds a fuck of a lot better than my job, so, cheers." Josh raised his beer can, and took a long, long swig.

"Speaking of, did you decide what to do about this problem you had, Josh?" Dan asked.

"No. Not really. I mean, I thought I did, but to be honest that's what fucked things up with Abeke."

"What problem was this?" Marco asked.

Whether it was beer, or disillusionment with work, or anger with BluJacket, or a combination of all three, BBA\Rowley's non-disclosure agreement seemed a lot less important now. Josh began to tell them about the BluJacket product, his suspicions that it didn't work properly, his conversations with Matt, and his utterly fumbled attempt to get information from Abeke.

"Holy shit." Said Dan, now not even pretending to be interested in the movie. "I can't believe you kept all this from me. So, what, you're working with this journalist?"

"I don't even know anymore, honestly. He keeps calling me, he even sent me..." Josh suddenly remembered the video, that he'd been ignoring all day. "...he sent me this video. I should probably watch it."

"Hell yes you should!" Exclaimed Dan. "Come on, it's got to be better than this garbage." He turned off the TV, and swept a space clear on the coffee table for Josh's laptop.

Josh, Marco and Dan clustered round and watched the video from start to end. They sat in silence through the parade of technical disasters, right through to the final chords played by keyboard cat.

"And they're actually using this shit? With real police officers and soldiers?" Dan asked, when it was over.

"Yeah, seems that way."

"And they're asking you to market it to the general

public?"

"Guess so."

"Well absolutely fuck these guys, right, Josh?" said Marco.

"Yeah," Dan agreed. "I mean, come on. You've got to get back to this journalist of yours. You've got to."

"Josh. Where've you been, I was worried?" Matt answered Josh's call on the first ring.

"I'm dealing with some personal stuff. I saw the video you sent me."

"Yeah. It's not good, is it?"

"What does it mean, though? Are you going to write a story about it?" Josh asked.

"Maybe, yeah. But it's not simple. We need corroboration, and we need more recent test footage. Otherwise BluJacket will just argue that Mickey Cook's footage is out of date and the product has improved since then. And honestly they could be right."

"Ok, so how can you get more recent footage? And if Mickey had this stuff, and he died, then isn't that proof that BluJacket are trying to cover this up?"

"It's… suggestive. But 'proof', no, I'm afraid it's not. Without direct evidence, I don't know what I can do."

Josh sighed. His reignited enthusiasm and righteous anger was being rapidly dampened again by Matt's cold logic.

"So what if I can get you recent test data?"

"Can you?"

"I don't know. But… like you said, I'm the closest thing you've got to an insider. I guess I'll see what I can do."

Josh did have an idea for how to get the evidence Matt wanted, but he was going to need some help, and it would take a lot of convincing.

33

"So," said Marco, "you want me to help you break in to a building?"

"No. I want you to show me how I can break in to a building. For a good cause."

Marco shook his head.

"This is insane, Josh. You're not the police."

"No, because the police aren't doing anything about this and I am."

Dan had stayed silent up until now. Josh wasn't sure if he was thoughtful, or angry, or perhaps both. Now he spoke.

"Ok, explain this properly. You want to break into BluJacket's offices?"

"Sort of. Well, yes. I need access to the footage from their tests, and I'm pretty sure that will be on their servers. So, if I can get access to their offices, maybe I can —"

"Let me stop you there," Dan said. "That 'maybe' is doing a lot of heavy lifting. Let's just pretend, for a minute, that you've got in to BluJacket's office. You think 'maybe' you can break their encryption and get on to their servers? That's mad."

"Well, have you got a better idea?"

"Yes, of course I do. My idea is… do nothing. Drop this. You told your journalist friend, so let him handle it."

"You know I can't do that." Josh said.

"Yeah," said Dan, resignation in his tone. "Ok. Well, in that case, let's at least help you come up with a plan that won't end up with you going to prison for no good reason."

"Be my guest." Josh said, extending his palms upwards.

"Right. Well, first thing, how can you even be sure this office has access to the footage? I thought all that stuff happened in the US office?"

"That's the thing. It does, but Abeke told me the CTO insists on working from an office in Edinburgh. It's just him… and a high-speed connection direct to their server. And none of the security they have at their Silicon Valley site."

Dan looked almost impressed.

"Ok," he said. "Yeah, well that answers that. Next one is a biggie though. Getting into the building gets you nowhere if you can't get into the IT, and you're still going to need to get through whatever security he has for his remote access."

"I'm guessing Marco doesn't do that kind of penetration?"

"No," said Marco. "I do not."

"But… maybe you know someone who does?"

Marco gave Josh a sour look.

"You know, I haven't agreed to help you yet, let alone roping in one of my colleagues to a criminal enterprise."

There was an awkward silence. Then Dan spoke again.

"*If* we can get direct access to their network room, it might not need that much in the way of hacking, as such."

"No?"

Dan explained.

"Ok," Josh said, enthusiastically, when Dan was done. "So, what's stopping us?"

34

"How did it go with Chris Adamson, then?" Luke asked, inevitably, when Matt called him from a bar in Palo Alto to provide an update.

"Ok. I didn't get much out of him, but things have progressed. I went to see a guy in Mission District –"

"Mission District? In Central San Francisco? Why?"

Matt explained, as quickly as he could.

"Hang on," Luke said. "You went into the city because some British kid says he watched a YouTube video about BluJacket –"

"Not actually about BluJacket, no, that was never published."

"Some British kid watched a video that's *not* about BluJacket, published by a guy who's committed suicide, but then someone with the same name as an imprisoned fraudster emailed him to ask if he was sure the YouTuber really *had* killed himself. Am I about right?"

"That sums it up. But then, he was clearly right, because I found the video…"

"Ah yes. You illegally accessed a device and account

belonging to a dead man and watched a video which alleged that the BluJacket product isn't very good. Again, stop me if I'm miles off."

"I accessed it with the permission of his next of kin," Matt said, which was at least somewhere in the same ballpark as the truth. "I get that you're unhappy. But we're on to something here. I just spoke to Josh, and –"

"Stop. Matt, just stop. I gave you rope, here, but you're embarrassing me. Do you have any single piece of firm evidence around which to write a story?"

"Not yet, but we're getting it." Matt thought back to times when Luke had supported him pursuing a tenuous but interesting story much further than this. He wondered if Luke had changed, or if Matt had just finally pushed his luck too far.

"We?" Luke said, exasperated. "Who is we? You're tasking someone the other side of the Atlantic, who you've never met, with finding evidence for you. You have nothing. For fucks sake Matt, why are we in this position again? Come back to Washington, we'll book you a flight."

Luke hung up without another word.

For a long time after his conversation with Luke, Matt sat and stared at his beer. It was hard to summon up the momentum to go anywhere or do anything. He was getting the sense that, if he returned to Washington now as requested, he might not have much of a future on the paper. On the other hand, what other options were there?

As he leaned forward to gesture to the barman for another beer, holding his credit card in one hand to indicate he was a paying customer, the hairs on the back of his neck prickled, and he had the sensation that he was being watched. He dropped his credit card and feigned a little drunkenness in clumsily trying to pick it up, taking advantage of the action to glance down to the far end of the bar. No one was looking at him, but he had the distinct impression that a bearded man sitting on a bar stool at the end of the bar had quickly looked away. His face was familiar somehow, but Matt couldn't place where he'd seen him before. He racked his brain. Had he been on the street where Mickey Cook had lived? Or at the BluJacket building earlier? Or did one bearded man in a baseball cap look much like any other?

The barman had certainly noticed Matt now, at any rate, and came to take his order. At the last minute, Matt made a decision.

"Just a tap water, please."

The barman nodded, and moved off. Matt held his phone in his left hand, and leaned forward as if watching the barman making his drink, but let the phone camera casually point towards the bearded man. Moving the phone around idly in his hand to make sure that at least one photo was pointed in the right direction, he pressed the volume key half a dozen times, taking as many photos.

Then Matt did some quick mental arithmetic in his head and figured he owed around $15. He slid two $10 bills under his now empty beer glass, and got up from his stool, acting a little more unsteady on his feet than he really was. He looked around for the restrooms. They were behind him, just inside the main door to the bar. He began making his way towards them and then, slightly theatrically, patted his back pocket and looked back towards his bar stool as though concerned he'd left his wallet there. As he did so, he spotted that the bearded man had also got up from his seat, and was moving towards the restrooms. Matt acted as though he'd discovered his wallet, and then pulled his phone out. He slowed down his pace, trying to maintain the air of somebody drunk and perhaps messaging an ex or flipping through social media, while in practice he was trying to see how quickly he could book himself an Uber.

He placed a booking, but the app spun and spun and spun, the 'we are finding you a driver' message just sitting there. Matt couldn't slow down any further than he already had, and now he was almost at the door to the bathroom and faced with a choice. Head out of the bar and into the street, probably revealing that he'd noticed he was being watched, and inviting confrontation. Or go into a bathroom that presumably had only one exit, but perhaps string things along just long enough for a car to arrive. As he took the last step towards the bathroom door, the app found him a car; it was seven minutes away. Shit.

He pushed open the door to the bathrooms and found himself in a small corridor; ladies on one side, gents opposite it, then further down a disabled toilet, and an emergency exit. Thank God. Matt wasn't sure how far behind him the bearded man was, but the second the door was closed behind him, he snapped out of his drunken shamble, and moved quickly. He pushed the door to the gents bathroom wide open, but then moved straight past it towards the emergency exit. It had a push-bar, and Matt wondered if it was alarmed, but there was no signage to indicate an alarm so he decided to risk it. He barrelled into the push bar, catching himself at the last second so that he opened the door the smallest gap possible, squeezed through it, and then forced it shut behind him. If his timing was right and luck was on his side, he hoped that his pursuer would enter the corridor to see a closed emergency exit, and a door to the gents still swinging shut. That might buy him a few extra seconds.

Matt found himself in an alleyway next to the bar. To his right were trashcans and stacks of cardboard boxes, and to his left was the high street that the bar was on. He checked his phone again, six minutes now until his Uber arrived. He turned right, running the other way up the alley towards the parallel street, and then took another left at the top. This was a more residential street, and it was almost empty at this time of night. He would stand out a mile if the bearded man figured out which way he'd come and pursued him up here.

Matt glanced around for anywhere to hide. The houses on the street had large front gardens, mostly bordered by low fences, though some had hedges. He could easily hide behind one, but he knew this type of neighbourhood well enough to guess that most of the properties would have security lighting. Crouching in a garden while lit-up by motion sensitive floodlights was not, Matt suspected, the most effective way to hide. Behind him, he heard a door slam, indicating that his pursuer had figured out that he'd taken the emergency exit. Matt hoped he'd turn left, the obvious route back towards the busy high street, but he wasn't willing to bet his life on it.

He began jogging down the road, looking for another side street or alleyway he could duck into to give him a bit of cover. A couple of hundred metres down the road, there was a narrow path between two houses, bordered on either side by high fences. Matt turned into it, and then paused to catch his breath. The path would take him back to the main street, which was where his Uber was arriving in – Matt checked – four minutes, but also where his pursuer most likely was. Matt clicked to change his pick-up location. It had to be somewhere within the grey circle that marked a set distance from the original pick-up point. Currently Matt was just outside that circle, but he could move the location to the quiet residential street he'd run onto, and hope that his pursuer didn't come this way. Or he could keep it on the busy main street, and trust to the crowds of late-night drinkers to give him cover to jump in the car and get away.

Matt hesitated, finger poised over the app. Then he made a decision, and moved the pick-up point to still be on the main street, but as close to his current location as the circle allowed. In less than four minutes the car would pull up just fifty or so metres from him, and all he would have to do would be get to it without being seen. Matt watched the little car icon making its way towards him, and realised that it was going to come right past the alleyway he was in. If, and this was a big if, he timed it correctly, he could step out, flag down his Uber and get in, and be away before his pursuer could even notice. Matt crouched low, and risked a hasty glance out of the alley and onto the high street. At first, there was no sign of his pursuer and then he spotted him, outside the bar and talking animatedly on the phone. He was pacing up and down, meaning that sometimes he was looking towards Matt and sometimes away.

Matt stared down at the Uber app, the car had just turned onto the high street. He looked up the street; there it was, a black Toyota Prius. Now, timing. He looked back round, the bearded man was facing away from him. Taking a deep breath, Matt stepped out into the street and walked briskly in the direction of his Uber while simultaneously raising the hand holding his phone in what he hoped was an unambiguous signal to the driver. To his immense relief, the car signalled to pull over. Matt risked a glance behind him and, as he did so, locked eyes with the bearded man who put his phone away and began running up the street. The Prius stopped in front of Matt, and he bounded over to it, opening the back door and throwing himself in.

"Matt Ibarra?" Said the driver, tapping slowly on his phone.

"Yes, but drive, please, I'm in a huge rush."

The driver looked puzzled. Matt hit the door locking mechanism on the passenger doors, and looked out of the window. The bearded man was just metres away. Abandoning all pretence of calm, Matt said, voice at least an octave higher than usual.

"Just DRIVE!"

Thank god, the driver finally chose that moment to pull away, leaving the bearded man almost within a hands breadth of grabbing the door handle. As the car pulled away, Matt saw the man pull his own phone out, and then finally lost sight of him as the Prius merged into traffic and began making its way towards the airport.

Matt spent much of the journey to the airport looking out of the back window, trying to identify any suspicious vehicles following him. Nothing stood out, but that didn't reassure him much. He could feel adrenaline rushing through his body, and he was glad to be sitting down as his legs felt cold and hollow. A couple of times he typed and re-typed the number for the local police, but already the terror of the escape from the bar was draining away and being replaced by uncertainty about what he'd experienced. What had really happened? Someone had made him nervous and, maybe, followed him out through an emergency exit. But maybe not. And, yes, he'd run towards Matt's Uber but that was hardly a crime. Perhaps he'd just mistaken it for his own. It was hard to imagine Palo Alto Police taking even the most passing interest in Matt's report.

Just as he got to his hotel, an email came into his inbox. A ticket for a flight back to Washington, first thing in the morning. Matt stared at it for a while and then put his phone away. He still hadn't decided whether to take the flight, but for now it didn't matter. For now, he just wanted the safety of his hotel room. Glancing around him for any sign of the man from the bar, he checked in to the hotel found his room, and closed the door behind him. Then, after moving the heavy armchair from the room to block the door, he began to feel somewhat safe again.

35

Josh, Dan and Marco took the train to Edinburgh. It felt slightly more anonymous than flying, although by the time they'd bought their tickets using credit cards and been captured by dozens of CCTV cameras at the station and on the train, that anonymity was probably just an illusion.

As they travelled up, Marco spent an hour peering at his laptop, clicking around, and occasionally scribbling notes on a tiny pad. Eventually he looked up, smiling wolfishly.

"These people. It's like they want to make it easy."

"How so?"

"The serviced office?" Marco said, whispering despite the carriage they occupied being almost completely deserted. "They have a whole virtual tour of the interior on Google Maps. I can see all the security cameras, I can zoom in on all the door locks, I've already got a plan of most of the building. Such ego, showing off their fancy office online, and no thought to how someone like me might use that."

"So you can get in?"

"Oh, I can get in. What's tricky, is not being spotted."

"I think," Josh said. "I have an idea for that as well."

"Go on?" Dan asked.

"Well, the whole reason we're going to Edinburgh is because BluJacket's CTO insists on mostly working from here."

"We know that."

"Right, but think about it. Even if he's working from here, he's bound to be mostly working on US time. In fact, on Californian time. That means he probably doesn't even get in until late afternoon and then works all night."

"Ahhh," said Marco. "I think I'm seeing your point. So we can go in during the morning, act like we're meant to be there, and get into the BluJacket office while it's empty."

"That's right. If we went at night, we'd stick out like a sore thumb. But during the day, it doesn't matter if anyone does see us, except if we're doing something we shouldn't be doing… but we can avoid that."

"I like it. This makes things a lot simpler for me," said Marco.

"Right. Not to mention it makes it a lot less likely we get arrested. I mean, worst case, we're maybe trespassing. I'm not even sure this meets the definition of burglary."

"That's comforting," said Dan.

When they arrived, the three of them checked into an AirBnB in central Edinburgh. Marco took over the dining area, laying out a series of items he'd brought with him while he checked them and assembled some pieces. There was a laptop, a flat black box with a cable, and a small stack of plain white plastic cards. Next to that, a metal tool that looked like a screwdriver except that the end was bent sharply 90 degrees and ended in a point, some sheets of acetate, and what looked like a roughly straightened out wire coat hanger with some string attached to one end. Josh looked at them in fascination.

"This is the stuff you use to get into buildings?"

"Yeah," said Marco, flicking through a bunch of assorted keys. "This should just about do it."

"Pretty cool. Ok. Pizza, beers, and some planning?"

"Sounds good to me," said Marco.

"Abso-fucking-lutely," said Dan.

Josh walked out to a Papa John's pizza not far from the AirBnB and bought pizzas, then stopped in a Co-Op on the way back to grab a couple of six-packs of beer. By the time he arrived back at the apartment, Marco had tidied his tools away and he and Dan were sitting together on the sofa, Dan's arm around Marco.

"Christ," said Josh, dropping the Pizzas on the coffee table in front of the TV along with half the beers. "As if it wasn't bad enough being the only spare part on this whole thing, now I really feel like a third wheel."

"Oh, cheer up," Dan shouted after him as Josh went to the fridge to deposit the other pack of beers. "And you're hardly a spare part. You're the brains behind this whole madness. Now come sit down and have beers."

Josh did as he was told, grabbing a slice of pizza and opening a can.

"Right," he said through a mouthful of ham and mushroom. "Here's what I'm thinking for tomorrow. Dan, you said you have to buy some stuff?"

"Yeah. Well, not a lot, just a reasonably high-spec router. Shouldn't be hard to find."

"Cool. So, you do that, and Marco and I will go and scope out the office building."

"Right," said Marco. "And if it all looks good, I'll nip in and do stage one. Otherwise, I'll go back this afternoon and do it."

Josh grabbed a pencil and started drawing on the top of one of the pizza boxes.

"Great," he said. "Then, part two is the following morning.

Here's the rough layout as best I can tell from their virtual tour."

He started moving a beer can out of his way and then changed his mind and decided to open and drink it.

"Only issue is, we don't know exactly which office is BluJacket's, but it's probably one of these here." Josh gestured with the pencil.

"Yeah. Here's where it gets a little tricky, though." Dan broke in. "For my bit, I need to know if Pete has his own wifi just for his room, or if there's a building-wide one that he uses. If I had to guess, he probably has his own."

"Is that good?"

Dan shrugged.

"Yes and no. I'm doing a man-in-the-middle attack. I'm going to turn off his wifi and replace his router with our own one, with the exact same network name. Almost guaranteed, he'll just stick his password in and reconnect to it without even thinking. And then we've got his password *and* we can see all his traffic."

"Right, so, if it's his own wifi?"

"Well, if it's his own, then it means we won't have the whole building suddenly finding they need to re-enter their wifi passwords one morning. Which is a good thing, as someone's bound to get suspicious. The bad news is, it means the router is probably in his own office, so we'll have to get in there, not just into the building's network room."

"Ok, well maybe I can find that out while Marco checks out the building," said Josh. "So, what else haven't we covered?"

There was silence. All three of them had drunk a little more and a little faster than they normally would; he suspected they were all making a similar effort to calm nerves but also quell excitement. It was a long time since Josh had felt even half this level of enthusiasm or sense of purpose about something, and the alcohol was helping to lift that buzz of energy and turn it into a feeling of satisfaction, contentment, and warmth towards Dan and Marco, his partners in crime.

The following morning, Josh didn't feel quite so enthusiastic about the four cans of beer, but he perked up considerably when he discovered that Marco had already walked out to a local coffee shop and come back with cappuccinos and croissants.

"I think I can see what Dan sees in you," said Josh, gratefully taking one of the coffees, and then dropping into a sofa. "Is he still in bed?"

"He was showering when I left. He'll be out soon."

Sure enough, Dan appeared a minute or two later and they drank their coffees and ate the pastries in companionable silence. When Josh had finished, he showered and got dressed, putting on the clothes he'd carefully selected for the day. When he returned to the living room, Dan stared at him.

"Who are you and what have you done with Josh?" He asked after a second.

"What?" Said Josh, doing a little spin. "You don't like it?"

"Is that my gilet?"

Aside from the grey puffy gilet, which was indeed borrowed from Dan, Josh was wearing slim-fit jeans and a checked flannel shirt. He'd also, and he suspected this was what was really attracting Dan's mirth, stopped at the Focus Point opposite Kings Cross station on the way out of London and grabbed some chunky-framed glasses with non-prescription lenses. He was hoping that the whole ensemble gave him the look of a start-up founder or freelance tech worker, the sort of person who might be looking for space in a shared office. It had to be better than his usual outfit, at any rate.

"First impressions matter, Dan."

"That's what I'm worried about," Dan muttered.

Josh ignored him.

"Right. Marco and I are going out. Call us if you need anything, otherwise we'll see you back here in a few hours."

"Have fun."

Josh and Marco headed out, Marco taking with him a soft satchel that he loaded with a couple of pieces of his kit and then slung over his shoulder.

As they got out into the fresh air, Josh immediately wished his costume had involved a slightly more substantial coat. The wind was bitterly cold, and his cheeks and ears were stinging within a few minutes. They walked briskly along Shandwick Place, Josh looking up appreciatively at the majestic Atholl and Shandwick Crescents as they walked past them and onto Princes Street. At first, looking into the park to the right, all Josh saw was the crisp reds and oranges of autumn trees, but then as they walked further the castle became visible, rising up into the grey sky and looming over them. Finally, they turned into an upmarket shopping street, lined with elegant stone buildings.

Part way down the street, the shared office had a narrow frontage that led into a lift lobby that, Josh knew from the virtual tour, took visitors straight up to the main reception area on the second floor. The rest of the second floor consisted of a small cafe, meeting rooms, and a large open-plan area with hot-desks that people could book by the day. Above that, the third and fourth floors were the private offices, varying in size from barely big enough for one person, to a space suitable for a 20-person company.

"Ok," Josh said, as they stopped a little way away from the front door. "My appointment is in five minutes, so I'll go in first. I'll meet you back out here in a while, alright?"

"All good. I'm going to go and wait in a coffee shop for a bit. It's too cold to be out here."

* * *

Taking a deep breath and trying to settle his nerves, Josh walked into the building and pressed the call button for the lift. Inside, there were buttons for each floor next to a flat black panel that looked like an RFID card reader. The button marked '2' also had the word 'reception' next to it, and there was a small plastic plaque that said 'Tap access card for floors 3-4'. Curious, Josh idly pressed the button for the third floor. Nothing happened. Then he pressed the button for the second floor; it illuminated and the lift immediately began to move. As Marco had suspected, there was direct lift access to the higher floors but it required a pass.

The lift came to a stop, and Josh stepped out into a bright, bustling space. White walls, exposed brick, and lots of pale wood furniture with a vaguely Scandinavian feel. Most of the space was the other side of a waist-height barrier with little glass doors. There was a long bar lined with coffee-makers with huge touch-screen interfaces and, beyond that, rows of desks. In front of him, and just about the only furniture this side of the barrier except for a small seating area, was a plain wooden table with a Mac screen on it, and a smiling dark-haired lady behind it. He assumed that was reception, and stepped forward to introduce himself.

"Good morning, I'm Mark Riley. I think I have an appointment about taking some office space?"

"Oh yes, hi Mark. If you just take a seat, someone will be right with you."

Josh settled himself into a soft, grey sofa and pulled his phone out, flicking idly through social media while he waited. The building seemed busy; several people arrived even in the few minutes while he was waiting. They tapped access cards to get through the glass barrier, and then most made their way to the coffee bar, while some headed straight to one of the few remaining hot-desks and drew laptops from their bags.

A door behind the reception desk opened and a young man dressed disconcertingly similarly to Josh stepped out. He walked over, extending a hand.

"Hi Mark, I'm Ali. I'm a resident experience support manager. Welcome!" He had only the barest hint of a Scottish accent. "So, I hear you're interested in our ten-person office space?"

"That's right, yes."

"Fantastic. We do also have a fifteen-person space available today. That extra bit of room can really make a difference, and of course saves you moving if your company expands, so we can take a look at that as well."

"Oh, sure. Thanks." Josh said, immediately annoyed with himself for knuckling under so easily to a sales pitch, and then annoyed with himself for caring in the first place. Arguably, a longer tour just gave him more of a chance to scope out the building.

"Great," said Ali, stepping round to the lift. "This way, then."

Ali called the lift and, when it arrived, they stood back to give space to another group of arrivals, and then stepped in. Ali pulled a white passcard that hung on an extendable cord from his pocket, tapped it on the RFID panel, and then hit the button marked 3. The lift moved, and the doors opened into a smaller lobby space. There was a kitchen area with another of the huge coffee machines, and three round tables surrounded by bright orange chairs.

"So, each floor has a breakout and kitchen area that's just for residents of that floor."

"Ah ok," Josh cut in. "So people using the hot-desks downstairs won't bother us up here?"

"No. Well they can't. Each floor is isolated so people with hot-desk-only passes can't access the higher floors."

"Oh I see. That's clever." Actually, it wasn't; it was fairly obvious. Obvious in retrospect, anyway, but Josh silently cursed himself for not having foreseen it. As Ali led him down the corridor away from the kitchen, Josh pulled his phone out and quickly tapped out a message to Marco.

'Hot-desker passes don't give access to the private office floors. Need a plan B to get passes for the building.'

The offices were arranged around the edge of the building, with meeting rooms, lifts, kitchens and some storage areas in the centre. Each office had a glass plaque next to the wall, behind which the occupants could put a business name or a printed logo. As they passed them, Josh looked out for BluJacket but didn't see it.

Eventually Ali walked up to one without a name or logo behind the plaque and tapped his card on the RFID panel next to the door. There was an audible click as the lock released, then he pressed the door handle and opened the door.

"All the offices are card-access, are they?" Josh asked, trying to sound nonchalant.

"They all lock with a key as well. It's up to each company if they use it. Most lock it with the key overnight and rely on the electronic passes during the day."

"I see, yeah, that makes sense."

"Anyway, here we are." Ali led them into a long, bare room. It had four windows giving attractive views down onto the shopping street and across to the buildings opposite, and there were pillars breaking the space up slightly.

"It's a good size," said Josh, not really knowing if it was or not.

"Oh, it is. This is actually on the larger side for a ten-person office, but it gives you scope to have a reception and waiting area if you want. Some of our tenants do that if they have a lot of visitors."

"Right, yeah. I expect we might do that." Josh said, casting around for anything to say. "How about the fifteen-person office you mentioned?"

"Absolutely. Let's go there now."

They went along another identical-looking corridor, passing toilets and then a room marked 'network room'. Josh paused.

"This is the network room?"

"Oh, yes. That's right. You shouldn't really need access to that but we do have an on-site IT department so if there is anything particular you need set up, they can assist with that."

Josh's phone buzzed. He forced himself not to look at it while he seized the moment to try and get some crucial information.

"Ok, cool. And, actually, how does that work with internet access and so on?"

"Well, there's wifi for the whole building. The hot-deskers downstairs use that. Our larger permanent tenants mostly have their own wifi, and of course we can help you get that installed."

"And… what about the smaller ones? I mean, do all the one- and two-person offices have their own wifi?"

Ali gave him a slightly puzzled glance, and Josh knew it was an odd question for someone who'd explicitly come here to look at larger spaces.

"It's about fifty-fifty. They're welcome to use the building wifi, but a lot of them do put their own routers in."

Josh felt his phone and watch buzz with another message. Worried that keeping glancing at his watch would give the wrong impression, Josh pulled his phone back out. It was another message from Marco.

'Ok, I have a plan B. But I need you to find a way to point out to me someone leaving the building who has a full building pass. Ok?'

Josh quickly messaged back.

'*I'll try*' and then put his phone away. He wasn't at all sure if that would be possible, but he'd cross that bridge when he came to it.

The larger vacant office was one floor up and this time they went up via a staircase, using the pass card to get back from the stairwell onto the fourth floor. Josh kept anxiously looking out for Pete's office, but none of the doors he passed had the BluJacket name or logo outside. As he passed one, he checked Ali was in front of him and still looking ahead, then took his phone out, letting it hang in his hand but angling it towards the doors and snapping several pictures of the locks and RFID readers on various doors as he passed them. He hoped that at least one of the pictures would show whatever detail Marco needed and hadn't been able to get from the slightly grainy images on the 3D tour.

By the time they got to the larger office, they still hadn't passed any marked BluJacket, and Josh was beginning to get concerned. Trying to sound as casual as he possibly could, he decided to risk just asking.

"I was actually recommended this place by a friend who works for BluJacket. They've got an office here, haven't they?"

It was far from ideal. Ali might see Pete later that day and mention that someone had been asking after him, but Josh had to try something.

"Blue Jacket? No… you sure they're in this building? I don't know the name."

"Oh. Really? Yeah, maybe I got the company wrong." Josh tried to keep a note of panic out of his voice. Could he have come all this way on a fool's errand? "Pete Taylor?"

"I don't know the name, but I've only been here a couple of months, and I only really see the company names, so yeah, maybe he works for a different company? Anyway, here's the larger office…" Ali went into another spiel about the size of the space, and all the things Josh could do with it.

36

Matt glanced at the armchair blocking the door. It didn't seem like much of a barrier any more. Accepting that a good night's sleep was probably out of the question, he plugged his laptop in and opened it up. Then he brought his phone out and looked back at the photos he'd taken earlier at the bar. As he'd expected, most of them were poorly framed, too dark, too blurry or otherwise useless. But the last couple had pointed nicely towards the man at the bar and had been taken as he began looking back at Matt, presumably thinking that Matt's attention was elsewhere. The result was a well-focused, if slightly grainy, full-face shot.

Matt transferred the photo to his laptop, and then logged in to Pimeyes. A facial recognition search engine, it did a frighteningly impressive job of taking any photo and turning up other photos of the same person anywhere on the public internet. It could be a very useful shortcut to finding out who someone was, if they had even one or two photos of themselves anywhere online.

In this case, Pimeyes came back with just one result. Matt looked at the photo returned and was certain it was the same person. A little younger, for sure, but the same eyes, same broad nose, same jawline. He clicked on the photo and it opened a blog post from 2015. He vaguely recognised the website; an anonymous blog that wrote exclusively about military topics but had a reputation even amongst traditional newspapers for its reliability and impeccable inside sources. This particular post was headlined *'Bill Ingram, Navy SEAL implicated in Tal Eltut war crimes, resigns.'*

It went on to detail how Ingram, already skating on thin ice within his team due to his enthusiasm for 'getting kills' with the custom Tomahawk he carried into combat, had been accused by no fewer than six other SEALs of shooting dead a family of Syrians in a vehicle approaching the SEALs location. While a handful of rightwing commenters were quick to defend Ingram, the special operator community itself seemed to have no such patience for his activities and he had been comprehensively disowned by a series of current and former operators. His position clearly untenable, he had resigned and now largely dropped from view. There was certainly nothing to link him to BluJacket or to Silicon Valley, and further searches on his name turned up nothing relevant.

Matt examined the photo in more detail. Ingram was handsome, rugged, an all-American hero. But his eyes were cold and angry, and it was somehow all too easy to picture him delighting in indiscriminate killing with a hatchet.

If, Matt thought, BluJacket hired enough ex special operators, then how hard would it be to eventually find someone violent and damaged enough to agree to do anything to clear some obstacles to multi-million dollar success? Including, perhaps, faking a couple of suicides. And clearing an inconvenient journalist out of the way.

37

When the tour was finally done, Ali brought Josh back to the lobby on the second floor.

"So, any more questions? Or, we can fill out the paperwork today if you're interested in taking one of the offices?"

"Thanks very much, but let me discuss it with my business partner and then I'll give you a call."

"Of course," Ali said. "Well, thanks very much for coming in."

They shook hands and Ali disappeared back through the door he'd come from. Josh was left with almost no option except to walk over to the lift. He had to figure out a way to identify someone with an all-floors pass, so he could point him out to Marco. If there was someone in the lift coming down from a higher floor, and they carried on down with him to the exit, then great. But if the lift was empty, or whoever was in it got out at this floor, it wasn't going to be easy to find another way to identify someone with the right pass. He could wait in the lobby but, at that point, anyone coming out of the lift could just as easily be a hot-desker with access only to the second floor. Not to mention that he'd look suspicious as hell if he stood waiting for the lift and then, as soon as someone exited, turned round and followed them out of the building.

He was about to just pray to blind luck and press the lift call button, when he spotted the red LED display above the lift door showing what floor it was currently at, and had an idea. Stepping back to the sofa he had sat on originally, he sat down, turning to the lady behind the reception desk and saying.

"Just waiting for my colleague - ok if I wait here, rather than down in the cold?"

"Of course," she replied, and Josh took his phone out as if waiting for a message to come through, but angled himself so he could see the display above the lift. Currently, it showed 3, and hadn't moved in a while. Suddenly it changed to 2, and then to 1, then stayed at 1. That was a missed chance, but he'd never have been able to catch that.

For another almost five minutes, nothing happened, and Josh began to wonder if anyone was going to come to or from the building at all. Then the display changed again. One, then two, then three and then – thank God – four. Hopefully that meant someone on the top floor had called the lift. If so, they could only be going down. Of course, they could be getting off at the third or, more likely, the second floor but at least he'd increased his odds a little.

Putting his phone away and jumping to his feet as if a text had suddenly come through, Josh quickly hit the lift call bell before the lift got to the second floor. After a moment, the doors opened and, sure enough, someone was in there. An overweight man in his thirties wearing a hoodie over a t-shirt with a character from a Marvel comic. To Josh's enormous relief, the man made no move to exit the lift. Josh got in with him, nodded politely, and then turned to face the door. As he did so, he glanced down and saw that the man, like Ali, had a white pass-card dangling from his waist on a retractable cord. This, hopefully, was exactly what Marco needed, although Josh couldn't help wondering what Marco's plan was. Was pick-pocketing among his list of skills?

When the lift reached the ground floor, the doors opened and Josh got out first. He walked quickly out of the front door to the building, glancing around for Marco who, to his relief, he spotted sitting on a bench just a few metres away. Ignoring him, he sent a quick text message.

'Guy walking out behind me.'

Then he began walking away, getting a decent distance down the street before he looked round. Marco was gone from the bench, and both he and the man in the marvel t-shirt had disappeared into the crowd.

Josh sent Marco a message with his location pinned, and then waited in the coffee shop for about half an hour, feeling increasing anxiety about the revelation from Ali that BluJacket didn't even have an office in the building. He searched online but there was no mention of an Edinburgh office anywhere. He realised this whole escapade was entirely based on Abeke telling him that Pete worked from a co-working space on George Street. This was definitely the only one on the street, but could Abeke have been wrong? Or could Pete have moved to different offices? Either option would mean they'd wasted a lot of time, and perhaps missed their chance.

Eventually, Marco came in, looking around for Josh. When he spotted him, he walked over, a big smile creeping across his face.

"It worked perfectly," he said, as he sat down next to Josh.

"It did? What did you do?"

"I followed him to Starbucks, and got into the queue next to him. Then while we are queuing, I just get a little too close, let my satchel bump against his key card for a few seconds…"

"I don't really get it," said Josh.

"I have a reader in my bag, it can scan one of these RFID passes and copy it. It just needs to be held close to it for a second, maybe two seconds. That's very easy in a busy coffee shop."

"Oh I see. So now you've got a copy of the card?"

"Close enough. I've got the code that's on the card, so when I get back I make as many copies of it as I like. As long as you're right that he's got a full-building pass, that gives us access to all the floors."

Josh didn't share Marco's grin.

"Ok. Nice work. But we've got a problem."

"What?"

"Well, first off, the network room is on the third floor, but the guy showing me round said it's fifty-fifty as to whether all the small offices would have their own wifi router or use the building's."

"Ok. So did you see the BluJacket office? Any idea which they use?"

"That's the problem. I asked my tour guide if BluJacket were in the building and he'd never heard of them."

"Shit. But you sure they work here, right?"

Josh shrugged, brow furrowed.

"I *was* sure. Abeke told me Pete worked from here, but it's all unofficial. Their website just lists the California HQ."

"Don't worry," Marco said. "It's one guy working from a cupboard, he probably registered under his own name. Maybe he preferred to keep BluJacket secret. Don't panic."

"Yeah." Josh didn't feel reassured. He'd convinced his best friend and a man he barely knew to take a huge risk on his confidence in his plan, a confidence that had completely evaporated in the last hour.

Marco could see his worried expression and, clearly trying

to change the topic, said, "You looked at the door to the network room, like I asked?"

"Yeah, I did. As best I could without arousing suspicion. It's got a lever door handle, with an inbuilt key code. That push-button type, you know?"

"Yeah, I know," Marco said.

"You can pick it, or hack it?"

"Maybe, maybe not. But I don't think I'll need to."

"Really? How come?"

"You'll see. What about the office doors?"

"I got some pictures," said Josh, sending them to Marco on WhatsApp.

"Nice work. Come on, let's see how Dan's doing."

Dan was waiting for them when they got back to the AirBnB.

"All go ok?" He asked, when they came in.

"Sort of" Josh said. "Had to switch plan from just booking a hot desk, as it turns out you get a pass that doesn't let you in to the rest of the building. But Marco's all over it."

"Yeah, all good," Marco agreed, opening his bag and taking out the little device with the cables attached that Josh had seen yesterday. It was attached to his laptop, which was also in the bag. He put both on the desk, opened up the laptop, and started working in a programme Josh didn't recognise.

"There's a bigger issue, though," Josh said, and explained to Dan about his conversation with Ali.

"Well, shit. That's not ideal," Dan said. "What do you reckon. Is he not there, or is he just not registered under BluJacket?"

"Abeke was definite he worked there," Josh said, thinking it through. "And Ali had never even heard of the name, so it's not like he *used* to be there and moved recently. So, most likely he's based there but just doesn't use the BluJacket name."

"Ok," Dan said. "Well, that's a start. But we're going to need to find his office either way, so we can check if he's got his own wifi network. We won't have much time to go hunting for it tomorrow... Isn't there any way we can confirm where it is?"

"I could go back and ask if they have an office under his name, but it's going to look a bit suspicious."

"Yeah," said Dan. "Could you ask Abeke?"

"What, just text her and say 'hey, where precisely in the building is Pete's office, just asking, no reason'? Not sure how well that'll go."

"Well, we need to think of something."

"Here's what we'll do," Josh said, trying to sound more confident than he felt. The small setback was already making him start to despair of the whole plan, and he had to actively fight the desire to simply give up and go home. "You need to get into the network room either way, right? So, while you and Marco get in there and do your stuff, I'll go and hunt down Pete's office."

"How are you going to find it?"

"We know it has to be one of the smaller ones, so that narrows it down. And Ali didn't recognise him by name, so whatever he's operating under it's a company name. Hopefully I can spot it. If I'm not sure, I can Google the business and see if they have a real online presence. Look, it's not perfect, but with a bit of luck I can narrow it down. Worst case, I'll give you a couple of options, Marco gets us into them, and then once we're in I'm fairly sure we can work out which is him just from looking around the office."

Dan looked skeptical. Marco spun round from his laptop, the screen of which was covered in user manuals and circuit diagrams for RFID readers. He looked surprisingly cheerful.

"It'll be fine, Josh. I like your attitude. Adapt and

overcome. Once we're in, we can figure it out."

That vote of confidence seemed to stop Dan from voicing his concerns.

"Ok then. Well that's the plan."

"Anything else we need to go through?" Josh asked.

"Not really," said Dan, flopping down into the sofa with his own laptop. "I need to get on and sort out this programme. I'd take a coffee, though, if you're making one?"

"I'm not. But I'll go out for one. Might as well leave you two nerds to it for a bit. Marco, want a coffee?"

Marco did, and Josh headed out. He'd spotted a nice looking place more or less opposite Haymarket train station, not far from where they were staying. Nomad Coffee had big welcoming windows full of plants and reclaimed-wood furniture. Inside, a long bar was stacked with pastries and baked goods, and chalkboards listed drink options.

Josh ordered three flat whites, and took a moment to appreciate the rich smell of the coffee beans and the surprising fact that the three coffees together didn't even cost £8. A far cry from GRND back home, he thought. That thought slightly ruined his mood, though. He wondered what Abeke was doing and whether breaking into her boss's office might be ruining any chance he had of rekindling his relationship with her.

38

Quite apart from the security it had given him overnight, Matt was grateful for the opportunity to shower and shave at the hotel when he woke up the next morning. He did, however, urgently need some clean clothes. He took a free shuttle to the airport terminal, where he grabbed a t-shirt and some spare underwear from one of the tourist shops in the departures terminal and changed into them in the bathroom. Then he picked up a coffee and stood for a while looking at the departures board with his flight to Washington on it. Finally, he turned, and walked out of the terminal and into the warm San Francisco air.

Feeling a little more human, he began to figure out a plan for the day. It was still early on the East Coast and it would be a good few hours before Luke would realise that Matt hadn't got on his flight. Not that it mattered necessarily, the Washington Record wasn't exactly going to send bounty hunters after him, but he wasn't looking forward to the embarrassment of trying to explain himself to an angry Luke, a man he respected.

As he rode the BART into downtown San Francisco, Matt

pulled out his laptop and started to do some research. He opened up LinkedIn and went to the people search page, then entered a search for people who had both BluJacket and the US Army or Navy listed in their past employers. A handful of hits came back, and Matt began looking through each in turn, trying to find someone who had served a long stint in the military before moving on to BluJacket, and had then left the startup. He found two good candidates, both of whom still seemed to be located in the San Francisco area, and both of whom had left BluJacket in the last six months. He sent each of them a message via LinkedIn, and prayed fervently that one of them would respond quickly.

To Matt's immense relief, by the time he had got into Downtown and had a cheap but delicious breakfast at a 24hr diner on Geary Street, he had a response in his inbox from one of the men he'd messaged. Jason 'Jase' Moore had spent twenty-five years in the US Army. His career was described with enough vagueness on his LinkedIn profile that, combined with his immediate hiring by BluJacket on leaving the Army, Matt suspected he'd spent a good chunk of his service in special operations. Moore spent just six months at BluJacket, before moving on to another tech startup with a minimal online presence and a lot of ex-military types on their management team.

'Ok - I'll hear you out. Come to Starbucks on 3885 El Camino Real at midday today. Come alone.'

Matt could easily make it there by midday. He took an Uber, arriving almost half an hour before the meeting time. The Starbucks was a nondescript single-story building in generic Californian style; pale brown walls and terracotta tiles. It had a wraparound drive-through and smoked-glass windows, behind which was exactly the kind of soulless and noisy seating area where no one would pay the slightest attention to other patrons or their conversations.

When Jase Moore walked in, Matt thought he would have spotted him even if he hadn't carefully studied the man's LinkedIn photo. Moore was barely six foot tall, but broad chested and with the chiselled, weathered kind of tan that seemed to suggest time spent in Middle Eastern villages, not Californian sun-loungers. Unlike many of the former special operators Matt had met, Moore was beardless, but his hair was long, slicked back, and topped with the ubiquitous battered trucker cap favoured by the community.

Moore immediately clocked Matt, and nodded at him, suggesting that he had been doing his own prior photo research. He didn't come straight over, though. Instead, he bought himself a coffee, and took his time stirring sugar and cream into it, before finally coming to Matt's table.

"Mr Ibarra," he said simply, as he took a seat. Matt was slightly wrong-footed by the formal greeting, and wondered if that was intentional.

"Uh, call me Matt. And, can I call you Jason?"

"Jase is fine."

"Ok, well thanks for meeting me, Jase."

Moore didn't say anything. He studied Matt intently. Matt, no stranger to awkward interviews, nevertheless stumbled over what to say next.

"So… um. You used to work at BluJacket?"

"I did. You know that, since you looked at my LinkedIn."

"Right. Could you tell me why you left?"

Moore sipped his coffee before answering.

"Matt, your message said *you* had something to tell *me*. So, please don't take offence, but why don't you get around to that and then we can decide if *I* have anything to tell *you*."

Matt half-shrugged, raising his hands slightly in a gesture of surrender.

"You're right. Well, did you know that BluJacket hardware

is being used by police forces? And that it's implicated in the death of a young Black man in Colorado?"

Moore just raised an eyebrow. Matt went on hurriedly.

"Ok, sorry, no questions yet. But, take it from me that both those statements are true and I have good evidence for them. I also have evidence that the BluJacket product failed testing with the Brits and that they saw 'dishonesty' from the company." Moore still said nothing. Matt played his last, riskiest card. "And, I'm starting to piece together evidence that a former Navy SEAL named Bill Ingram may be implicated in at least one murder to hide evidence of all the above. And probably two."

Moore finally spoke.

"*That's* a big claim, Matt. You have evidence of that?"

Time, Matt decided, to finally push back.

"Your turn now. You left BluJacket after only six months. And you agreed to meet me, at less than a day's notice. That tells me there's something going on there that you're not happy with. Help me fill in the blanks."

Moore said nothing for a few seconds, his eyes never leaving Matt's face while he thought.

"I can fill in some blanks. Only some, though. And you need to back all this up without using my name, ok?"

"It's all off the record, guaranteed."

"So, like you say, BluJacket hired me straight out of the army. I'd signed their contract before I even left, actually. I turned in my uniform one day and started at BluJacket the next."

"What was your role?"

"Product Performance Improvement Consultant," Moore said, the virtual scare quotes audible in his tone. "Most of us ex-military were doing that. The whole point of the software is it learns to identify threats, right? So, you need people to teach it. People who've been there, done the job, and know what threats look like. That was us. We reviewed footage, highlighted threats, and corrected errors when the software made them. It was all about improving the AI. At least that's what we were told."

"What do you mean?" Matt asked.

"After a while, it started to feel like making the AI work stopped being the real goal."

"So, what was the goal?"

"Making it *look* as if the AI worked."

"Right," Matt said, leaning in. "But this is what I can't figure out. If it *doesn't* work, how has BluJacket managed to fool so many people?"

"You ever heard of a company called SpinVox?"

Matt wracked his brains. It rang a bell, but he couldn't pin it down.

"Maybe. I can't recall anything about it, though."

"It's another tech startup. I looked it up because I saw Pete talk about it on the chat system we used. That dude was never really one for OpSec in chat messages, and this one time he mentioned 'the SpinVox approach' in a public channel. I might not even have paid attention if it wasn't for the fact that he deleted it really quickly, like, within 30 seconds. It's just luck I was looking at the channel when he first sent it. Anyway, that obviously made me curious."

"And? What does it mean?"

"Well, SpinVox claimed to have software that could automatically transcribe your voice mails and send them to you. Probably not that hard now, but back then it was fairly cutting edge. Anyway, it seemed to work pretty well, but then it came out that most of the time it wasn't their software that was doing it. It was people. Just cheap labour, doing it the old-fashioned way."

He paused, letting Matt join the dots on his own.

"So," Matt said slowly, "the SpinVox approach is… having

people watch the footage coming on on the BluJacket cameras and flag threats. In real-time?"

"That's what I figured. It made sense. There were so many of us, all supposedly 'training the AI' but when they ran exercises or customer demos it was pretty clear the whole thing was reliant on our input. Half the time we were fighting just to correct the AI's mistakes quickly enough."

"So it doesn't work at all?"

Moore shrugged.

"It works sometimes. Under ideal circumstances, in a controlled environment, on a good day, you know, it's actually pretty impressive. But, funnily enough, it's not designed to be used in ideal circumstances or controlled environments. Or on good days. And when you're relying on something to keep you safe, how often are you happy for it to be wrong? One percent of the time? Ten percent? Well, some days BluJacket fucks up more than fifty percent of the time. Putting that shit in the hands of operators or cops, it's not just useless. It's *worse* than useless. It's a false sense of security *and* it's mis-identifying threats. It's fucked up both ways. That endangers our troops, and anyone that happens to cross their path."

For the first time, Moore's icy-calm facade seemed to slightly slip and his lips tightened with anger.

"That's why you quit?"

"That's why I quit. I don't mind helping build something that isn't ready yet. Hell, the product's a good idea and maybe in five years it'll absolutely change the game. But the top brass at BluJacket weren't willing to wait that long. Or maybe they just couldn't afford to. VC funding doesn't last forever these days, you know. When I realised they were faking the tests, and then they started rolling it out for live trials, I had to get out."

Moore glanced at his watch, and Matt realised his window

to get information was rapidly closing.

"So the kid shot in Colorado. What do you think happened there?"

"How should I know. I left months ago. And, let's face it, cops have been shooting innocent people for years without the help of BluJacket. Maybe it's pure coincidence."

"You believe that?"

"Doesn't matter what I believe. Look, I've told you what I know. We're done here, and don't forget your side of the bargain – I better not see even a hint of my name anywhere near this."

"You've got my word. Can I reach you if I have more questions?"

Moore shook his head, already half way out of his chair.

"No. The more you contact me, the more the risk. Leave me out of this now."

And with that, he stood up and walked out.

Matt debated whether to update Colonel Rogers with what he'd learnt. He didn't feel any particular obligation to keep the officer informed; if anything, he actively preferred not to let Rogers believe that he had Matt at his beck and call. On the other hand, having the inside view from the very people who'd been deceived by BluJacket would only enhance his story. And, he wanted some kind of comment on the plausibility of what Jase Moore had told him.

A little reluctantly, Matt dialled the number he'd saved for Colonel Rogers. It was answered after only a couple of rings.

"Matt. What've you got for me?"

"We're on the record still, anonymous military source, right?"

"Sure. But I want to know what you've found out."

Matt stifled a frustrated sigh.

"I have a credible source who tells me BluJacket were still

faking their tests and demonstrations the whole time they were selling to you."

"What source?"

"You know I can't tell you that. Like you said, we protect our sources."

"Someone at BluJacket?"

"It's credible. And they told me how they were doing it."

"Go on."

"I want you to tell me if this is plausible. As an expert in the testing process. Could they have successfully faked the trials by having human operators watching the video footage in real-time and providing responses, because the AI was making too many errors?"

Rogers exhaled a long, thoughtful hum.

"It's plausible. I'd need to look into it further to be sure. I really would like to know who this is coming from, though."

"Not going to happen. So you didn't have any kind of countermeasures that would prevent that?"

"Why would we?" asked Rogers, a defensive note entering into his voice. "We don't anticipate outright fraud."

"I'm not blaming anyone. Just trying to be clear on the facts."

"That's not how this is going to come across when it's made public. Who else knows about this?"

"For now, just me. But this is coming out, Colonel, I'm sorry. It might be a day or two, maybe a week, it depends how much more evidence I need, but it's going to be a story. You'd better be ready for that."

After a second's silence, Matt realised Rogers had already hung up.

39

Dan, Marco and Josh woke early the next day. Josh had slept badly; a combination of nerves and beer, and it looked as if the other two hadn't slept much better. Marco went out for coffee, but the cheerful, almost holiday feeling of the day before had gone and been replaced by a mood of serious work. Or, Josh thought, the mood he remembered from university when he saw his friends on the morning of a particularly important exam.

After they'd finished their coffees, they walked together back to the shared office building on George Street, arriving just a little before eight in the morning. Early enough that the place would be almost empty but not, they hoped, so early that they'd attract unwanted attention or have to ask a security guard to be let in. As they arrived, Marco drew a stack of three plastic cards from his bag, and gave one to each of Dan and Josh, then put the other in his pocket.

"If Josh got the right guy yesterday, then this card should give us access to all the floors. We'll go up together, but keep the cards in case we have to separate."

They walked into the lobby, and called the lift. Inside,

Marco tapped his card on the RFID panel, and they all silently held their breath. A little light flashed green and, when he pressed the button marked three, the doors closed and the lift began to move. The cloned cards worked.

To Josh's relief, the lift didn't stop at the second floor. He was anxious about running into Ali again, although he had discarded the glasses, shaved the designer stubble he'd grown for yesterday's persona, and changed his outfit for a beanie and a scruffy hoodie. He hoped that, at a very quick glance, he wouldn't immediately be identifiable as the same person who had been in the day before.

When they arrived at the third floor, they stepped out into the little coffee and seating area. At this time in the morning it was empty and the surrounding corridors were quiet, with lights off in most of the offices. Marco pulled two yellow hi visibility vests out of his bag, along with a clipboard. He handed one of the vests to Dan and put the other on himself.

"Universal disguise," he said. "You can do almost anything if you're wearing a hi-viz vest and carrying a clipboard, and it's a brave person who'll ask what you're up to."

As the two of them disappeared in the direction of the network room, Josh set off on his own mission. He started near the lifts, where there was a fire plan of the floor. Although the offices weren't individually labelled on the plan, it gave him a sense of where the larger and smaller offices were. This floor seemed only to have large offices. He could identify on the plan the ten-person office Ali had taken him to the day before, and saw that few of the other rooms were much smaller than that, certainly not small enough to be a one-or two-person office. He decided to try the fourth floor first, and see what the layout was there.

Using the pass card Marco had made him, he used the stairwell to go up a floor, and found the fire plan in the same location near the lifts. The overall shape of the floor was the same, but the offices were subdivided differently, with the whole of one side of the building seeming to consist of much smaller rooms. That was definitely the place to start.

Holding his laptop as a low-key disguise, and praying he didn't run into Ali, Josh moved quickly down the corridor. It had a lot more doors along it than the equivalent corridor on the floor below, and he could look through the little window in each door to see small offices, most with just one or two desks and many piled high with stock of various kinds. As on the third floor, each door had a glass panel next to it where a name or logo could be put, and it was these he studied as he passed the doors. To begin with, he ruled out those that seemed to have a properly-designed logo. Not that he necessarily put it past Pete to have an entirely fake business, but the set-up didn't seem to be about that level of secrecy or disguise. Of the non-logo panels, he first did the obvious scan for 'Pete Taylor', but there were none with that name on. Then he excluded the offices that seemed to be full of products ready for shipping. After that, he excluded any that appeared to have two or more occupants, based on the amount of desks, chairs and IT equipment. He couldn't be completely sure that Pete didn't share the office, but everything he'd heard suggested that Pete worked there alone.

That still left half a dozen options. Josh glanced at his watch. It was almost quarter past eight now; the first people would be bound to be arriving at their offices any minute. He tried not to imagine the consequences of the three of them getting arrested, and focused back on the row of offices and the names on the doors.

Two of them stood out to him simply because of how deliberately generic they sounded. *Flux Deliverables Ltd* and *Cognitive Performance Ltd*. He Googled both. The first had a very simple website; it looked as if it sold refurbished classic video game consoles. The latter turned up nothing but references on companies house and other company profile websites. Josh clicked in to one of these to find a list of directors.

Sure enough, it was listed with just one director; Pete Taylor. The company had been founded almost ten years earlier, when Taylor was still doing his PhD, and Josh wondered if he'd had this office all that time. Peering in through the little glass panel, Josh could see the space was small but tidy. It had a large L-shaped desk stacked with computer monitors, a tiny sofa barely larger than an armchair, and a low bookcase. The window at the back was cut in two by a dividing wall that had clumsily been put in to make these smaller spaces, but there was a sliver of a view across the rooftops to the south, and to Edinburgh Castle in the distance. The castle was bathed in pale light and deep shadow as the sun rose over the city. A part of Josh started to understand why Pete might have refused to leave this place no matter how attractive the offer to go and be part of the company he'd founded in Silicon Valley.

Turning away from the door, Josh pulled out his phone and messaged Dan.

"Ok, I've found BluJacket. Fourth floor, meet me in the coffee area and I'll show you."

Dan and Marco came up the stairs just as Josh had, letting themselves into the fourth floor with their cloned pass.

"How'd it go?" Asked Josh.

"Piece of cake," said Marco. "I knew it would be. That combination lock on the server room just has a handle on the inside, so you can't get locked in. But, I have a tool; long bit of bent wire, long piece of string, slip it under the door and then twist it up, hook it over the handle, pull the string. Boom, you're in."

"Nice," said Josh, and looked at Dan. "So does seeing how easily your boyfriend can break into places make you fancy him more, or less?"

"Oh more, definitely more."

"Will getting into BluJacket's office be that easy?" Josh asked.

"Unlikely, I'm afraid," Marco replied as they started walking quickly round to the office Josh had identified. When they got to the door, Marco looked at it briefly, and made a little sucking noise with his teeth.

"Can you get in?"

"Yeah, I can get in. Just deciding what to… ok, let's give this a go."

He took the tool Josh had seen earlier, the thin screwdriver with the bent tip, and carefully inserted it into the gap between the door and the frame, just above the keyhole, jiggling it and trying to rotate it.

"Nope, no good."

"What are you doing?" Josh asked quietly, glancing up and down the corridor.

"This tool, sometimes I can just poke it into the bolt, and push it back. You know, a bit at a time. But this lock, is fairly new and is installed well. It has a deadbolt button." Marco was already reaching into his bag for something else, this time he brought out a little leather wallet, and fished in it as he explained. "When the door is closed, the deadbolt button is pushed, and then the bolt can't be moved except with the key. So my little tool is no good. But it's fine, we'll try something else."

He opened the wallet and took out two small pieces of metal. One was flat and bent into an L-shape, the other was a long thin strip with the last third of it bent into a wavy shape, with three little peaks. He took the L-shaped piece and inserted the short end into the lock at the bottom, then pressed a finger against the long piece, rotating the lock very slightly. Next he pushed the wavy end of the other piece of metal into the keyhole, lifted it, and dragged it sharply out. He did the same movement again three times and, on the third time, grunted with satisfaction as Josh saw the keyhole rotate completely. He used the L-shaped piece of metal to rotate the keyhole all the way around, 180 degrees, and then took both tools out and put them away.

"Cheap locks. Very easy to open, you don't even need to pick them, really. Just rake the pins and eventually they usually all get into the right place. Ok, now the RFID. This is the tricky bit."

"Tricky?" Said Josh. "Not sure I like the sound of that." He looked at his watch again. 8:30. He was amazed no one had yet arrived on their floor, but it was only a matter of time, and he doubted that hi-vis jackets would protect them for very long if anybody started asking questions.

"Tricky compared to the lock. Don't worry Josh, it's simple. These RFID panels, they're a common type, and once I saw your photos I found the circuit diagrams online."

Out of his bag, he took a magnet and a small Phillips screwdriver. He used the screwdriver to undo a single screw at the bottom of the RFID reader, but didn't yet take the cover off.

"Inside this cover," Marco said, pointing to the RFID reader, "there is a little magnet. The magnet is attracting a little piece of metal, and stopping it from touching a circuit. So, if I take the cover off – magnet is gone, metal can move, circuit forms. Maybe an alarm will go off. But, I put my own magnet here –" He held his magnet to the top left hand side of the reader. "– And now when I take the cover off, it will never know."

"And if that doesn't work then the alarm goes off, right?"

"Well, yeah," Marco admitted. "But it almost always

works." He didn't sound quite as relaxed as he had before.

With one hand holding the magnet, Marco used his other to apply a little pressure and slide the RFID box up. It came off the wall-mount, still with a series of four coloured wires attaching it to the wall. For a second, all three of them held their breath and listened for the sound of an alarm, or approaching footsteps, or any other indication that they had been detected.

Nothing.

Keeping the magnet in place with one hand, Marco carefully rotated the reader so he could see the back of it.

"Ok, so the door is held closed with an electromagnet, too strong for us to pull the door open. Here, you see," he said. "Blue and orange wires, they are the ones that tell the electromagnet to stop holding the door closed. Normally, they are not connected, so there is no signal. If I tap the RFID card, it sends a signal. But also, I can just connect them… here, hold the panel."

Still using one hand to keep the all-important magnet in place, Marco passed the RFID panel to Josh, and then reached into his pocket and took out a paperclip. He twisted it open, then bent it round so that the two ends were almost right next to each other. Finally, he inserted each end into the circuit board, one next to the blue wire and one next to the orange. Josh heard a click, and the door moved very slightly as the electromagnet released.

"There," Marco said. "Hey Dan, open the door, then I reassemble all this. Quick as you can."

Dan pushed the door open, Marco put the paperclip away, then replaced the RFID reader on the wall and put the screw back in. Finally, he returned the magnet to his bag.

"Told you, simple. These little offices, they never take security seriously. Ok, Dan, you want us in there?"

"Nah," Dan called back. "It's crowded enough as it is. Just

keep an eye out."

As Marco and Josh stepped back away from the door, Josh heard the ping of the lift arriving all the way down the other end of the corridor. He looked at Marco.

"Someone's here."

"It's fine. Nothing for them to see now."

"Still. I'd rather not be seen."

Marco shrugged.

"Nothing we can do. Just be cool."

Down the corridor, Josh heard the distinctive noise of the coffee machine grinding beans and frothing coffee. If whoever had arrived worked on this corridor, they'd be walking down here any minute.

"Come on," Josh muttered. Another thirty seconds passed glacially slowly, then finally Josh heard the door release again, as Dan pressed the button on the inside. He slipped out, turning the light off behind him, and Marco used his little lever tool to quickly re-lock the door. Then, taking a deep breath, they walked back down the corridor and into the kitchen area.

As they stepped in, they almost collided with a small, grey-haired woman carrying a coffee and a laptop. She apologised in a thick Scottish accent, but seemed otherwise almost oblivious to their presence. All three breathed a sigh of relief, and walked over to the lift, pressing the call bell.

They stepped out on the ground floor just as the first real flow of people was starting to arrive at the office, and there was a little queue for the lift as they left. None of them said anything until they were out in the chilly morning air. It was a beautiful morning; crisp and cold, with clear blue skies, and autumn sunshine lighting the street. Almost in unison, Dan and Josh burst out laughing at nothing in particular, just the release of tension and delight in the success of their escapade. Marco, perhaps more used to this sort of thing, just grinned.

"Well, what now," Dan asked, looking around at the busy street. "Everyone else is off to work, and seems like we're done for the day."

"There must be a pub open, right?" Said Josh.

"Must be."

40

"Where've you been?" Matt asked, when Josh called. "I've got some stuff to tell you."

"Yeah, well, hold your horses Matt because *we* have got some crazy shit to tell *you*!"

The kid sounded a bit drunk, Matt thought. But who could blame him, really.

"Ok, go on."

Matt was holed up in one of the many cheap, anonymous motels that lined the main drag of El Camino Real. Cheap and anonymous was what he wanted, given that he was stretching his credit card to the max with every passing night, and was still twitchy after the near miss at the bar. He was fairly confident there was no trail Bill Ingram could follow to find him at the motel but, then again, he still wasn't sure how he'd been found in the first place so it was hard to relax.

"Right," Josh was saying. "Well, we found a way to get the most recent footage from BluJacket's testing."

"How did you do that?"

"You don't want to know. We've been downloading it for almost a full day now, we had to wait for Pete Taylor, their

CTO, to log on to work, because of... well, reasons, never mind. Anyway, we've got stuff literally from the last few days, way more than Mickey ever had."

"And?"

"I mean, there's a *lot* to look through here, Matt. I hope your newspaper has a lot of interns in need of some work."

Matt didn't think now was the moment to tell Josh that he probably didn't work for a newspaper anymore.

"Have you looked at any of it, though?" He asked, instead.

"Of course. And, the stuff Mickey had is honestly pretty representative. Like, maybe the algorithm is improving, but it still keeps fucking up. Every clip we watch, just about."

"Ok, well, that's good news. If they've put this on soldiers on operations, and if they're trying to sell it to the public, and it's as bad as you say... that vindicates what I've been saying."

"Right," said Josh. "But there's more. Like I said, we've got *all* the footage, right up until yesterday, looks like."

"You mean...?"

"Yeah. We've got the Nathan Adams footage." Josh said, sounding suddenly a little more sober.

"And? Don't keep me in suspense!"

"I'll send it to you. Hang on."

Matt opened his laptop, and stayed on the line with Josh while he waited for the email to come in. When it arrived, there was a dropbox link, which opened the video straight away. Like the videos he'd seen on the footage from inside the BluJacket office, this consisted of two widescreen shots, one representing the front view and one the back. It started with both showing views of a suburban street. Matt squinted at it, trying to make out distinguishing features. He spotted a car that he recognised from the iPhone footage of the shooting, and a brightly painted blue gate leading to one of the houses. Just visible occasionally on one or other of the shots was a figure in a SWAT uniform, presumably walking to the left of Deputy Weston.

For the first thirty seconds or so, nothing much happened. The two SWAT officers walked up the street. Then another figure appeared on the rear view camera, some way behind Weston. Matt assumed it was Nathan Adams, although he was too distant to be able to make out his face in any detail. He was dressed in running clothes, and hopping a little from one foot to another as he stood on the sidewalk. For the first few seconds he was on the screen, there were none of the icons that Matt had seen in Mickey Cook's or Arturo's footage, then suddenly an amber box appeared around him, and the text 'Possible Threat'. Matt squinted; there was nothing to justify that, surely.

For another second, all was calm, the SWAT officers carried on walking away from Adams, who was looking down at his wrist. It was impossible to tell from the footage, but Matt knew from speaking to witnesses and from his own experience that the runner was just waiting for the satellites to connect to his watch, so he could track his run accurately. Then suddenly, Adams moved both hands together, right hand reaching towards the watch on his left wrist. At that moment, the box around him changed from amber to red, and the text 'Threat Threat Threat' appeared above it. The footage reeled nauseatingly as deputy Weston spun around, and now Adams was visible on the front camera. Weston's rifle was starting to appear in the bottom of the screen and, as it did so, a new icon appeared at the top left of the view. Blood red, a stylised outline of a pistol, flashing and accompanied by the words 'GUN GUN GUN'.

There was a moment when everything seemed to freeze. Just a heartbeat, and Matt stared at the figure of Adams, just barely beginning to register the movement down the street from him. Then the screen went white as Weston's rifled fired, two or three times. As the light cleared and the world became visible again, Matt could see Adams's body crumpling to the ground, and then the whole view bounced and shook as deputy Weston began to run over.

"Well? You saw it?"

Matt had forgotten he was still on the phone with Josh.

"Yes," he finally said. "Fucking hell."

"I know."

"What the hell happened there?"

There was silence for a second.

"Looks like it had Adams pinged as a threat right from the start," Josh finally said. "Then it went on high alert when he pressed a button on his watch. And then… am I crazy, or did it identify Weston's *own fucking rifle* and flag that there was a gun?"

"That's what it looked like. Jesus Christ, no wonder they're worried about this getting out."

"They are?" Josh asked. "What do you mean?"

Matt filled Josh in on what had been going on for the last few days and, especially, his run-in with Bill Ingram.

"Be careful, Josh. I'm hoping you're a bit safer, over in the UK, but if they find out you're looking into this, if they were happy to kill Mickey Cook, and a police officer… you'll be nothing to them."

"I'll be careful. So is that the stuff you wanted to tell me about?"

"No," said Matt, who had almost forgotten his own discoveries. "There's more."

He explained about Jase Moore, and everything he'd told him about the so-called 'SpinVox approach'

"I've come across this sort of thing previously," Matt said. "Although I've never heard it called that before. It's not actually that uncommon. Start-ups come up with ideas but struggle to build the technology, there's pressure to make it work for investors or even for customers, and honestly there are a lot of automated tasks that can be done just as well by humans… if you're willing to throw a tonne of money at it."

"And they get away with that?"

"Yeah. Well, sometimes. It's not necessarily even that bad, if you're using a shortcut to temporarily fulfil a feature while you build it out, then fair enough. It all depends what you're telling customers. But imagine if BluJacket literally have a room full of people watching live feeds while the army is doing a test, and they're the ones highlighting threats. You could give a passable impression of AI, but completely mislead customers about the actual state of your tech."

"Is that even possible?" Josh asked.

"I think so. It ties up with why they're hiring so many ex-special forces guys. I just assumed they were doing consultancy, or maybe helping sales using their contacts and knowledge, and early on that's probably all they *were* doing. I'm guessing they realised that, for early demos, these guys had the experience and the reflexes that they could stand in for the AI – at least for the purposes of a brief test. What I couldn't work out is why they went from having half a dozen of those guys six months ago to having around thirty now."

"That's a big increase… You're thinking using the ex-military isn't just a temporary fix now, it's the whole approach?"

"That's what it feels like. Like even BluJacket have stopped believing they can make the tech work anymore."

"It does raise a question, though."

"What's that?" Matt asked.

"On the Nathan Adams footage, was that the AI that fucked up, or a person?"

Matt was silent for a second.

"Or maybe both? The AI flags the gun, and no one reacts fast enough to correct the mistake? But either way, there's no way this should be on the streets."

After Josh had hung up, Matt watched the footage two or three more times. He thought about Weston's supposed suicide. If he'd been planning to tell Matt about how badly BluJacket had failed in the seconds before Weston had shot Nate Adams, then it made a lot of sense why BluJacket would do almost anything to cover it up.

Finally, Matt reached for his phone. He had a dozen missed calls from Luke, all of which he'd ignored, but now he finally felt in a strong enough position to call him back.

"Matt. Where, the *fuck* are you," Luke said, as soon as he picked up.

"I'm in Silicon Valley. Luke, I've got something."

"You've got nothing, Matt. Nothing. Why didn't you come back to Washington when I told you to?"

"I couldn't do that. This investigation is too important."

"Bullshit," Luke spat. Matt had never heard him this angry. "I think we need to talk about your future at the paper. Come back to Washington. Now."

"Wait, Luke. Just wait. I've got the helmet camera videos from the Nathan Adams shooting."

There was a long pause.

"That's wrapped up, Matt," Luke said eventually. "It doesn't matter what footage you've got. It's not going to show anything that the world doesn't already know."

"I think it might," Matt said. "It shows that it was BluJacket's algorithm that highlighted Adams as a threat from the moment it saw him, it was their algorithm that misidentified his hand movement as dangerous, and it was their algorithm that triggered a high alert based on the deputy's own weapon appearing in the footage. So, not just a stupid algorithm but, maybe… a racist algorithm? We've seen those before, but normally they don't get people killed."

"And you have that footage?" Luke sounded a lot calmer now. He was back to his usual thoughtful and interested self, already discarding the frustration at an insubordinate journalist and thinking five steps ahead to circulation figures and front pages and awards.

"I have it."

"Where did you get it from?"

"A source. I can't reveal that."

"Ok." There was a long pause, while Luke thought. "Fine. Come back to the office, bring the footage, get this written up. If it is what you say it is, we'll go big. Front-page story, inside story, explainer story, editorial, follow-up, the whole thing."

"Alright."

"I'll get a car sent for you, and I'll have Melissa book you a flight. What address are you at?"

Matt gave him the address for the hotel, and then ended the call. He breathed out deeply, a sense of relief washing over him at being back in the fold again. He packed his bag with what little stuff he had with him – mostly the same few items of clothing he'd been wearing for several days now – and then put his phone on charge while waiting for the car to arrive.

About fifteen minutes later, a text from Luke popped up on his phone. *'Car booked, plane tickets will be with you soon. Car is a black Lincoln Continental. Should be ten minutes away. See you tomorrow.'*

As he waited, a thought occurred to Matt. Normally when he was in DC he'd stay with Lori, his friend in Georgetown, so the paper knew not to book him a hotel. Except he realised that by now Lori would have left on her long trip to Europe. She probably wouldn't have minded him staying at her place anyway, but he didn't know if she left keys anywhere accessible and it seemed unfair to interrupt her trip and ask her. He was much better off just making the newspaper pay for a hotel for him.

He dialled the number for the Washington Record switchboard, trying to remember the name Luke had said would be making the bookings. Melissa, was it? When someone picked up, he just went for it.

"Hi, it's Matt Ibarra, I need to speak to the lady who's booking my flight back from San Francisco… Melissa I think?"

There was an awkward pause.

"Yes, that's me. Melissa Vega. But I don't know about any flights."

"Are you sure? Luke should have requested them. Maybe he asked someone else? I need to get a hotel booking as well, you see."

"I can book you a hotel, but I promise, I'm Luke's assistant and I do all the travel bookings. He hasn't sent me a request."

A cold prickle formed at the base of Matt's neck. He wondered again how Bill Ingram had found him so quickly or, for that matter, had known that Myles Weston was about to talk to Matt.

"What about a car, has he booked a car, in Palo Alto?"

"Again, I'd normally do that sort of thing for him but he hasn't sent me any request. Shall I speak to him?"

Outside his motel, Matt heard the swish of a car driving through the large puddle by the entrance as it pulled into the motel parking lot, and his room was briefly illuminated by headlights. Trying to move the curtain as little as possible, he glanced out. A black Lincoln Continental had stopped outside. Its headlights were turned off now, and it was impossible to see into the driver's seat.

"No, it's ok," Matt said quickly. "Don't mention it to him, I think I've made a mistake and I don't need to make him any more angry with me. Thanks Melissa."

He hung up the phone, and glanced out of the window again. The car was still there, and as far as he could tell no one had got out. He didn't think he'd heard a door closing. Perhaps whoever was in the car was banking on him voluntarily getting into it.

First job was to get out of his room. He was too easy to find here, and he doubted that the motel staff were going to take guest privacy too seriously if anyone asked them which room he was checked in to. Grabbing his bag and peeking quickly out of his room to check the corridor was empty, he stepped out. To the left, the corridor ran towards the main staircase and then down into the lobby, which led directly to the parking lot. To the right, it ran towards a fire exit which, Matt was fairly sure, led onto an external fire escape leading down to the back of the building. Matt went that way, pushing open the fire door and stepping out onto a metal staircase.

It was raining heavily now; the loud pings of rain off the staircase and the splash of drops falling in the puddles on the concrete below masked almost all sound. Matt went down a floor to where the fire escape reached the ground, at the base of the building. He looked around. The whole motel lot was surrounded by a high fence, making it impossible to leave the site anywhere except through the parking lot. Matt reached for his phone and opened the Uber App. He could try the same trick here that worked at the bar, except that this time whoever had come for him had a car too, and could all too easily just block the exit from the parking lot. He closed the app again.

There was an alternative, which was to try and create a distraction and then just sneak away on foot. The dark and rain would create a decent cover, if the driver's attention was occupied for long enough. Matt opened the phone app and dialled 911.

"911 what's your emergency?"

"Yes, hello," Matt said, trying to sound frightened and realising that it didn't require much acting effort. "I'm at the Travelodge at 5325 Camino Real. There's a car outside and I saw men in it wearing masks and carrying guns. I'm worried they're going to rob the motel! It's a black Lincoln Continental. Please come quickly!"

"Ok sir, I'm dispatching units. Can I take your name, please?"

Matt hung up the phone. Then he began to carefully move around the side of the building, positioning himself so that every so often he could peer round the corner and check on the car, and so that he was as close as possible to the exit, and the street beyond. He waited, praying that any minute now he'd see flashing lights and responding patrol cars.

Five minutes passed like an absolute eternity. He knew if he left it too long, the driver would start to get suspicious. Surely police would respond quickly to a potential armed robbery? How much longer could they be? He repositioned himself to lean out again and check there was no movement from the car, and was just about to peer out when he finally saw the flash of blue and red lights and two patrol cars pulled aggressively into the parking lot.

Seizing his moment, and knowing it might not take long before the officers realised the car wasn't full of masked men, Matt simply walked to the parking lot exit and out onto the street. The police officers, jumping out of their cars with weapons drawn, barely even registered him but he felt the piercing eyes of the driver of the black Lincoln on him every step of the way.

41

Josh found it hard to settle back into work when he arrived back in London. The buzz from the trip to Edinburgh, from the excitement and risk of stealing the footage, had worn off. Now, despite all the risks he had taken, he felt as if his part in the investigation was over and all that was left was for Matt's newspaper to publish a story, while Josh went back to churning out dreary ad campaigns.

It wasn't just the comedown from the adventure, though. Josh was unable to shake a particularly deep bout of anxiety and depression. Both, for once, had fairly identifiable causes. He'd still heard nothing back from Abeke. And, as for the anxiety; the simultaneous threat of possible police investigation as well as potential death at the hands of a rogue ex-special forces operator would make anyone anxious.

He was supposed to be populating the half-built BluJacket website with copy and photographs using their content management system, but knew that he was making slow progress.

Out of a sense of guilt at his inefficiency with the project, Josh stayed in the office until well after 6pm, making sure to look suitably buried in a series of project plans and client presentations. Only after he'd seen Jamie head for the lift, Josh closed his own laptop and headed for the locker room to change into running kit and set off on a gloriously, painfully fast, run home.

As he approached his flat, he barely noticed the figure standing outside and wrapped in a thick coat with a hood – it was a busy street, and a busy building, and it was hardly unusual to have someone waiting outside. It was only as he stopped running and pressed the pause button on his watch, then looked up again, that he realised who it was.

"Hey Josh."

"Abeke… what are you doing here?"

42

Matt paid for his own flight back to Washington DC. It landed late in the afternoon, and he took the metro to Downton, then walked slowly towards the Washington Record building, thinking about his next step. He and Luke had known each other for years but, unlike Matt, Luke had always been well-connected in DC. Even as a relatively junior reporter, he and his wife had been a feature at dinner parties in Georgetown and Foggy Bottom, and now that he was a managing editor at the Record with several best-selling books to his name, he was on the invite list of senators, senior military officers and foreign diplomats. He'd always seemed more than able to keep his web of personal relationships separate from his reporting, or that of his juniors. Now Matt wondered if this was the first time he'd crossed the line or if he'd been building up to it over years of smaller transgressions.

By the time Matt got to the building, it was almost 5pm. He knew Luke tended to leave promptly at 5:30. He would cycle home and work there for another hour or two in his neat, book-lined study before either going downstairs to join his wife for dinner, or going out to one of the several dinner parties he attended each week.

Matt waited opposite the side door of the Record's office; the door that he knew led down to the underground parking lot and secure bike park. Sure enough, at 5:40, the door opened and Luke appeared, clad in expensive lycra and wheeling a bike worth slightly more than Matt's car. He was focused on tightening up the straps of his backpack without dropping his bike, and didn't see Matt at first. Matt stepped right in front of him, putting a hand on the handlebars of the bike and gripping them firmly.

"Hello Luke."

Luke snapped his head up to look at Matt, but quickly recovered from the shock.

"Hello Matt," he said, calmly. "You startled me. What are you doing here?"

"Well quite, Luke. What *am* I doing here. You never booked my flights."

"Did I not? God, I can only apologise. I am sure I emailed Melissa, but perhaps the email got stuck in my outbox." He pulled his bike free, and began to wheel it away, cleated shoes clicking on the sidewalk. "Still, looks like you got a flight. Be sure to claim it back."

Matt grabbed the seat of the bike, and pushed it, toppling Luke off balance and forcing him to take a step and let go of the bike with one hand.

"You didn't book my car either. But the funny thing is," Matt said, "a car showed up anyway. And I'm pretty sure the driver was a man called Bill Ingram. A former Navy SEAL who's been following me for days."

"My God," Luke said, as he recovered his balance and regained control of the bike. "Are you sure?"

"Oh yeah, pretty damn sure. What I'm wondering is how this individual knew where I was. Or knew where I was the first time I ran into him, in Palo Alto. And actually, Luke, I have a feeling he killed Myles Weston, which makes me wonder how he knew I was about to talk to him."

"These all sound like interesting questions but perhaps we should talk properly about your story tomorrow." Luke pulled on the bike, but Matt held on firmly to the seat.

"They're rhetorical questions, Luke. I know the answer. Every move I made, I told you, and you told BluJacket. What I don't know, is why?"

Luke gave up pulling on the bike, and fixed Matt with a cold stare. In the yellow glare of the street lighting, Luke's skin colour looked even more unhealthy than last time Matt had seen him.

"I don't have any contact with BluJacket, Matt."

"Don't lie to me," Matt said, barely keeping his anger in check. He looked at the man in front of him, trying to reconcile the two versions he saw; his long-time mentor and friend, and someone who had willingly given him up, quite possibly to be murdered.

Luke sighed, and his body seemed to slump. He let go of the bike altogether, and leaned against the wall.

"All I did was talk to a friend of mine. I didn't expect any harm to come to you, I promise."

"Bullshit. If you thought I was getting out of Palo Alto, you'd have booked my flight."

"He told me not to. He told me they'd warn you off, and then get you back home to New York, out of the way and off the story."

Matt stared at him. Luke was many things, but he'd never been either naive or gullible. Perhaps, Matt thought, even he could successfully pull the wool over his own eyes when he simply didn't want to accept the truth of what he was doing.

"You can't be that stupid, Luke," Matt hissed, taking a step towards Luke so that the other man had to back away from his bike and up against a wall. "You didn't think that after what they did to Myles Weston and Mickey Cook, the same thing wouldn't happen to me?"

"I had no idea anyone did anything to Weston, or to the YouTuber, I promise you. I've never heard of Ingram. My friend just told me he wanted to keep an eye on the investigation so he could prepare for any awkward questions."

Matt looked at him, searching for signs of deceit and not finding any. He'd always thought he could spot when his old boss was lying. But then, Matt thought, maybe he'd never been as good at spotting Luke's lies as he'd imagined.

"Who's 'he'? And why were you giving him information?"

"Why does anyone do anything. Money. I'm sick, Matt. Brain tumour. I'll be lucky to be alive by next Christmas. I want my wife and my girls to be taken care of."

"Christ, well... I'm sorry to hear that. I am. But you've got insurance, haven't you?"

"Insurance, and almost half a million dollars of debt."

Matt tried to keep the surprise off his face, unsuccessfully, it seemed.

"Don't look at me like that," Luke went on. "Do you know how expensive it is keeping up appearances in this town? The lifestyle that people expect an editor at the Record to have? We have generals and senators round for dinner just about every night of the week –"

"So, you're being paid for info?" Matt cut in, unable to stomach any more of Luke's self-pitying justifications.

"God no. Just, this friend, he heard about my... health issues. So, he gave me an investment opportunity. A sure thing. Little company, about to get approval from the Armed Services Committee to roll their tech out across the whole army, but hardly anyone knows that yet. What little remains of my life savings and entire 401k now, turned into millions of dollars in a couple of years time when I'm six feet under. Can't fail."

"BluJacket. That sounds like insider trading to me."

"Grow up, Matt. A tip from a friend, that's all. Anyway, then you started digging into it, and my friend just asked to be kept apprised of your progress. That's all, I promise. He doesn't even work at BluJacket. I'm truly sorry you got hurt, that was never what I wanted."

"So, who's the friend?" Matt asked..

"I can't tell you that, Matt. I'm sorry."

Matt looked at him. His rage, not so much evaporating, but being redirected. Luke started to look pathetic, worn and grey and heartbreakingly skinny in his stupid lycra. Perhaps he was a victim in his own way, taken advantage of by the people who really circulated the halls of power. Talked into a Faustian bargain that he didn't even stand to personally benefit from.

"What now, Matt?" Luke asked, eventually.

"I'm publishing what I have. Stay out of my way, and I'll keep your name out of it. That's the best I can do."

"It's my life savings. It's everything I was supposed to leave for Julie." His voice cracked.

"I don't know what to tell you, Luke. Your money's gone. Whether I publish or not, that investment is never going to be worth anything."

"Jesus Christ." Luke said, softly. He looked down at his bike. "Well. Are we done here, then?"

"We're done. Am I going to see you in the office tomorrow?"

"We'll see," Luke said, taking his bike gently from Matt's grasp and swinging his leg over the saddle. He clipped his left foot in and pushed off. Matt heard the other foot clip in, and then he was away, a small fragile figure weaving into the sea of traffic.

* * *

Matt was walking to his hotel when his phone began buzzing in his pocket. Pulling it out, he recognised Brian Rogers's number, although he hadn't saved it in his phone.

"Hello?"

"Hello Matt. I heard you were back in DC. We need to talk."

"Ok, well, I'm listening."

"No, face to face. I've got something you'll want to hear, but I'm not saying it on the phone."

"Fine. But I'm going to print any day now, so if you want this in the story we'd better meet soon."

"Tomorrow morning. I'll text you a location."

"Alright."

Matt ended the call.

43

Abeke sat on the sofa in Josh's living room, while he perched awkwardly on a footstool opposite. She rapped her fingernails absent-mindedly against the mug of coffee he'd made her, and then finally spoke.

"I'm sorry about what happened before," she began.

"No, don't. *I'm* sorry. I didn't mean to accuse you of anything."

"Forget it. The thing is, you weren't completely wrong."

Abeke paused. Her fingernails rapped anxiously on the mug again.

"How do you mean?" Josh prompted her, eventually.

"After we spoke last time… well, I was pretty angry. I FaceTimed one of my friends at BluJacket. He's one of the ex-army guys. Been there since almost the very start, and we've always got along. Anyway, I thought he'd cheer me up, but he was even worse than I was."

"Worse, what… angry?"

"Angry, sad, disappointed. I don't know. He didn't want to talk about it for ages. Just said he was thinking of leaving the company. Then he told me to get out while I still could."

Josh was about to say something, then stopped himself. Abeke clearly had to tell her story her way.

"Obviously I wasn't going to let that go," she said. "So I kept pushing. And eventually… well, he pretty much confirmed what you said. About the cop shooting that kid."

"He knew about it?"

"Oh yeah. Said he'd been warning them for ages that something like this could happen, that 'The Mind' was constantly misidentifying threats, and even with human oversight they couldn't pick up the errors fast enough. He said it was only a matter of time before the you got the wrong error, in the wrong place, in the hands of the wrong cop. And now it had happened. Then he sent me the footage."

"So you saw what happened? The Mind flagged the cops gun?"

"How did you know that? Never mind, I get it, you've been digging. Fair play to you for not letting this go, I guess." She smiled slightly. "That's probably one of the things I like about you. Anyway, sure, the AI fucked up badly but that's not what really freaked me out."

"It's not?"

"No. Watch it with me again and I'll explain."

"Ok," said Josh cautiously, wondering how to broach this. "But, look, there's someone else you should probably explain it to at the same time."

"Who?"

"This journalist I've been talking to. He started investigating the original shooting, and… well, it's a long story, but he needs to hear anything you've found out."

Abeke looked thoughtful.

"Ok. Fine. I guess I should have known you'd have spoken to a journalist, and if you trust him then that's good enough. You going to call him, then?"

Josh dialled Matt's number. It rang a few times before Matt

picked up.

"Josh, I'm glad you called," he said, before Josh could say anything. "I wanted to let you know I'm expecting to have a story on the front page day after tomorrow. It looks as if I've got an interview lined up with one of the Army guys responsible for assessing the product. Either way, we've got enough now that it's time to go to print."

"You don't sound as happy as I thought you'd be."

"No I am," Matt said, wearily. "It's just… it's not the whole story."

"What do you mean?"

"My editor, Luke, he wasn't in touch with BluJacket directly. He was feeding information about me to some friend, the same friend who gave him a tip to invest in BluJacket. If I had to guess, I'd say it's someone on the Armed Services committee that are supposed to be assessing it."

"So, make that part of the story!"

"I would. I will. But, the Record doesn't print allegations against US Senators unless it's got some rock-solid evidence. And there are other unanswered questions here. For one thing, I still want to understand why Nate Adams was tagged as a threat right from the start."

"I might be able to answer that," Abeke cut in.

"Who's that?" Matt asked.

"That's my friend Abeke, the one I told you about? That's why I called actually. She's figured something out and you need to hear it."

"Abeke who works for BluJacket? Ok, go on."

Josh put his mobile on the table between him and Abeke, and switched to speakerphone.

"Nice to meet you Abeke," Matt said. "We definitely need to talk."

"We sure do," said Abeke, leaning in towards the phone. "I think there's a problem with the BluJacket technology that you may not have realised."

"Well," said Matt, "we know the AI flagged the cop's gun."

"Yeah," said Abeke. "But you've got to look further back than that. Why is Adams flagged as a threat in the first place?"

"He moves his hands to start his watch?" Matt said.

"Sure, but even that wouldn't have been an issue if the AI hadn't identified him as a potential danger from the very start."

"I see your point. It highlights him in amber right from the beginning, so everything escalates from there. But *why*? That's what's killing me. I've done stories before about AI that ends up getting programmed to be racist, but I couldn't find any evidence that happened here."

Abeke nodded her head, though of course Matt couldn't see her.

"Yeah, it's actually worse than that, I think. I figured it out talking to my friends in the PPIC team." She pronounced it pee-pick.

"PPIC?"

"Product Performance Improvement Consultants. A bunch of ex-forces guys, mostly special operators of some kind."

"Right, I met one of them. They were supposed to be training the algorithm, although it seems like lately they were faking it more than improving it…"

"I heard that. But, that's the thing. It's the training. They're hired for their instincts and quick reactions, at least in part, right?"

"Sure, and their ability to spot threats."

"Ok. So then, they react to stuff. Video footage, old and new. Training exercises, live stuff, recorded stuff. Over and over again, see and react, as quick as possible."

"Ok. I'm still not sure I see where…"

"So, the AI, no one can open it up and look at its rules for what is or isn't a threat. No one's programmed it to consider Black people more of a threat. It's not even the opinions of any one person. But it's been made into an amalgamation of all the most instinctive responses of a bunch of people. The judgements they make before they even really think about it."

"Shit," Matt said, quietly. "I think I see where you're going with this."

"I'm not sure I do," said Josh, cutting in.

"These guys, they're your stereotypical ex-operator, right?" Abeke explained. "As a group, they're one hundred percent male, probably ninety percent white, definitely more conservative than average. They're good guys, don't get me wrong. A lot of them were my friends. I'm not saying they're racist, not consciously."

"But?"

"But… most people's racism *isn't* conscious. It's the assumptions they make before they have a chance to think. Before they even know they've made them. If you're a decent person your conscious brain kicks in and corrects you. But, BluJacket's managed to take all the most instinctive, unconscious, assumptions and reactions of a bunch of conservative, white, ex-special operators, and mash them together into an artificial intelligence."

"And then make that artificial intelligence responsible for identifying threats for police officers and soldiers…" Matt cut back in. "And no one can even look at it and *see* the problems or change the programming somehow. And they're about to roll it out to even more live deployments…"

"Are they, though?" asked Josh. "Isn't your article going to stop them?"

"Honestly… I don't know. You'd like to think so, but companies have survived much worse PR problems than this. Right now, they can chalk it all up to bugs, defects and honest mistakes. They'll say, at worst, maybe they pushed out a product a bit before it was really ready. And what tech company hasn't done that?"

"So we need proof. Proof they knew it didn't work, and knew it was dangerous."

At his side, he felt Abeke stiffen. She began to speak, then closed her mouth again.

"What is it?" Josh prompted.

"Ok, so I *might* have an idea," she said, thoughtfully. "But I'm not at all sure how I'd go about it."

"What are you thinking?"

"I was thinking about phone records. And then I thought, well, at BluJacket we didn't communicate much by phone."

"You didn't?"

"Not really, no. It was all Chat, all the time. And Chris was always getting fed up with Pete for saying things he shouldn't on Chat and email. I mean, if he was accidentally dropping info like that into a public company chat… imagine what he was saying in private rooms and direct messages."

Matt thought for a moment.

"Yeah, I'm with you. But how are we supposed to get the messages?"

"Ok, so that's where I said I'm not sure how I'd go about it. But, you know, we want their chat logs. And Josh here works for their digital agency. There's got to be *something* we can do."

An hour later, and long after they'd finished the call with Matt, Josh didn't feel much closer to a plan. He and Abeke sat in his living room surrounded by a laptop, both their phones, a bottle of wine and two glasses, and various scribbled notes and ideas.

"I can't believe Pete isn't an admin for your Chat deployment," Josh said, for what he realised might be the third or fourth time. "The one bloke in the company whose password I think we've got…"

Abeke shrugged.

"Setting up Chat was all Chris's idea. He thought it made us seem like a proper tech company. He's probably an admin, but the main guy who runs all that stuff is Sonnie, our head of IT."

"Right. So we're back at, we just need Sonnie to export all the company's Chat messages for the past few years, and send them to us."

"Simple."

"Or give us his password."

"Right," said Abeke. "Which seems unlikely."

They fell silent again. They'd gone round multiple times and always ended up back at this point. Sonnie, Abeke had assured him, was unlikely to be able to be bribed, begged or cajoled into either giving up his password or exporting all the company's Chat messages for them. And he was certainly tech-savvy enough to have a strong password that he wouldn't blindly give out, or enter into a website if he didn't trust it.

If he didn't trust it. Josh thought, suddenly. *But what if he did trust it?*

"I might have an idea. It's going to need both of us, though. And it's going to need a simple little webpage. Don't suppose you know how to build one, do you?"

"Not really. Do you?"

"I can probably manage enough for what we need… and if not, we'll get Dan to do it when he gets home."

Josh pulled his laptop over and started work. As he did so, he explained his plan.

44

Chris Adamson paced in his office, looking down again at the print-out of an email from Matt Ibarra. The bullet pointed, itemised list of allegations stared back at him as though it was already a charge sheet or indictment.

He dialled and redialled his contact on the Armed Services Subcommittee. He had failed to take Chris's calls for almost two days now. Finally giving up, he called Pete.

"What is it?" His CTO answered, grumpily. Chris checked his watch; he was pretty sure he hadn't woken Pete up, but it was impossible to tell when the man slept, so anything was possible.

"Have you seen this email? It's a request for comment from the Washington Record, before they publish a story. I forwarded it to you."

"I've seen it."

"And? Is that it? How the fuck did they get all this?"

"I don't know. I thought you were taking care of Ibarra? Why is he even still working on the story?" Pete's voice had an accusatory tone that immediately irritated Chris.

"Yeah, well, there were some complications there. Last I

heard Ibarra made it back to Washington so I guess that didn't work out."

"What a fucking mess."

"It's fixable. He's got nothing we can't explain."

"What about the Nate Adams footage? How the fuck did he get his hands on that?"

"I don't know. But I'm planning to find out."

"Don't just find out. Get it back."

"I'm trying," said Chris, doing his best to remain calm. "But I'm about to fly to London to meet a potential investor. And I need you to get to grips with the technology. Either make it work or make it *look* like it works."

"What do you think I've been doing?" Pete asked, and hung up.

45

"Not sure I'm looking forward to being back in the office after all this." Said Josh, sliding his laptop into his backpack ready for the commute the following day.

"Me neither. But I have a feeling we're going to be looking for new jobs after all this so... I guess enjoy it while it lasts."

"Well, thanks. That makes me feel loads better." He paused, then said. "You think this'll work?"

"Course it will," she said, with surprising confidence. "It's a good plan."

Josh headed for the underground station and began the same commute he'd done a thousand times before, while Abeke headed off to her WeWork.

When he arrived, he logged into his workstation and then accessed the content management system for the BluJacket website. He'd been spending days in the system recently, adding pages and copy-pasting content in, getting the site ready for the big launch in a couple of weeks. This time, instead of creating a new page using one of the many templates crafted by the agency's designers and built by their web developers, he created an entirely blank page. He uploaded the files that he and Dan had spent an hour or two hacking together the night before. Finally, he hit the publish button and checked how the page looked.

Perfect.

Then he drafted an email to Abeke. Courteous, polite, perhaps a tiny passive-aggressive edge of frustration at being asked to do some last-minute task. In other words, a convincing email from a marketing agency executive to his client.

It mentioned an entirely fictional conversation about a new requirement to have a customer services chat function on the website home page. That, Josh said, would be best powered by a Chat widget so that customer services agents could easily use it. The only hiccup was that he'd need someone with admin privileges on BluJacket's Chat instance to approve the widget. All they had to do was visit this webpage, log in using their Chat username and password, and hit approve.

Simple. And, by the time Abeke forwarded the email to Sonnie, pretty convincing. It would take an unusually suspicious man to question an email from his company's marketing agency, forwarded to him by their own marketing manager, with a link to a page that sat on their own draft website.

Josh just prayed that Sonnie wasn't an unusually suspicious man.

Josh had to wait less time than he'd expected before Sonnie responded to Abeke's email. Knowing that the head of IT, like most of BluJacket, worked in California he'd expected to get nothing until almost the end of the day. Clearly, though, Sonnie started his day early because it was barely lunchtime when an email from him popped into Josh's inbox. Seemingly, without a hint of suspicion on Sonnie's part, it agreed to set up the widget.

A few minutes later, another email popped into his inbox. This time it was generated by the page he'd created on the BluJacket website, and did little more than forward him any username and password that anyone happened to enter into the form. In this case, the username and password were Sonnie's admin details for Chat.

Armed with those details, Josh entered the URL for BluJacket's internal Chat instance, and was met by a login screen. Nervously, and half-convinced that doing so would surely set some kind of alarm bell ringing at BluJacket headquarters, he entered the details he'd received from Sonnie. A second later, and with no fanfare, he was in.

The next part was a little trickier, and really did risk setting alarms off. As Josh had discovered from the user guide he and Abeke had looked at online the night before, as an admin of a Chat Pro+ account, Sonnie could easily export all of the conversations that had happened in the BluJacket workspace, including seemingly private DMs. The only problem was that when he did so, Chat would do the export in the background and then email him with a link to the file once it was ready. An email which, of course, would go straight to Sonnie.

Except that, now Josh was logged in, he could simply change the email address associated with Sonnie's account. Then, to be on the safe side and make it a little harder for Sonnie to lock Josh out when he inevitably realised what was going on, Josh changed the password too. He wasn't sure how much time that would buy him, but he hoped it would be enough.

Remembering the steps from the user guide, Josh navigated to the settings and administration area, and found the 'export data' option just where it was supposed to be for an administrator. The next option was a date range. He knew that the more he selected, the longer it would take. But if he didn't select enough, he risked missing exactly those critical early conversations that would prove who had known about BluJacket's fraud and how long for. Praying it would be enough, he chose a date three years earlier, and hit export.

As expected, the next screen was a download progress indicator. Josh had no idea how long to expect it to take, and watched anxiously as the 'estimated time' jumped around, starting at four days and eventually settling at around forty minutes.

That was still far too long, as far as Josh was concerned, but there was nothing he could do but wait. The office seemed eerily quiet; oblivious to the massive act of computer piracy Josh had just committed against one of his agency's most important clients. He had a feeling the BluJacket office wouldn't be quite so oblivious – Sonnie would presumably have been notified that someone had changed the email address on his account. And if he'd then tried to log in to find out what was going on, he'd have discovered he was locked out. After that, it wouldn't take him long to figure out that something was seriously wrong.

Josh quietly started gathering up his belongings and slipping them into his bag, ready to make a quick getaway as soon as the download was done. Or sooner, if needed.

46

As soon as Chris landed at London City Airport, he reactivated data on his phone. WhatsApp and Chat messages that he'd been sent during his overnight flight began to fill up the notifications screen. As he queued for immigration, he started going through them all; relieved to be plugged back in to his network.

He had a habit of reviewing his inbox from oldest email to newest, meaning that he'd just about reached the front of the queue before he got to the fourth email to the top. When he read it, he was confused for a second. Sonnie, his head of IT, seemed to be upset about something to do with their corporate Chat instance. He read it again, trying to decipher the meaning in the jumble of jargon and barely-disguised panic. Was Sonnie saying they'd been hacked?

That made him pay attention. He'd had a nasty feeling for a while now that the company's Chat instance could be a weak spot. They'd used it since the earliest days of the company, and he'd tended to treat it as a secure and safe place to speak almost as unguardedly as he would in person. Pete had been even worse, frequently speaking without any regard for who else might be in a Chat channel. Chris had meaning for a while now to have the whole history purged, but simply hadn't got round to it.

Noticing the signs prohibiting the use of mobile phones in the immigration queue, Chris opened WhatsApp and fired off a message to Sonnie.

'What the fuck is going on? Should I be worried?'

The response came back almost straight away.

'Yes, you should be worried. I think someone has taken over my Chat account.'

'Who?'

'This is going to sound crazy, but I think it's that marketing agency in London. And I think Abeke's helping them.'

For a second, Chris was stunned, but his mind quickly caught up, and then went a few more steps ahead to realise the possible consequences of what he was being told. He swore under his breath, and quickly typed another message back to Sonnie.

'Call the agency. There's someone there stealing our data. They need to find who it is, and stop them leaving the building. And I want their name.'

'Then what?' Sonnie replied.

'Then I'll deal with it. I'm going there.'

At that moment, the Border Force officer called him forward, and Chris stepped up to the counter, trying not to let his frustration and impatience show as he answered a tedious series of questions about his reasons for coming to the UK.

The minute he got through immigration, he broke into a jog, ignoring a few surprised glances as he made his way towards the car hire desk.

47

When Matt woke up, he had already received a text from Brian Rogers.

Pentagon. 10am. I'll meet you at the visitors entrance. Wear a Washington Nationals cap so I can recognise you.

It was only just gone seven. Matt had plenty of time. He showered, shaved, and put on the smartest and cleanest shirt he could find in the handful of possessions he'd been lugging around with him for the last week. Then he took the metro out to the Pentagon, stopping for a coffee and a bagel on the way, and picking up a Washington Nationals cap from a stall near his hotel.

He arrived at the Pentagon just a little before ten, and walked the short distance from the metro station to the visitors centre. For a moment he wondered whether to go in, or how he'd recognise his contact, but then, as he scanned the people lingering around the entrance he locked eyes with one. A tall, shaven-headed man in green service uniform decked with multiple rows of ribbons, and various metal badges and emblems indicating achievements and qualifications that Matt barely recognised. He did know enough about the army to recognise the single star insignia of a brigadier-general on the collar, and was briefly surprised at how senior his contact was. He'd imagined a more junior officer, or perhaps a captain commissioned from the ranks near the end of a long career.

"Matt Ibarra?" the officer said as he approached Matt.

"That's me." Matt stuck out a hand. The officer took it and shook it.

"Brian Rogers. Nice to meet you. Come this way." He gestured into the visitors entrance, and followed Matt inside. The doors led into a room that resembled airport security, with uniformed guards and a few rows of X-ray machines and metal detectors. Matt put his phone, keys and watch into a tray, and then walked through a metal detector. The officer followed him, ignoring the detector beeping as he did so.

Matt was about to retrieve his possessions and return them to his pockets when the officer reached out and stopped him.

"Secure area. You'll need to leave your phone here I'm afraid. There are lockers you can put them in."

He gestured to a wall of small lockers, like those found in a swimming pool or gym, but each only about the size of a shoe box. Matt reluctantly put his phone into one of them, locked it, and put the key in his pocket.

"That everything?" Rogers asked. "They've got detectors so don't try and sneak a second phone in. You'll make me look like an asshole, and that's the end of our deal."

"That's everything. I promise."

"Alright. This way."

Ignoring the bank of doors directly ahead of them, Rogers turned left and led Matt through a smaller door that led them back out of the building, and along a path that ran along the outside of the huge wall of the Pentagon, down towards the southern tip of the building, and the huge car park there.

48

As Josh watched the download progress timer ticking into the last few minutes, he heard Jamie's phone ringing a few desks away. Jamie answered it, listened, and then glanced over at where Josh was sitting. Josh looked hastily away, and back at the download progress. It was down to two minutes now.

Behind him, he heard Jamie put his phone down and jump up from his chair, starting to walk over to him. Josh picked up his laptop and, carefully leaving it slightly open so that it stayed active and connected to the office WiFi, slid it into his bag. He stood up, and started to walk away from his desk.

"Josh, where are you going?" Jamie asked.

"Popping out for a coffee, why?"

"Uh, I'm not sure what's going on, there's some issue with BluJacket…"

"What issue? I've not done anything."

Jamie gave Josh a careful look, and glanced at his backpack on his back. He hesitated for a second, but evidently whatever information he'd had from BluJacket didn't give him a reason to physically manhandle another member of staff.

"Look, don't go anywhere until I've straightened this out, ok. If you want a coffee get one from the machine."

Josh shrugged.

"Ok, sure." He carried on walking, swerving the lifts and heading in the direction of the little kitchen area, with its bean-to-cup automatic coffee machine. When he got there, he risked a glance back, and saw that Jamie was now in the office of Susan, his boss, talking animatedly to her.

Josh altered course, and quickly opened the door to the staircase. As soon as he was through it and into the stairwell, he pulled his laptop out of his bag and re-opened it, praying that the download had continued and completed. His shoulders sagged with relief as he saw the message 'download complete' on the screen. He shoved the laptop back into his bag and started heading down the four flights towards the exit. As he half-jogged down, he grabbed his phone and called Abeke.

"Is everything alright?" She said as soon as she answered.

"I hope so. I think I've got the files. But I'm pretty sure they're on to us. You're not anywhere they can easily find you, are you?"

"Hell no. I've holed up in a coffee shop in Covent Garden. I'm staying offline. Can you make it over here?"

"I'll do my best. See you soon."

"Hang on," Abeke said quickly, before Josh could hang up.

"What is it?"

"I had an email from Chris's PA. Suggesting that he and I have dinner."

"What?" Josh asked, puzzled.

"Dinner. Because he's here, in London. Apparently he flew in this morning, to meet an investor."

Josh hesitated. He was just arriving at the bottom of the stairs, and was about to push open the door into the lobby.

"Does that matter?"

"Probably not. But still, just… be careful, ok?"

Josh used his pass to exit the staircase into the lobby. The security guard at the desk was on the phone and looked right at Josh as he came through the door.

"Yeah, he's right here," Josh heard the guard say, and then, "Hey, Mr Collins. One second please, don't go anywhere."

Josh ignored him and, twisting quickly on the shiny floor of the lobby, turned towards the door, breaking into a run as he hit the green exit button, pushed the door open, and stumbled out onto the street. Without stopping, he turned right and sprinted towards the river, attracting a couple of surprised glances but no attempts to stop him. After a second, he glanced back. No one had followed him; the security guard wasn't paid nearly enough to chase down runaway account managers, and Jamie was still five stories up.

It was raining hard outside, and Josh wished he'd grabbed his coat. His t-shirt and jumper were soaked through in seconds.

Behind him, he heard the angry blast of a car horn and looked around. Half way up the street behind him was a small SUV in the generic grey favoured by hire car companies. It wouldn't have stood out at all, were it not for the fact that it had pulled around the corner a little too quickly, cutting off a black cab. Now Josh gave it a closer look. The driver had a thick beard, but it was hard to make out other features through the reflection on the windscreen. There was something about the way he was looking at Josh, not at the cab driver they had just enraged, or at the no entry sign he was about to violate, that made the hairs on the back of Josh's neck prick up.

Josh began to run again, turning left onto the pedestrianised Southbank where the car could not follow.

Behind him, he heard a loud revving of engines and then a

car door slamming, followed by another furious horn blast, but he didn't stop to look around. He turned the corner around the Coat and Badge pub on the riverbank and sprinted up the steps onto Blackfriars bridge, weaving to avoid a cluster of schoolchildren. When he got to the top, he turned left onto the bridge and took a second to look back down the way he had come, from his new vantage point. Behind and below him, the men from the car was just reaching the bottom of the steps. He looked up, and locked eyes with Josh. This time, his features were easy to make out and Josh recognised him instantly. Chris Adamson.

Ahead of Josh, as he turned back to the bridge and started running, a number 40 bus had pulled into the stop a hundred metres from him. There was one person waiting to get on and, as Josh sprinted towards the bus, he saw them step on and fish out a debit card to pay with. If he could get there before the doors closed, the bus would pull away before his pursuer could get to it. But if Josh missed it, he'd be stuck on the bridge with, literally, nowhere to turn.

Josh waved at the bus as he ran towards it, praying that the driver would see him and be considerate enough to wait. As he got to the bus stop, he saw the doors start to close and swore loudly. Then, to his enormous relief they opened again just as he slid to a stop on the wet pavement next to the bus.

"Quick as you can then, mate," said the bus driver, already eyeing the road and looking for a gap to pull out into traffic. As soon as Josh was on board, the driver closed the doors and started to move off, leaving Josh to hang on to one of the bars while he brought up a contactless card on his phone and tapped to pay for the journey.

As the bus drove off, Josh looked backwards out of the window. Chris Adamson was standing at the bus stop, black raincoat shiny with rain. He looked at the bus, expression impassive, and then took off running again, almost keeping pace with the bus's slow progress through London traffic.

Josh swore under his breath. The next stop was only just the other side of the bridge. If his pursuer could beat the bus there, Josh would be a sitting duck. Perhaps he was safer staying onboard anyway, with driver and CCTV cameras to protect him, except that he'd lived in London long enough to have no confidence that anyone would raise a finger to help if someone dragged him screaming off public transport. He stood by the exit door, anxiously watching the progress of the bus relative to the man in the black raincoat running along the pavement.

Josh thought back to all his frustrations with London traffic over the years, but never before had the walking-pace progress of a bus seemed like such a life and death matter. Chris had pulled ahead of the bus now, and Josh could no longer see him out of the side window. He turned to look forward out of the front windscreen. Chris was almost at the next stop, while the bus had barely even got off Blackfriars bridge and was now stuck at the lights at the junction with the Northern Embankment.

Josh made a decision, he reached up and flipped open the plastic cover on the 'emergency exit' switch, and pushed the red button. The door slid open and, ignoring the shout of protest from the driver, Josh stepped out and took off running down Victoria Embankment, away from the bus and the bus stop it was headed towards.

Josh wondered how long it would take Chris to realise he'd got off the bus. Not long, probably. He'd surely have been carefully watching the bus's slow progress through traffic and would have seen the door open and Josh step out, so Josh wouldn't have much of a lead. He turned right into the maze of roads leading up to Fleet Street, and then began taking rights and lefts at random, just hoping to get away from anyone following him. As he rounded a corner into Salisbury Court he slowed down, glancing behind him and listening for footsteps. Did he hear running on one of the nearby streets, or was it his imagination? The streets and alleys here in the dignified heart of London's legal quarter were quiet, but the sound of rain and the swish of heavy traffic through puddles on nearby Fleet Street helped to mask and distort any sound. He suddenly felt very isolated in these quiet back streets, and began walking quickly towards Fleet Street in search of crowds to blend into.

The rain wasn't as heavy as before but it was freezing cold and Josh shivered in his soaked clothes. He turned the corner onto Fleet Street, looking up and down the busy road anxiously but not seeing any sign of Chris. Desperate to get off the street and out of the rain, he ducked into the first café he spotted, enjoying the blast of warm air as he walked through the door.

He bought a coffee, using his phone again to pay, and then found a seat in the back, well away from the windows, but with a good view of anyone coming in through the door. Then he opened up his laptop, and called Abeke.

"Josh, are you ok? You weren't answering my calls."

"I'm ok," Josh realised his voice was shaking slightly, and it wasn't just the cold and the exertion from running. He tried to get his breathing under control. "I got out. And I think I've got the messages. I'm just going to look at them now. But, you were right, Chris is here and he came after me."

"You're kidding. How did he find you?"

"He must have come straight to the office, maybe saw me leaving, or maybe just got lucky. Are you somewhere safe?"

"Yeah. They're definitely on to me, though. Sonnie's been trying to call. And my BluJacket email and Chat accounts have been disabled."

"Better hope the stuff we downloaded is worth it, then,"

said Josh, double-clicking to open the folder.

49

"We're not going inside?" Matt asked, as they got to the car park and began walking down the rows of cars.

"Nope." Rogers said, shaking his head. "I'm based at another site – it's not far away, but we'll be safer talking there. This place is a madhouse. Here's my car."

They arrived at a grey chevy suburban, and Rogers unlocked it as they approached.

"Jump in."

Rogers got into the driver's seat and, after a second's hesitation, Matt climbed in next to him.

"You want to tell me where we're going? We could just as easily talk back there, or in the car."

Rogers shook his head.

"Nope. Two reasons. First, this is some seriously classified stuff and call me old-fashioned but I discuss classified information in a secure location. And, secondly, I want you to meet some of the rest of the team. Some of us have spent the last five years working on the BluJacket project so if they've been lying to us, and that's still a big 'if' in my book, people want to hear about it."

He pulled out of the car park and onto the highway. For a minute Matt assumed he was headed across the bridge into central DC, but then he came off again and headed north along the Potomac. Eventually, after ten minutes or so of driving, they turned onto a tree-lined residential road, and then onto a rough track leading into a wooded area. The car bumped along for a few more minutes before stopping in a clearing surrounded by trees. There was one other car already there, and Rogers pulled up behind it, making it impossible for Matt to see any more of the driver than the outline of the back of his head.

"Wait here. My colleague is kind of… sensitive. I should have a word with him first."

Rogers got out of the car, and walked over to the other vehicle. He crouched down next to the drivers window and exchanged a few words, then looked back at Matt. He straightened up, and beckoned Matt over. Matt opened the car door, got out, and began walking over towards Rogers and the other car. As he did so, the driver opened his door and got out to meet Matt.

50

Josh read the chat messages with a level of excitement that was out of proportion to the mundane exchange he was actually looking at. It didn't surprise him that the file he'd opened at random showed nothing but a dull chat between two engineers about some project. It was the fact that it showed *real* messages, between real people at BluJacket, that gave him confidence. Somewhere in the thousands of other such files he had there were, surely, bound to be far more incriminating messages.

"Found anything good?" Abeke asked, on the other end of the phone.

"Nothing specific, but it's definitely going to be here. I just don't even know where to start with this stuff."

"We should just get them to Matt. Newspapers know how to trawl through these sorts of things and pull out what matters."

"I guess you're right. One sec, though."

Josh had an idea. He clicked the search icon on the folder containing the emails, and typed in 'Ingram'. That would instantly find every file that contained that word anywhere in its text. The search took barely a second; just one file was returned. He clicked into it. It was a series of direct messages between Chris Adamson and someone whose name Josh didn't recognise.

There was only one mention of Ingram within it. In a message from Chris.

'I met your guy, Ingram. I can't say I like this. Let's talk offline.'
Josh read it to Abeke.

"Well, shit," said Abeke. "I think that answers that question."

"Yeah… it does," Josh said, slowly, staring at the conversation.

"What?"

"Who's he talking to? Someone's recommended Ingram to him but he doesn't sound completely onboard…"

Josh scrolled further back in the chat history.

"Who does it say the other person is?" Abeke asked.

"It doesn't, that's the thing. Their username is just random letters and numbers… hang on."

"What?"

"Ok, so there's a message here, about a month before the mention of Ingram. Looks as if he's giving Chris advice on how to run a demo for the military. He's literally telling him the best ways to get through the demo without exposing the product issues."

"Who do you think he is?"

"Whoever he is he knows his stuff. Knows exactly how the demo's going to run, knows how the military will be assessing…" Josh stopped abruptly.

"What?"

"In the messages, he refers twice to 'my guys', and in another one he even mentions he'll be there on the day."

Josh breathed out softly.

"He's serving military. Got to be. And senior, by the

sounds of it. Matt said the army wouldn't like having the wool pulled over their eyes… well, it sounds like at least some of them were the ones doing the pulling. Making damn sure it passed all the tests. But why?"

"Self-protection?" answered Abeke, thoughtfully. "Maybe they'd bet too much of their own reputation on it to see it fail. Thought they could just paper over the cracks long enough for the problems to get fixed."

Josh nodded.

"Money too, perhaps. Matt seemed to think there were senators on the committee who'd invested in BluJacket early on, and were making sure to get it approved. Want to bet there might have been a senior military officer who'd done the same… oh *shit*!" Josh broke off and swore suddenly, reaching for his phone.

"What is it?"

"When we spoke to Matt, didn't he say he had a senior military contact he was going to meet?"

"Yeah but, I mean, that could be anyone. The Army's a big organisation…"

"Sure. But still, it doesn't feel right. I should give him a call. And I'll come and meet you. Where are you?"

"I'll send you a pin. See you soon."

Josh hung up, picked up his laptop, and stepped back out onto the street. As he dialled Matt's number, he walked back towards the river, ending up on the quiet pedestrian path that ran from Blackfriars all along the northern embankment past the Tower of London and beyond.

As he walked, he glanced around occasionally, seeing nothing more threatening than the occasional jogger or a city banker scurrying towards the train station sheltered by an umbrella. When Matt didn't answer his first call, he dialled again, and then looked down at his phone to start typing a message. As the path passed underneath Blackfriars railway bridge, he looked up a second too late as a shadow stepped out of the gloom. Before Josh could react, a powerful hand reached out and grabbed his phone, knocking it into the gutter.

Chris Adamson stood on the worryingly-deserted path. He reached out again, this time gripping Josh's shoulder and pushing him back against the low railing that was the only thing between Josh and the fast-moving, swollen river below.

"Word of advice, Josh. Don't use your bank card to pay for stuff when you're on the run. Guys like me have all *sorts* of contacts."

51

Matt recognised the driver instantly. Bill Ingram was wearing a black raincoat and a baseball cap, and carrying a handgun in a low, one-handed grip. He wasn't even bothering to point it at Matt. It was angled towards the ground, but they both knew that he could raise it and fire a dozen shots before Matt could take more than a couple of steps in any direction.

"What the fuck is this?" Said Matt, feeling panic grip him, and looking desperately at Brian Rogers. The officer just shrugged.

"I'm sorry, buddy. But you haven't exactly given us much choice. Give me your locker key."

"What?" Matt said, confused.

"The locker, from the Pentagon. With your phone. Give me the key."

"Fuck you."

Ingram, expression unchanging, slowly raised the pistol.

"Ok, ok," Matt said, his courage ebbing away as he stared down the barrel of Ingram's pistol. He fished in his pocket for the key and threw it to Rogers.

Rogers turned to Ingram. "Ok, I'm off. Give me an hour,

alright."

As he walked back to his car, Matt shouted desperately after him. "Come on. You think you can get away with this? I'm booked in under your name at the Pentagon."

Rogers ignored him, getting in his car and turning the engine on, but Ingram answered.

"You sure are. And in about half an hour, you'll book out again. The CCTV will show you leaving. Shame your face isn't very visible, but then you *did* choose to wear that stupid cap. You'll even pick up your phone on the way out, and it'll be found out here with you."

Ingram's baseball cap and scruffy beard gave him an almost friendly, avuncular impression. An impression that was destroyed as soon as Matt looked into his eyes. They were cold, hard, and empty. He didn't look merely unemotional, but completely detached from his own actions or those of anyone around him, like someone observing ants fighting over a leaf. A man like that wasn't open to bargaining, or threats, or even begging. It was the eyes, more than anything, that made Matt feel truly afraid.

"I know who you are, Ingram." Matt said, trying anything in search of an opening. "Real brotherhood, isn't it, the SEALs? Doubt you're invited back to the team barbecues now though, are you? That must hurt."

"Fuck those guys." Ingram answered shortly. If Matt's words had caused any emotional response, it certainly wasn't visible there.

"Shame though. All those years of service, and now you'll spend the rest of your life in prison."

"Oh? How you figure that?"

"Murder? Especially of a police officer. And if I turn up dead as well, that's really going to turn the heat up."

"You reckon? Deadbeat reporter has a meeting with a well-respected Army officer, makes a load of wild accusations, is shown convincing evidence he's wrong, and ends up going off into the forest and overdosing on whiskey and pills. Sounds to me like that'll get a full five minutes of investigation. Right, walk ahead of me," Ingram ordered, when Rogers's car had disappeared from view down the track. Keeping the pistol low at his side, and Matt ahead of him, he propelled Matt down a narrow footpath until they arrived at a three-sided wooden shelter, presumably intended for hikers.

"On your knees. Hands out in front of you, palms together," Ingram said, when they got into the darkness of the shelter and well out of sight of anyone who might chance to stray off the road for a late-night hike or assignation.

Matt did as he was asked. He struggled to take his eyes off the pistol. He remembered all the bold escape and resistance attempts they had made on the HEAT course, and how foolish that all felt now. He realised that no matter how much the instructors on the course had shouted, or how many smoke grenades they threw or blank rounds they fired, they just couldn't replicate the paralysing fear generated by having a loaded gun pointed at you by someone who was completely willing to pull the trigger.

With Matt on his knees, hands outstretched, Ingram pulled from his back pocket a neatly folded pair of heavy-duty disposable handcuffs. Matt had seen them on the body armour of SWAT officers and soldiers. They were made of thick plastic and locked like zip-ties, but were far more robust. Keeping his pistol hand free, Ingram used one hand in a practiced manoeuvre to slip them over Matt's hands and then pull them tight. If there had been an opportunity for escape anywhere in those few seconds, Matt thought, it had completely passed him by.

"Lie down," Ingram ordered. Matt, clumsily using his tied hands to try and break his fall, sat backwards and then rolled onto his side. Ingram then repeated the zip-tie manoeuvre with Matt's feet. He lay there, bound and helpless, frustrated at his own helplessness. He began twisting his wrists in the zip-ties, not in any hope of getting out, but simply in the hope of creating enough marks on his wrist that his death might not be immediately ruled a suicide after all. It was a pretty small victory, but any victory was enough in that moment.

Ingram leaned over him.

"Now, Matt. You have some videos. Videos that you stole. What I need to know is, where are they, where are any copies, and who gave them to you?"

"Go fuck yourself," Matt growled, lifting himself up on his elbow to look Ingram in the eye.

"I won't, but thanks." He reached down, and picked up Matt's bag, which was on the ground next to him. In the darkness, and distracted by the pistol, Matt hadn't even realised that Ingram had carried it with them. He squatted down next to Matt, reached into the bag, and took out Matt's laptop. He opened it, studied it for a second, then reached for Matt's bound hands, grabbing one finger and forcing it onto the fingerprint reader that unlocked the MacBook.

"Shall we look at your emails, then? Quite a lot from someone called 'Josh'. Who is that?"

Matt said nothing, but he looked in despair at the series of emails from Josh, culminating in the one where Josh had sent over the footage from Nathan Adams. Now Ingram clicked on that, opened it, and saw the footage.

"Well. Naughty Josh."

Ingram walked out of the shelter again. Matt heard his footsteps retreat towards the car.

Matt rolled onto his back and looked up at the mottled tin roof of the shelter. He thought about Josh, not really all that much older than Matt's son, and how Matt had put him in harm's way. He'd been more interested in getting the story he wanted than in the ethics of asking a complete stranger to participate in a dangerous investigation.

Matt levered himself around, and into a sitting position. He recalled a technique that they'd been shown on the HEAT course. He'd successfully practiced it, but only once, and only on a thin commercial zip tie. Still, he wasn't willing to go down without a fight and, if he was going to die here in this car park, he'd rather make it as difficult as possible for Ingram.

Matt reached down awkwardly with his bound hands, and undid his shoelaces. Then he worked one side of his left lace out through the eyelets until it was hanging freely from his shoe. Working clumsily with his fingers, he fed the end of the lace up through one of the cuffs around his wrist, then took the tip of the lace in his mouth. He applied a little tension between his foot and his mouth, pulling the lace tight, and began moving his hands rapidly up and down it, using the lace against the plastic cuff like a saw.

For a while, he couldn't tell if it was having any effect at all, but then it started to get a little harder to move the cuff, and he realised that was because the lace was starting to burn a slice into the plastic, and now it was part-buried in the cuff. He kept on going, and then suddenly his head jerked back as the tension on the lace was released. For a second he thought he'd got through the cuff, and then he realised the opposite had happened; the lace itself had snapped. Matt felt with his fingers for the cut he'd made on the cuff; it was deep, but not even close to half way. Trying to calm his pounding heart and stop his hands shaking, Matt began to undo the other side of the lace on the same shoe, and repeat the trick.

Outside the shelter, he could hear Ingram's voice, indistinct, on the phone. He was still over by his car. Matt carried on cutting with the other half of his left lace, and made more progress, before it too snapped. Again, he felt with his fingers, all too aware that he was half way through his laces, and more than able to do the math. Surely, he thought, it felt as if he'd cut through more than half the cuff. Surely.

Practiced at the technique now, Matt quickly undid one side of the lace on his other foot, and began again. He heard Ingram's footsteps coming back towards the shelter, and carried on sawing as they got closer and closer. Finally, at the very last moment, he dropped the lace from his mouth, lay back and rolled over. He let his arms drop under his body, hoping that any damage to the cuff was well-hidden in the gloomy interior of the shelter.

"Leave Josh out of this, Bill," Matt said, partly out of a sincere desire to protect Josh and partly in the hope of distracting Matt and reducing the chance that he'd look too closely at Matt's restraints. Or his now mostly laceless shoes. "He's not involved."

"Of course he is. I don't know how he got hold of those files, but that's some sensitive shit. He didn't just trip over them, did he. He stole them, and there will be consequences. And, speaking of consequences, I'm afraid our time together is pretty much at an end."

Matt realised Ingram had a bag with him, that he'd obviously picked up from the car while he was making the call. He crouched down and opened the bag, drawing out a bottle of whisky, and two pill bottles.

"Now, Matt," he said, holstering his pistol for a second while he pulled the foil off the top of the whisky. "There's an easy way and a hard way to do this. I strongly recommend the easy way, but really either one works for me."

A lot of thoughts went through Matt's mind at once. He thought about the holstered pistol, and Ingram's temporarily-occupied hands. He thought about his laptop, a faint silvery shape on the dark floor just an arm's length away. And above all, he thought about the scratchy feel of the cut plastic against his skin, and wondered how much he'd weakened the cuff. He'd only have one shot at this, and if the cuff held, it was game over.

Matt raised his arms, slowly enough that Ingram barely even registered what he was doing, and then in one swift motion brought them down. Elbows past his body, cuffed wrists slamming hard into his chest, just like they'd practiced on the HEAT course, where they'd broken out of cheap zipties with ease. Ingram looked up, startled by the movement, and relief flooded Matt's body as he felt the weakened plastic snap, and his hands come free.

Ingram dropped the whisky and went for his pistol, at the same time as Matt rolled over and grabbed his laptop with his freed hand. Then his swung it with as much force as possible at Ingram's head, hitting him on the temple with one corner. There was a sick thud, and Ingram reeled backwards, but didn't immediately go down. Matt, unable to move far with his legs still tied, struck Ingram again, hard, and then leapt onto him, reaching for his pistol.

Despite the two heavy blows, Ingram fought back hard. Matt felt powerful hands scrabbling to stop him pulling the pistol out. With strength born of fear, anger and adrenaline, Matt fought for grip with one hand and landed another blow to Ingram's face with the other. Almost to his surprise, he found the pistol suddenly sliding free in his hands, and he rolled back away from Ingram, pointing the pistol at the figure lying there in the darkness.

52

"I don't know what you think you have there, Josh," Chris hissed, reaching for the laptop. "But you've committed a *whole* bunch of criminal offences by obtaining them."

Josh twisted in Chris's grip, pushing the laptop behind his back, and pinning it against the railing with his body. He silently cursed himself for not having thought to send the chat logs on to Abeke or Matt.

"Maybe I have. Not quite as bad as conspiring to sell the army a duff product, though."

"Don't be stupid. It's just business. Now give me the laptop, tell me who else has seen those messages, and I'll let you walk away. I can't promise you'll keep your job, but you're a smart kid. I'm sure you'll find another."

"Or what? How about I shout for help? You going to kill me right here?"

Chris shook his head slowly. He wasn't trying to grab the laptop anymore, but he didn't release his hold on Josh's shoulder.

"Go ahead, shout for help. Pretty sure that laptop is BBA\Rowley property and has a sticker to prove it. Once they let the police know about your activities, I wouldn't fancy your chances of getting the laptop back."

Josh looked desperately up and down the empty footpath, prompting Chris to do the same. He seemed to be weighing up the chances of someone coming, and the risk, growing with every second that passed, that whatever passing Londoner interrupted them might take Josh's side over his.

"You know what, fuck it. Too many loose ends here."

He loosened his grip slightly and then, taking advantage of Josh's surprise, suddenly pushed him back against the railing again, this time lifting him so that almost Josh's whole body toppled over. The laptop dropped to the ground as Josh desperately clung on, fighting to prevent himself from falling backwards. Chris reached down for one of Josh's legs, pulling it up, and robbing Josh of the last of his balance. For a second he felt himself teetering on the edge of tumbling over the side and into the river, and then he felt Chris's hands release.

Recovering, he slumped down to the pavement, leaning back against the railing, then he looked up. In front of him, with Chris in an effective-looking chokehold, was a short, wiry man with a black beard and thick black hair combed back with what looked like a tonne of hair gel.

The man spun Chris around, and released him with a push and a "fuck off, pal."

"Wait, don't let him go! He tried to kill me."

"I know he did," said the man, reaching down to help Josh up, and then again to pick up the laptop. "But we don't need to get tangled with the old bill right now. And if he was that worried about what's on that laptop, a little attempted murder is the least of his problems. Come on, let's make ourselves scarce. I've got a car around the corner."

"Wait, who the fuck are you?"

The man laughed.

"Oh yeah. Sorry. I'm Smudge. Tim. Tim Smith. I knew your

dad."

Josh gaped at him. None of this was making any sense. He faintly recognised the name, and thought back to his conversation with Paul, about the former rifleman turned Special Forces Sergeant Major who'd asked after Josh and his mum.

"What on earth are you doing here?" Josh asked.

"I'll explain. But, come on, we don't want to hang about."

Once they were safely ensconced in Smudge's car – a huge silver Range Rover – Josh reiterated the question.

"Look, you're not going to like it. But... I work with some very smart and tech-savvy characters. Their whole job is finding people."

"You had me tracked?"

"You had yourself tracked, frankly, just by carrying a smartphone. I just misused some of our technology to help me pull your phone data out of the noise. But aren't you glad I did?"

"I guess so. I mean, yes, of course I am. I think Chris had decided that just dumping me and the laptop in the Thames was the quickest way to make the problem go away."

"He'd have been right, too. Not many people who go into that river come out alive."

"But *why* where you tracking me?"

"Because I was worried about you. I've been emailing you. I'm 'James McCormick'. You said you wanted more information and I asked about a meet, but then I didn't hear anything from you. I was pretty fucking concerned if I'm honest, knowing what you've got into."

Josh struggled to take the information in. What meet? Then he remembered. The email from James McCormick that he'd deleted after his disastrous conversation with Abeke. Shit. He'd completely forgotten about that.

"Oh. Right, yeah. Sorry about that. But, why did you email me in the first place? Why did you send me that document? I thought it was Paul at first, to be honest…"

Tim shook his head, not so much as if disagreeing or unhappy with the questions, but as if just unsure where to start.

"Paul? Hell no. He's far too by-the-book for that. But he did tell me you'd been asking about BluJacket. He was worried and digging into it and because of where I work… you know I'm at Hereford now, right?"

"Yeah, Paul said."

"Ok, so yeah, he spoke to me. Informally, of course. I told him I couldn't help but…" Tim sighed. "The whole BluJacket thing sat really badly with me. I was there when we were testing it, and it was a fucking shitshow. Excuse my language, but seriously. They shouldn't be issuing that kit to traffic wardens, let alone fucking SWAT teams and Navy SEALs. I just couldn't let it lie, and I thought, maybe if I fed you a bit of info… I'm sorry, I ended up putting you in a tough spot and that wasn't my intention."

"Nah, you didn't. I chose to dig, you just gave me a spade. I'd have ended up in this spot either way."

"Yeah, maybe."

Tim was silent for a bit.

"Your dad could never let something drop, either. He looked after people. I know he'd be proud of you for caring about this. For not letting it go."

Josh couldn't answer straight away, his vision was blurred slightly and he was worried his voice would shake. When he was a bit more confident in his response, he mumbled, "thanks, Tim. I appreciate that."

"Yeah. Well. I'm sorry I've not seen you over the years. I never really knew what to say to your mum and then, after I went to Hereford, it feels like I've barely been in the UK."

"Nah, I get it. You guys had your careers to get on with."

"So," Tim went on, clearly trying to push past the awkward moment. "When you emailed, you were asking how we knew BluJacket didn't work?"

"Yeah. I mean, assuming I'm even right that it didn't work. I've actually seen some footage of the testing. It doesn't look good."

"You have?" Tim looked startled. "Shit. How did you get that? Never mind, you can tell me later. That sounds like a story. Anyway, in that case you probably get what the issues were. The idea was great, our chain of command was really up for doing trials, but the tech just wasn't there. Early on, it seemed ok. Like, not perfect, but it was definitely adding some value. We might have stuck with the trials and funded BluJacket to improve it. But then we figured out they'd been faking the tests."

"How did you work it out?"

"Well…" Tim laughed. "It's kind of funny in retrospect. And there's no way I should be telling you this. But, I guess I've gone this far. And, out of respect for your dad, right."

Josh stayed silent. He didn't want to say anything that would make Tim change his mind about opening up.

"So, when we do training, we believe in exercising multiple capabilities at once. It's like, value for money I guess. Maybe comes of our army being the size it is, I don't know. But, case in point, when I did my close protection course, years ago, on our final exercise we had guys off the surveillance course doing *their* final exercise, surveilling us. Double whammy. See what I mean?"

"Um, yeah, I think so," Josh said, not at all sure where this was going.

"Ok, well, you know about my mob, right? But there's another unit, Special Forces as well, but signallers. Radios originally, but these days it's anything cyber and IT-related.

Real dark techy stuff, some of it. I don't understand it myself. Sometimes they work alongside us and Poole, sometimes they do their own thing."

"Ok."

Tim paused for a second while he navigated a roundabout, then went on.

"So this signals unit, they got interested in the BluJacket tech because firstly, if we're going to be using it, they'd need to make sure they can secure the signal that goes between the lads wearing it, and wherever the AI server is, right? Can't have Russia hacking into it, seeing where our blokes are, seeing what they're looking at, sending false info, all that. But of course, the same goes in reverse, our lot also want to learn how to hack the signal themselves, in case enemy forces end up buying it as well. So, when we were exercising with the kit, the signals lads were kind of secretly doing their own exercise…"

"You're joking. So you were hacking the signal without BluJacket knowing?"

"Yeah. I mean, we probably should have told them, but honestly it didn't seem like it would be a big deal. The signals guys weren't planning to disrupt anything, they just wanted to see if they could access it and read the data. That would be more than enough to be getting on with, from a combat point of view."

"And it worked?"

"It worked. They got into it, and that's when they started looking at the data feed in detail. And what they realised is that in a lot of cases, you get an initial bit of data from the AI, and then it gets overridden by *another* signal, but this time from a live user. So, let's say, the AI identifies a football as a bomb, but then suddenly a real person jumps in and switches it to 'nah, it's just a football'. Or the AI doesn't spot the bloke with a gun, but the live operator hits a button and flags it.

That's how they were keeping the whole thing so that it just about worked well enough for us to progress with trials and not tell them to fuck off after the first test."

"Yeah," said Josh. "I kind of heard about that, but… shit. I didn't realise it was quite that bad."

"It was bad. We looked at the logs and realised that if we took out the human overrides, and just went with the AI results, the performance would have been absolute garbage. Worse than garbage. Fucking dangerous. And, more than that, we just don't like being lied to. So, yeah, that ended that. They were formally fucked the fuck off."

"How come you didn't tell the Americans?"

"Oh we tried," said Tim. "It went up the chain, and… just disappeared. Next thing we knew, the Yanks were deep into trials, and we'd been banned from even discussing it. Oh, and I'm pretty sure BluJacket made some changes to their feed, so now it's a lot harder to spot the human operator stepping in. I guess they learned from their mistakes with us, and now they're winning over the bigger customer."

Josh was about to ask to be dropped off somewhere when he suddenly remembered one of the other emails Tim had sent him, and a realisation formed in his mind.

"Hang on, how did you know about Mickey Cook? Did you send him the footage?"

Tim grimaced.

"Yeah. Fuck. I feel fucking awful about that, but look, when I did that I knew these guys were absolute chancers but I didn't think they were going to go around topping people. And when I contacted you I didn't know that either, or I'd never have put you at risk. I came across Mickey when I was doing some digging, trying to understand how this whole artificial intelligence shit even worked. I saw how he liked having a pop at companies making crap products. So when our trial ended and it seemed like BluJacket was going to skate off to some big US contracts, I thought, yeah, that's a nice fit, send him some footage anonymously, he can publish a video, and with any luck that'll be enough to bring the whole thing crashing down, with no one the wiser. Then weeks pass, no video, and finally when I do a bit of digging, I hear he's dead. Jesus."

"From what I've heard, he's not the only person who's mysteriously died."

Josh filled Tim in on his and Matt's investigation, and what he knew about Myles Weston and the circumstances around his death. He went on to explain about the trip to Edinburgh, and getting the footage. Tim laughed out loud at that, and grabbed Josh's shoulder.

"See, I fucking knew you were your dad's kid. He'd have loved that. Look, you can't link any of this info back to me in your friend's newspaper. But if it helps you get the truth out, and you can tie it to an anonymous source, then be my fucking guest."

"Thanks Tim. For everything, really."

53

Bill Ingram rolled over, breathing heavily. In the dim light, Matt could see a black slick on the side of Ingram's face, and it took him a moment to realise that it was blood. After a moment, Ingram managed to lever himself up onto his elbow and look at Matt.

"Put the gun down, you stupid fuck," he spat, his voice horse and pained. "Do you even know how to use that?"

Matt wasn't sure. Living in New York City, he didn't have much contact with firearms, but had once spent a very enjoyable morning on a shooting range in Charleston, South Carolina, with a friend who knew an extraordinary amount about them. He knew that there were really only three things he needed to worry about; was the gun loaded, was it made ready with a round in the chamber, and was the safety off. He could be pretty sure it was loaded, and he highly doubted that Ingram had been threatening with a gun that wasn't made ready but, just to be sure, he racked the slide. A round popped out. Clearly it had been cocked. But that was fine, now he was sure.

Ingram laughed horsely, but he looked less confident of his

position. Matt looked at the pistol for a second, he couldn't identify a safety lever in what he was fairly sure was the usual place by his thumb. Then he realised he was holding a Glock. It was one of the pistols he'd fired on the range, and his friend had explained several times that it lacked a manual safety, but had a trigger safety meaning that it required a positive pull on the trigger to fire the gun.

"Looks like I know how to use it, then," he said. "Or do you fancy your chances?"

Ingram stared at him. The blood on the slide of his face was spreading.

"You've never shot anyone," he said eventually. "You don't have what it takes. Maybe I'll just get up and walk away."

Ingram had a point. Matt might be able to shoot him in self-defence, but he certainly couldn't shoot him just to stop him getting away. He threw a look over his shoulder at Ingram's car and tried to think through his options. He wriggled up onto his knees, still unable to move freely with his ankles bound, and kept the pistol trained on Ingram while he pulled his bag over towards him. He put his laptop back in it, trying not to think about the dented and bloody corner of it, and then looked back at Ingram.

"Give me your phone."

Ingram said nothing. But, keeping his gaze locked on Matt as if daring him to shoot him, he reached into his pocket and pulled out a phone. For a second, Matt thought he was going to pass it to him, but then, keeping that cold, steady stare on Matt, Ingram unlocked it and dialled a number.

Shit. Thought Matt. Of course, he probably had some kind of backup and, even if he didn't, it sounded as if BluJacket had close links with local law enforcement. Matt didn't fancy his chances if the cops showed up and found him holding an injured ex-SEAL at gunpoint.

Spurred into urgent action, he lunged forward and

knocked the phone out of Ingram's grasp, then reached with his left hand to grab it from where it had fallen on the floor. Ingram, moving almost as quickly, grabbed Matt's right wrist, twisting it hard to try to free the pistol. Matt, startled, fell backwards and, as he did so, the pistol went off. Ingram's hand released, and Matt fell backwards onto the dirt next to him. He quickly rolled away, Ingram's phone in one hand, pistol in the other.

At first, Matt was certain that the shot had hit Ingram, who was lying still on the dirt, then Ingram started laughing.

"You fucking idiot, Ibarra. You haven't a clue what you're doing, have you."

"And yet here we are, and I've got the gun," Matt replied, the release of fear coming out as anger. He had Ingram's phone as well, he realised, and an idea began to occur to him.

He looked back at Ingram again, and noticed the multi-tool pouch on his belt. He put the phone in his pocket and, pressing the barrel of the pistol right into Ingram's stomach to dissuade any further heroics, reached over and took the multitool. He rolled quickly away and used the knife on the tool to cut his feet loose. Finally, he stood up, and took a few steps back, pleased to create a bit of distance between him and Ingram.

"Give me your car keys."

"Come and get them."

Matt had no desire to go back within striking distance of Ingram. He picked up his bag and, backing slowly away from Ingram with the gun still pointed at him, began to move back down the footpath towards the car. Once he got almost to it, and had lost sight of Ingram, Matt turned to the vehicle. He did a few things in quick succession. First, he fired a shot from the pistol into each of the front tyres and watched them rapidly deflate. Then he removed the magazine from the pistol and threw it as far as he could into the low scrubs and bushes on the edge of the woodland. He racked the slide again, retrieved the ejected round from the ground, then threw that after the magazine. Finally he wiped the pistol down and dropped it next to the car.

Matt gave one last glance back up the footpath towards where Ingram was. There was still no sign of him, and Matt wondered if Ingram had slipped into unconsciousness. It had been hard to see the extent of the injury, but the damage to Matt's laptop made it easy to guess at the damage to Ingram's skull.

As he walked away from the scene as fast as he could, Matt looked through Ingram's phone. The last few calls, incoming and outgoing, were with a number he recognised. Rogers. Matt scrolled further back, finding the day that he and Deputy Weston had been supposed to meet. Sure enough, there were a couple of calls between Rogers and Ingram that morning. There was another, just 30 seconds long, at five minutes to five that evening. Less than five minutes after Weston's neighbour had heard the single gunshot from his apartment.

Matt used Ingram's phone to dial one of the few phone numbers he knew by heart – the Washington Record's switchboard. When someone answered, he asked for Brett; an old friend on the crime desk.

"Brett, it's Matt. Listen, I need you to do something for me and I don't have time for a tonne of questions."

There was only the briefest hesitation.

"Alright, go on."

"Do you have a contact at Virginia State Police? Someone you trust and, more importantly, someone who trusts you?"

"I guess… probably."

"Well, if not, find someone and make them trust you. Do whatever you need to do to convince them, but tell them to get some units to a hiking trail in Langley Oaks park – I'll send you a pin."

"You going to tell me what all this is about?"

"I don't have time. But they're going to find an injured guy there, and if they hang about a bit, an Army brigadier-general is going to show up. He's going to have my phone and my watch on him."

"What the fuck, Matt?"

"They need to arrest both of them. Conspiracy to murder. I've got evidence that'll make the charges stick."

Brett breathed out softly.

"Fine. I'll do it. But first, you'd better not make me look like an asshole here and secondly, whatever this story is, I'm writing it up."

"Deal. Now make the call," Matt said, and hung up.

54

Three weeks later

Josh stepped out into the bustle of the arrivals terminal at Washington Dulles airport, and looked around for Matt. He was fairly sure he'd recognise him but, in the event, he didn't need to - Matt was holding a sign with his name on it, and smiled broadly as Josh gave him a little wave and walk over. Matt gave Josh an unexpected bearhug, and then grabbed his bag and insisted on carrying it.

"It's so good to meet you in person, Josh." Matt said, as they walked to his car.

"You too. Thanks for bringing me out here. I've never been to Washington."

"It's my pleasure. I mean, I convinced the paper to cover your flight and hotel, but it's still my pleasure. My new editor wants to meet you tomorrow, but I know what the jet lag is like so for tonight I thought I'd let you take it easy if you want."

"Ah, thanks. I don't feel too bad right now but I guess it's, like 9pm my time so that's going to hit soon."

"I'm sorry Abeke couldn't make it. I'd have liked to meet her too."

"Yeah," Josh hesitated. "She's had a tough time of it. It's her friends and colleagues who've been hauled in for interviews with the FBI. The whole senior team has been arrested."

"She's ok, right? Personally, I mean?"

"Oh, yeah. I mean, they accept that the vast majority of the company had no idea what was going on. And Abeke's done more than enough to prove her cooperation. I think she's worried if she'll ever be employable again, though."

They got to Matt's car and Josh put his bag in the back then got into the front passenger seat while Matt drove.

"Abeke'll be alright," Matt said, with reassuring certainty. "It's not easy being a whistleblower, but the tech world has a certain respect for people who've done the right thing when a company comes crashing down."

"Yeah, I hope so. I think she's looking for a new direction."

"And, what about you and her, huh?" Matt cast Josh a sidelong glance as he drove. "You figure things out?"

Josh smiled.

"I guess, we're *figuring* things out? She's back in the US and she doesn't have a UK work permit but… yeah, I think we're going to try and make things work."

"I'm glad to hear that. You seem like a good fit."

Matt was silent for a minute, and then spoke again.

"So, have you thought about trying to come and work over here?"

Josh looked at him, but Matt kept his eyes on the road, giving nothing away.

"Hell yes. I've got no special attachment to the UK, and at least one good reason to be over here. Why? You got a job going?"

"Let's talk properly over a beer. While you're still awake. I know a good place."

Matt navigated into central Washington and stopped at a hotel on Rhode Island Avenue.

"This is where the paper is putting us both up. I'll park here and there's a great bar almost next door."

He pulled the car up to the valet parking booth and handed his keys over, a uniquely American process that Josh had seen so many times in films that even that simple transaction fascinated him. Then the two of them walked around the corner onto 14th Street and Matt directed them over to a slim, two-story grey building with a handful of tables outside. They stepped in to a space that, though narrow like the building, was deep. Industrial pipework and trunking ran across the high ceiling, and metal I-beams intersected it in a couple of places. Down the left-hand side was a long bar with seats all the way along and screens above it playing an American football game, while down the right hand side were a dozen or so booths. Josh tried not to grin to himself. To him, this was, somehow, *the* American bar. The one he'd seen in every movie, the one he'd imagined Americans all spent their evenings in, and now here he was; a stone's throw from the White House, and with a real Washington Record journalist, discussing a front-page investigation they'd worked on together.

Matt saw Josh's expression and clapped him on the shoulder.

"It's a cool place, isn't it? Let's get a booth."

They took a seat and each ordered a beer, Josh noticing that several of the beers were as strong as 12 or 15% ABV and deciding it might be best to shy away from those - jet lag being what it was.

When the beers came, they clinked glasses.

"You must be pleased with how your investigation's panned out." Josh said, trying to play it cool and let Matt work back in his own time to the hint he'd dropped earlier.

"Oh, I am. It'll buy me another year or so at the paper, anyway. If that's what I want. The paper pulled through in the end, we had nearly fifty people looking through those Chat messages, digging out the relevant stuff."

"It seemed to do the job. I was reading the stories. Every bloody day, a new front page revelation."

"That's what does it. That's the benefit of all those messages. Day after day, another smoking gun. Keeping it in the public's mind."

"What about General Rogers? And Bill Ingram?"

"Virginia State Police picked them both up. They handed Rogers over to Army CID for now, but they're both probably going to end up facing Federal charges." Matt grinned tightly as he said it. That one, after all, was personal.

They both sipped their beers.

"So, Josh, what about you? What will you do now?" Matt asked.

"Well, I think I've burnt my bridges in advertising. They won't fire me, but they don't want account managers who go around leaking customer secrets to the press. I don't know what I'll do now, to be honest."

"Journalism?" Matt asked, smiling.

"Nah, that's a mugs game," said Josh, taking a swig of beer to hide his grin. "I'm kidding. Maybe, I'd consider it. I don't know if it might all be downhill after this, though."

"It might be." Matt suddenly looked more serious. "But, you know, if this is something you're interested in, there's a whole lot more to dig into."

"What do you mean?" Josh asked, wondering if Matt was finally going to get back round to whatever he'd been talking about in the car.

"I got a call a few weeks back, after I dropped the first story. My old editor from New York. He's long-since left newspapers. He runs a Substack – a kind of individual newsletter that people can subscribe to. Makes an absolute killing. That's the way journalism's going if you ask me. Most of the basic daily news will be written either by AI or by underpaid writers doing the minimum of research. But for the people who do real, deep, investigations… there's a market for that. People love it."

"Ok," said Josh, a little uncertainly. "So where do I fit in?"

"Asking the right questions, Josh. See, that's why we like you."

"We?"

"My old editor and me. He's jacked up some VC funding to start a little team. Deep investigations, quality journalism, putting out Substack articles, podcasts, YouTube videos, whatever. There's a lot of money to be made if you get the content right."

"And what's the content?"

"Tech… AI specifically, perhaps. This BluJacket thing, it's just the start."

"You think there are other start-ups making shit up? Enough of them to keep us busy investigating them full-time?"

"Actually yes, but that's not the point. It's not the ones making shit up that I'm so worried about."

"I don't quite see what you're driving at."

"Well." Matt hesitated, assembling his words. "What's worse than an artificial intelligence that claims to be able to identify threats but can't really do it."

"I don't know," said Josh, confused.

"An artificial intelligence that claims to be able to identify threats and *can* really do it."

Josh looked down at his beer, thinking about that one.

"I don't know about that. I mean, given the choice…"

"Are you sure about that? So, here's a story I worked on

back in 2013. It's, like, three or four months after the Boston Marathon bombing, ok?"

"I remember that."

"Yeah. And you remember they used bombs made from pressure cookers, and hidden in backpacks? Ok, well, there's a lady who lives in Long Island. She wants to cook lentils, so she's searching for pressure cookers online. And her husband wants to go hiking, and he's searching for backpacks. And her son, well, he's just fascinated by the news so he's searching for information about the marathon bombings."

"Ok I think I see where this is going."

"Yeah, you do. So she gets raided by the FBI. Questioned for six hours. Treated like a terrorist. They insist there was a tip-off, but she's pretty sure their searches have tripped some algorithm. Maybe we'll never know. Anyway, my point is that even the simplest attempts to do policing by algorithm can fuck up people's lives. And BluJacket *isn't* impossible. A working version probably isn't even that far off. AI is here to stay, and it's only going to get faster and cheaper and more powerful. Then what? How long until someone puts BluJacket-style AI into a robot and says they've made an automatic police officer that can replace our messy, expensive human ones? How long until someone realises that AI is far better at analysing evidence and making decisions than a jury, and can do it in a fraction of the time?"

"You're a pessimist, Matt. Maybe we'll end up with police officers who *don't* racially profile anymore, or shoot innocent kids, because they get a really great AI algorithm giving them unbiased prompts. Maybe we'll get unbiased juries, doctors that don't make mistakes, cars that don't crash… I dunno. Utopia."

Matt shrugged.

"I hope you're right. But BluJacket isn't the first clever piece of tech to get people killed, and I guarantee it won't be the last. And we both know the government won't keep up with investigating businesses, and businesses sure as hell won't regulate themselves. So, come on board, help me look into them. Keep an eye on them. If we expose the dangerous ones, then the safe ones can thrive. *That's* how you'll get your utopia. Worst case, I can offer you a salary and a working visa for a year. Best case, a job where you'll be doing something useful. Making a difference."

Josh had to laugh.

"You see right through me, don't you," he said, shaking his head.

"So you're in?"

"Of course. With a pitch like that, I'd be crazy not to be."

Matt paused a second.

"Good. Because I think I've got our first story."

"Of course you do," Josh said. He rolled his eyes theatrically, but he was hanging on Matt's every word. Despite the jetlag, he didn't feel even slightly tired anymore. Quite the opposite; he was fired up, excited, eager to hear more. And above all, eager to get started.

Printed in Great Britain
by Amazon